Praise for Robin L. Rotham's
FrankenDom

"A very edgy and intense read that may cause a few eyebrows to raise and faces to blush! The search for a balanced three-way relationship that is described provides a mesmerizing and sensual read."

~ *Night Owl Reviews*

"A book like nothing I expected, more on the darker kinky side of BDSM so be prepared, but also left me breathless for more. [...] My first step into the world of Robin L. Rotham and I have to say I was so glad that I took it and look forward to the second book."

~ *Guilty Pleasures Book Reviews*

"I will be reading this book again in the future and recommend this be added to every BDSM book lovers bookshelf, if for no other reason than it is a great story."

~ *BDSM Book Reviews*

Look for these titles by
Robin L. Rotham

Now Available:

Carnal Compromise

FrankenDom

FrankenDom

Robin L. Rotham

To Delphine –
Please write faster –
my autobuy finger is
getting restless!

Robin L. Rotham

SAMHAIN
PUBLISHING

Samhain Publishing, Ltd.
11821 Mason Montgomery Road, 4B
Cincinnati, OH 45249
www.samhainpublishing.com

FrankenDom
Copyright © 2014 by Robin L. Rotham
Print ISBN: 978-1-61921-705-8
Digital ISBN: 978-1-61921-656-3

Editing by Heather Osborn
Cover by Kanaxa

This book has been previously published and revised from its original release.

First Samhain Publishing, Ltd. electronic publication: April 2013
First Samhain Publishing, Ltd. print publication: April 2014

Dedication

To John Yossarian, for making me laugh. This book wouldn't be the same without you.

And to my fans, for being so patient and encouraging.

I promise, aliens are coming...

Acknowledgments

R.G. Alexander gave me the idea for this book and reignited my passion for writing.

Anne Calhoun and Eden Bradley critiqued and helped ensure *FrankenDom* was as good as I could get it.

Sher is my original crit partner. I wouldn't dream of publishing without her amazing insights.

Cookie got it out there faster than I had any right to expect.

Dawn is a promo machine and I'm very lucky to have her.

The Smutkedettes' enthusiasm makes me feel like I can really write.

The music of VAST continues to take my mind incredible places.

My heartfelt thanks to all of you.

A Note to Readers

FrankenDom is a fast, intense ride through a fictional world in which the characters engage in all sorts of kinky BDSM games. The characters observe the rules of safe, sane and consensual play throughout. However, the heroine skips a few safety precautions along the way because she already knows and trusts her Doms (most of them, anyway), and she has a safe word (most of the time, anyway), which she uses and her Doms respect.

If you decide to explore the lifestyle, please exercise considerably more caution than my heroine does. Before you jump in with both feet, do your own research in real life, not in fiction. Get involved in the community. Observe the players and get to know them. Ask questions. Make sure someone knows where you are. And always, always, always use a safe word.

Chapter One

October 13

When someone pounded on my apartment door like they meant business, I fumbled one of my mother's second-best teacups and almost dropped it.

If I'd had any idea who was doing the pounding, I might have let it fall and bitten my knuckle in suspense. Instead, I blew out an annoyed breath and finished wrapping the delicate cup in newspaper before answering. I would have ignored the rude summons altogether but I needed boxes too badly.

"I'm glad you're here," I said as I threw open the door. "I need some... Colin?"

He grinned. "I'm just in time then." When I blinked at him in shock, the grin widened. "Good morning, Rachel."

"I thought you were the movers," I said blankly. The last time I'd been this close to Dr. Colin Carter, he was pulling his underwear up over his spectacular ass. Why was he standing on my doorstep five years later, fully dressed in blue jeans and a black leather jacket?

He looked into the living room. "May I come in?"

After a moment's hesitation, I stood back, tugging self-consciously at the stretched-out hem of my faded purple UW sweatshirt. Then I glanced at the living room, which was a shambles and not just because I was moving. Organization had never been my strong suit. Boxes and books and stacks of medical journals made an obstacle course of the floor, and piles of paper covered every horizontal surface.

I flushed. "Sorry, I wasn't really expecting company. It's a bit of a wreck."

"Not a problem." He wrapped one arm around my shoulders in a loose embrace and brushed a kiss over my cheek before walking past.

My lungs collapsed in a nostalgic paroxysm of pure lust, leaving me practically gasping in his wake. Oh God, he still smelled like... *Colin.* Wind and leather and unrepentant sex— mind-bendingly dark sex that satisfied me on some unfathomable level, even as it left me craving more.

I was wet and ready to go in an instant, something that hadn't happened in a depressingly long time.

Feeling exposed, I demanded, "What are you doing here?"

He turned, wearing an ironic smile, his hands in his pants pockets. "Never were much for small talk, were you? Just..." his blue eyes skimmed down the front of my body, "...get right down to business."

"Please do," I said acidly as heat gushed into my cheeks. "As you can see, I've got a lot going on."

"You certainly do," he murmured, his gaze fixed on my breasts as if he'd never seen a pair before.

I crossed my arms. "Colin!"

When he dragged his eyes up to mine, the feral hunger radiating from them took my breath away.

Then he blinked and all I saw was the gleam of a challenge. Had I imagined it?

"All right," he said in a portentous tone, "I'm here to offer you a fellowship."

My eyes just about popped out of my head. "Really? You leave town without a word, show up unannounced five years later to leer at me and then offer me a fellowship? Gee, how can I resist? *Oh wait*, I've already got a fellowship, so fuck off, Colin."

"Not like this one. Trust me, Rachel, you want this one."

Reluctantly intrigued, I scowled. "What's so special about

this fellowship?"

"You'll be working with Julian Kilmartin."

Everything in me stilled. *Julian.* I hadn't seen him since before Colin left, and yet, even now, his name alone had the power to make me...pliable, somehow. Boneless.

Obviously I still had a weakness for arrogant young doctors.

Swallowing, I said, "I didn't realize you were still associated with him."

Actually, I had no idea what had happened to Colin after my second year of residency. He'd just...disappeared. My occasional Internet searches never turned up anything current, and the few times I'd swallowed my pride and asked after him, no one had heard a word about him.

"I leave the limelight to Julian," Colin said with a dismissive wave. "We've spent the last few years working on some cutting-edge research—I'm talking *razor's* edge, Rachel—and we're on the verge of accomplishing something truly miraculous. We need a good vascular surgeon on the team and your name was—is—right at the top of Julian's list."

"Why?" I asked baldly. I may have been a damn good surgeon, but I was hardly God's gift to modern medicine. Julian Kilmartin could afford his own dream team of world-class surgeons.

Colin gave a little half shrug. "He trusts you."

"Oh, well that explains everything." I rolled my eyes. "You know, we doctors are, by and large, very trustworthy. That's why they give us licenses to play Operation with real people."

"But you're the only one who's you."

I stared at him. "This is crazy. I can't believe he even remembers me. It's been more than five years since he left UW and went into private research, and we were in different departments, so it's not like we even had much contact."

"You're a memorable woman, and Julian knows a good

11

thing when he sees one." At my snort, he added, "He's kept tabs on you over the years, Rachel. You have plenty of credits in some impressive vascular journals, and that paper you did on endovascular repair of complex abdominal aortic aneurisms was particularly well received. He's even got a podcast of you on the vascular panel at the Women's Comprehensive Health Conference in Atlanta last spring."

Slack-jawed with amazement, I continued to stare.

"We'll double EVI's financial incentive," he tossed out.

"Holy— *Double?*" My jaw dropped even farther. The offer from Early Vascular Institute was already what most people would consider exorbitant. I could afford to pay off my student loans right away. Buy a nice house. Maybe even buy into one of the better surgical practices.

But this...

"What in the hell are you guys working on that's worth that kind of money?" I asked suspiciously.

"Ah-ah-aaah." He shook his head with a secretive smile. "Not until you've signed the contracts. And if you need a little more incentive, this project is based in Montaneva. You always wanted to travel, didn't you, Rachel? Have you made it to Europe yet?"

I could tell from his tone that he knew I hadn't, damn him. And he knew enough about EVI's offer to double it. Good Lord, as if they needed more incentive than the opportunity to work with the illustrious Dr. Julian Kilmartin.

"What's the catch?" Because there always was one. Nothing worth having came without a price.

"No catch. You agree to work for Julian for a minimum of two years, keep your mouth shut until the end of time—unless we renegotiate the nondisclosure agreement at a later date— and you'll get your salary and all expenses paid, plus a percentage of the income from any patents that result from research you're directly involved in."

It was an astounding offer, but I was wary.

"Why Montaneva?"

"Let's just say the government there is a little more receptive to outside-the-box thinking and trusts Julian to know where to draw the line."

I frowned. Less governmental oversight could be a good thing, as long as scientists were scrupulously honest. If they weren't...

Jesus, was I really thinking about this?

"I've already signed a contract with EVI," I hedged.

Just moments ago, I was thrilled to be joining the Early Vascular Institute all the way across the country in Maryland. It was an offer beyond anything I'd dared to hope for—not that I wasn't a damn good surgeon, but the competition was stiff and we all knew it took more than surgical skill to start out at such a prestigious practice. Connections were everything, and not only was I far from adept at making them but I'd never been comfortable taking advantage of the few I had, so why cultivate more?

Nevertheless, after three relatively painless interviews, the vascular surgery fellowship at EVI was mine and I had the signed contract to prove it. Bailing on it now could not only burn bridges, it could nuke any number of potential career highways.

"Julian will take care of it. You must be aware that money is really no object for him, and he has a lot of influence in the upper echelons of the medical community."

All too aware. Kilmartin BioTech had made the news with astonishing regularity over the years, and Dr. Kilmartin himself was a medical visionary, a revolutionary. How could one man have been blessed with so much drive and intelligence and sheer, unadulterated personal power?

God, the offer was so tempting, but I couldn't help hesitating. Already a headline-making neuromuscular fellow when I was still a green resident, Julian Kilmartin had intimidated the hell out of me. But he'd also cut an incredibly romantic figure with his aloof, pale Britishness, exacting standards and steel-eyed intensity, and like many of the residents on staff, I'd crushed on him pretty hard. He'd lost his father to Bain's atrophy when he was in high school and dedicated his life to finding a cure for the aggressive lower motor neuron disease. Literally his entire life. As far as anyone knew, he didn't exist outside a hospital or lab setting—his name had never been linked to a woman's, which made him the target for many female rescue fantasies.

Not that *I'd* wanted to rescue him. I'd just yearned to have him eviscerate me with that rapier stare until I collapsed in on myself like a dying star. In countless daydreams, I'd made some clumsy or careless mistake in front of him and he'd dragged me by the arm to his office and given me a stern dressing-down. I was in tears long before he finished, but that didn't stop him from bending me over the desk and pulling down my panties to reinforce the lesson with a stinging, bare-handed spanking.

And that was just one of the many twisted fantasies about Dr. Julian Xavier Kilmartin I'd entertained—not to mention masturbated to—over the two years we were at UW together. I couldn't even keep him out of my thoughts when I was in bed with his protégé.

And to my everlasting shame, Colin had known it.

The last morning we were together, he'd called me on it while he was still lying over my back, one hand buried between my legs and his softening cock buried in a place I'd never imagined allowing any man. I hadn't even had an orgasm yet— he'd delighted in making me wait for it, which frustrated me in the moment but was ultimately worth the suspense.

Not that time.

"You were imagining Julian in here again, weren't you, Rachel?" he'd panted, flexing his slippery fingers inside my vagina and grinding his palm against my supremely sensitized clit. If he'd said anything but that, I might have finally gone over the edge.

But this was the second time he'd skewered me with the uncanny insight, and feeling embarrassed and a little betrayed that he'd make fun of me in such an intimate moment—not to mention resentful that he was familiar enough with Dr. Kilmartin to call him by his Christian name—I'd bucked him off. "I was not, you asshole."

"Come on, admit it—you're only sleeping with me because of him." He laughed when I screeched. "I don't mind, honestly. You want me to ask if he's up for a threesome?"

That's when I told him to get out. And he'd done it, still chuckling as he walked out my front door.

For the last time, as it turned out, which hadn't been my intention at all.

"I wasn't making fun of you that morning," Colin said, looking at me intently.

Good God, he was *still* a mind reader.

"If you want me to even think about your offer, I wouldn't mention that incident again," I managed coolly. "Let's keep this strictly professional, please."

"Julian would have turned me down," Colin persisted, "but only because he felt he had no choice."

"Goodbye." I marched toward the front door.

"He wanted you in the worst way, Rachel McBride."

I froze, keeping my back to him. "What?"

"Julian wanted you," he repeated. "But he wouldn't let himself have you."

Stunned, I turned to gape at him and he met my eyes without flinching. "Why not?"

"Because you were a newly minted resident and he was a fellow in the hospital. He's an ethical man, Rachel." Colin sighed. "I owe you an apology. I should never have said what I

15

did. It was cruel to both of you. My only excuse is that I was jealous."

And I'd thought my jaw couldn't drop any farther. "Of *what*? You were his protégé, his *pet*."

He gave me a puzzled look and then shook his head as if to clear it. "Yes, but you'd caught his attention and I was still insecure enough to resent it."

"That's why you slept with me—to get back at me?"

"No," he said, "I slept with you because I was a horny senior resident and you were a sweet-smelling little doctor-girl who only had eyes for Julian."

"So I was a challenge. Nice."

He sighed. "I'm not winning any points here, am I?"

"You must be joking."

"Look, I thought it was best to be as honest as I could and clear the air between us. I'm very sorry, Rachel, and I hope I have the chance to make it up to you. I was a complete assmunch and, believe me, I've regretted it ever since."

I was still trying to get a handle on Colin's uncustomary humility when he added darkly, "Julian was livid."

"You *told* him?" I hissed.

He nodded somberly. "As soon as the words left my mouth, I knew I'd fucked up and I thought he'd better hear it from me first."

"Really? You thought I'd go running to him?" Had Colin even known me at all?

"No, but word gets around in hospitals."

"Not from me, it doesn't." When he didn't say anything, I couldn't resist prompting, "And?"

"And...he made sure I'd never again say anything without thinking about the potential consequences first." When I looked at him curiously, he said, "None of your beeswax."

Although my imagination was going wild, I shrugged. "If

you say so."

"So do you think you're mature enough to let bygones be bygones?" he asked, raising his brow.

I returned the look. "My maturity clearly isn't the issue here, Dr. Beeswax."

Colin grinned. "Touché, Dr. McBride. So what about it—are you going to reach out and grab the chance of a lifetime?"

Confused and torn, I looked out the window. It would be awkward enough working with Colin again after everything that had happened between us. But knowing Dr. Kilmartin had once wanted me as a woman, and had now sent for me as a *surgeon...*?

I shook my head. No way would I flatter myself that it was just an excuse to see me again, because men like him didn't hide behind excuses. They just took what they wanted.

So why had Colin dangled that bit of information in front of my twitchy little nose and then moved right along as if it had no relevance now?

Because it probably didn't.

And even if it did, I couldn't let it affect my decision. It would be one thing to give up the fellowship at EVI in favor of a better offer—*that* was marginally justifiable. But Julian Kilmartin was the one deliciously frightening fantasy I'd never outgrown, and my heart still gave a jerk whenever I saw his photo on the Internet or read some news story about him. Finding out that my attraction to him might have been reciprocated, at least on a physical level, pitched my stomach into free fall, and everything in me longed to explore what might still be possible between us.

That would be a totally *un*justifiable reason for passing on EVI. Not to mention unprofessional as hell, and likely a tiny bit insane. Even if the attraction were still there, why should I expect it to unfold differently this time? Julian Kilmartin was clearly married to his research.

If I accepted the offer, it would have to be for strictly professional reasons. I couldn't let myself hope there might be more to the offer or I'd be setting myself up for disappointment of epic proportions.

"If I have to get down on my knees and beg your forgiveness, I will." The intensity of Colin's voice startled me. "I'm serious, Rachel. What we're working on is so big..."

He blew out a huge breath and ran his hand through his short brown hair, which had lost none of its tendency to curl boyishly. Then he looked at me again. "If you pass on this, sooner or later you're going to hate yourself. I guarantee it."

I bit my lip. "Can I have a few days to think about it?"

"We have an experimental procedure scheduled on the thirty-first, and that date is set in stone. We need you there as soon as possible so we have time to bring you up to speed." Unzipping his jacket, he pulled out a manila envelope and handed it to me. "It's all explained in the contracts."

"What—"

"I'm due back in Montaneva tomorrow morning so all I can give you is..." he glanced at his watch, "...five hours. My cell is on my business card. If I don't hear from you by three o'clock, I'll have to make the offer to our second choice."

Second choice. So much for there being anything more to the offer.

"No pressure there," I grumbled.

"Julian's personal assistant will take care of all the details for you—moving and storage, travel arrangements, mail forwarding—"

"Is she going to break the news to my parents and sisters?"

"If you want *him* to, yes, he will."

I rolled my eyes. "I was kidding, but no thanks. If I accepted, could I at least tell EVI who I'd be working for so they'd know I wasn't making the decision lightly?"

"Of course. Julian will be contacting Brian Duff personally anyway."

Well that made me feel a little better. Dr. Duff would probably jump ship himself to work with Julian Kilmartin.

"You have a passport," he said, as if a negative answer were unthinkable. If he'd shown up here two months earlier, that's what he would have gotten, though.

"Yes. I did make it to the Turks and Caicos last month."

"I know. How was the diving?"

He *knew*? What the hell did that mean? And what the hell else did he know?

"Great," I said in a defiant tone.

"Excellent. So all you have to do is fill out the paperwork, sign the contracts in front of a notary and pack your bags. Julian will have your work visa expedited."

"I haven't said yes yet."

"You will." He checked his watch again and headed for the front door.

"I'm not going to sleep with you again," I threw out desperately.

"I'm not going to ask," he threw back with a gleam in his eye.

That shut my mouth, first with embarrassed annoyance and then with confusion. Exactly what did he mean by *that*?

Standing on the threshold, he said, "Five hours, Rachel—don't be late."

It didn't dawn on me until the door closed softly behind him that I was holding my breath. I'd always felt slightly at sea with Colin Carter, and clearly that hadn't changed a bit. After just ten minutes in his company, I felt as though I were on a small boat in the middle of a rolling ocean and hadn't gotten my sea legs under me.

And yet Colin *had* changed. He'd been genuinely humble

and earnest, qualities I would never have ascribed to him five years ago. He'd apologized for his behavior back then, something I'd never known him to do. He'd even offered to get down on his knees and beg for my cooperation, something the hotshot senior resident I'd known would *never* have done.

Dr. Colin Carter had obviously matured quite a bit, and he'd made me a straightforward professional offer with no apparent strings attached. So why did I still feel like we were playing some kind of game and he was the only one who knew the rules?

God, was it me? Was I reading subtext in his words that wasn't there? Was I the one who hadn't changed, who hadn't managed to move on after he vanished from my life?

It was a humbling thought.

Sighing, I pushed over a pile of papers and slumped onto the couch. From a professional standpoint, I'd have to be insane to pass up such an offer—I knew I had the diagnostic instincts, the surgical skills and the competitive drive to play with the big boys, and this project could be history in the making.

But from a personal standpoint, I was hopelessly outclassed and likely to make a complete fool of myself.

I'd have to be insane to accept.

After going round and round with myself for hours, I finally gave up the fight. There were some things a woman just couldn't live without knowing.

"I'm in," I said when Colin answered.

I could hear the smile in his voice when he replied, "Welcome to Kilmartin BioTech, Dr. McBride. I'll have a messenger there at three o'clock."

Kicking myself for dithering so long, I filled out all the forms, skimmed over the employment contract and rushed to the bank to sign all the documents in front of a notary, barely making it back to my apartment before the messenger arrived to pick them up.

The next couple of days passed in a blur of shopping, packing and visiting. My parents and my older sister, Clarissa, were thrilled for me—they'd already adjusted to the idea of my living almost three thousand miles away, so what was another four thousand? They spent the evening crowded around Dad's laptop with Clare's husband, Art, looking up information on Montaneva, a picturesque little speck of a country sandwiched between Hungary and Romania, and planning a family vacation there the following summer.

My younger sister, Breanna, used their distraction to drag me off to the kitchen and grill me like a cheese sandwich.

Though Clare and I were closer in age, Bree and I were each other's best friends. Clare tended to be a little domineering and a lot demanding, which made her the perfect army staff sergeant and worked very well for her and easy-going Art. But it had been a challenge for the rest of the family when we were growing up.

Bree had been a bit of a challenge for my parents too, just because she was so daring and outspoken, so completely at ease with herself and others. I'd worried about her a little, especially during her teens, but I'd also secretly admired her boldness and wished I were more like her. She was the only one I'd ever said anything to about Colin—though she got the heavily edited kid-sister cut—and she had plenty to say about the matter at the moment.

"Are you crazy?" she demanded, plucking a bit of ham from the mostly denuded bone in the roaster and popping it in her mouth. "You're going to let that douche canoe sweep you off to some foreign country nobody's ever heard of and make you live in a place called *Bangenschloss*?"

We both snickered—again—but I sobered immediately and said, "I've heard of Montaneva. And don't talk with your mouth full. It's gross."

She stuck her ham-laden tongue out at me. "How do you

know he's really taking you to Dr. Kilmartin? You said he fell off the radar years ago—what if he's some serial killer who's never caught because he lures women to foreign countries before he rapes, tortures and kills them? Maybe he'll make you bang *his* schloss for a year and then grind you up and serve you as Wienerschnitzel."

I rolled my eyes. "Do you even know what Wienerschnitzel is?"

"Or wait! Montaneva is right next door to Romania, and Transylvania's in Romania, right?" Her eyes grew round. "Oooh! Maybe Dr. Kilmartin is a vampire and Colin the Cockhead is his human servant, scouring the world for tender-skinned blood slaves to take home to his Master."

"Bree, where in God's name do you get these insane ideas?"

"I can read," she sniffed.

"Well you're twenty-six years old now, for crying out loud," I told her severely. "It's time you started reading something a little more edifying. Pick up some biographies at the library or something."

She blew a raspberry at me and I grimaced, brushing imaginary bits of ham from the sleeve of my sweater.

"Seriously, Rae, this doesn't feel right to me. You shouldn't let someone who already hurt you once take you so far away from the people who can protect you."

"What, like you're Buffy or something?"

"Hey, I can kill a man with nothing more than an air bubble," she said with a narrow look, "but that's not what I'm talking about."

"I know," I said in a conciliatory tone. "Come on, you know it was mainly my pride that was hurt, and I'm the one who told Colin to get out, remember? If anyone should be worried, it's him."

"You didn't mean forever and the cockhead knew it," she said doggedly. "And you had feelings for both of them."

"I had a fangirl crush on Julian, just like every other resident in the building, and Colin was just a—"

"Substitute?"

"Fling." I flung a piece of ham fat at her. "He was great in bed, that's all."

"That's it. I'm coming to visit you for Christmas. I have three weeks coming to me, and all the nurses on the floor owe me big-time because I'm the only one who's single."

Uh-oh. I wasn't allowed visitors for the first three months. "That might not be the best idea. We're going to be really deep into this project."

Her blue eyes narrowed. "You can't have visitors, can you?"

"It's a top secret project." It sounded weak, even to my ears.

"Well there's nothing that says I can't meet you in town, is there?"

"Of course not," I said brightly. "Maybe I can get a day or two off and we can do some sightseeing while you're there."

"Okay then," she said, marginally pacified.

"Hey, are you girls eating all the ham?" Art said, pulling up a chair and taking a defensive stance over the ham bone.

Bree put up her hands. "Easy, boy, it's all yours."

"You only say that because you know it's true." He looked at me. "The name of that place you're going to, Bangenschloss?"

Bree and I both snickered.

"Grow up, girls. *Schloss* means castle. We looked it up on a German translation site. And believe it or not, Bangenschloss really is an ancient castle."

A vision of me emptying a chamber pot out the castle window onto the heads of unsuspecting peasants below made me shudder. "I assume it's been updated with indoor plumbing?"

"I'd think so. A couple of articles mentioned extensive renovations."

"Of course. They wouldn't have put in labs with no bathrooms. Cool, then I'm down with a castle. Were there any photos?" I asked eagerly.

"As a matter of fact, no. We couldn't find a single one, which is really weird in this day and age. Not even a Google Earth image."

"Money buys privacy," Bree said in a disgusted tone.

"Yeah, that's why the tabloids are filled with pictures of movie stars without makeup or Spanx."

It was Art's turn to receive a hammy raspberry.

"So what does *bangen* mean?" I asked.

"Well, apparently it could either mean fear or awe."

Bree stared at him. "You're shitting me. Castle of Fear? Really?"

"Castle of Awe, with a mote of awesome sauce," I said decisively. "I can't wait to get there."

Chapter Two

By the time the limo passed through the little village of Kander and started the last leg of the journey deep into the woods of Montaneva, I was wired for sound. I'd slept for three or four hours—a good night's sleep for me—at a London hotel when my connecting flight was cancelled due to weather, so rather than battling fatigue, I'd spent most of today's trip trying unsuccessfully to dial back my excitement a little. Dr. Kilmartin had hired me as a surgeon. Period. End of story. If there were something more personal on his agenda, Colin would have said so, right? Or the man would have come himself.

Right?

Yeah, that's what I kept telling myself, but I couldn't help vibrating with nervous anticipation.

"Pardon me, Dr. McBride, but we are arriving at Bangenschloss."

Startled out of my reverie, I jerked upright. "Awesome. As much as I enjoy it, I'm ready to be done with traveling for a while."

The handsome, brown-haired limo driver, who'd introduced himself simply as Dirk, nodded knowingly as he turned in between two imposing wrought-iron gates and headed up a rutted gravel drive. "I have been to the States many times in my life," he said, meeting my eyes in the rearview mirror. "It is a long trip."

That explained his excellent English.

"Very long," I agreed. My eyes widened as we rolled to a stop, then I blinked repeatedly. "Are you sure this is it?"

"I'm sure. I've been here many times."

He hopped out and hustled around to open my door while I stared out the tinted window at the pile of rough-hewn limestone that was to be my working home for the next two years. Bree and I had laughed because the name sounded kind of dirty, but I wasn't laughing now.

Bangenschloss *was* dirty, and not in a fun way. Square, squat, and as gray and foreboding as the storm clouds boiling up behind it, the castle had an eternity's worth of filth drizzling down its mottled façade.

Good God, maybe I *would* be emptying a chamber pot out my window.

Assuming I could get it open without sending a bunch of baby birds plummeting to their deaths. The sills of the narrow mullioned windows bristled with nests.

And the two crenellated towers visible from this angle were riddled with holes and gouges, as if they'd taken a blast from God's own shotgun. Hopefully that wasn't their idea of air conditioning.

"Dr. McBride?" Dirk was standing there with his hand out.

Bemused by the courtly gesture, I hooked my purse and laptop over my shoulder and let him help me out of the limo. A quick glance around revealed that the grounds were almost as neglected as the castle. A jungle of weeds had pushed their way up between the cobblestones of the courtyard, the scattered ornamental shrubs were overgrown, and if there were any flower beds on the gently rolling grounds, I couldn't see them for the grass, which had long since gone to seed. The whole place looked unkempt and unwelcoming, and so far from the sparkling Disneyesque palace of my imagination it was almost laughable.

"No wonder there are no pictures on the Internet," I murmured. "The poor thing is probably embarrassed to be seen."

When I caught Dirk's haughty look, heat prickled in my cheeks. "Sorry, that was tactless of me. I was told the castle had been renovated."

"The interior *was* extensively renovated," he grunted as he grappled with the larger of my two bags. "And the castle was reroofed. It is now a palace fit for a king and all his minions."

"I'm sure you're right," I said quickly, though I had a feeling his idea of a palace and mine might be worlds apart. *Note to self: Don't diss the palace in front of the minions.*

But I knew there had to be a state-of-the-art research facility in there somewhere. Dr. Kilmartin's personal assistant Vince had said during our brief phone conversation that I could bring whatever electronics I wanted because the entire castle had been rewired with 110-volt outlets—which was why I'd anticipated lots of glass and steel, with immaculately manicured, if utilitarian, grounds. Why would he go to all the trouble and expense of renovating the interior and then let the exterior go to hell like this?

Something must be wrong. The exacting neurosurgeon who'd made all the residents quake in their sneakers when he walked by would never let anything in his possession deteriorate this way.

Thunder rumbled in the distance, and I shivered as a gust of rainy-smelling wind whipped up a funnel of leaves in the barren courtyard, plastering my pleated skirt against my thighs. Fortunately, I'd worn black tights and ankle boots so I didn't have to worry about flashing anyone.

Dirk finally got my bag over the edge of the trunk and let it thump onto the gravel next to my guitar. I'd brought everything I could possibly fit into two bags, and that one was so overweight it would have cost an arm and a leg to get it on the plane if I hadn't been flying first class.

He strapped the smaller bag to the larger, then picked up my guitar and turned. "If you will follow me, Dr. McBride."

Wow, talk about service. A cabbie—especially one I'd offended—would have dumped my bags on the ground and left me to haul them in myself.

I followed him through the courtyard and was surprised when he veered away from the badly weathered front doors. He rolled my bags along a cobblestone path at the foot of the castle and disappeared around the corner.

When I caught up with him, I had to stop and gape. There was a tremendous white wind turbine practically right there in the backyard, its slender blades spinning lazily in spite of the blustery wind. How had I not seen that? It towered over the castle and the surrounding forest of trees, looking very out of place in the primeval setting.

"Dr. McBride, this way, if you please."

I tore my eyes away to find Dirk waiting for me, gesturing impatiently up a short run of steps with a framed ramp for wheelchair access on the side. He was certainly arrogant for a limo driver, but then it seemed like really good-looking men always were, no matter how lowly their occupation. His erect bearing and strong Slavic features radiated command, and I wondered if he might have spent some time in the military.

Another rumble of thunder, this one louder, had me hurrying up the steps to the small wooden deck and ringing the doorbell. It took a few minutes, but the door finally opened and a cheerful young redhead with a Van Dyke beard emerged.

"You must be Dr. McBride. I'm Vince Price, Dr. Kilmartin's personal assistant. And before you ask," he said with a grin, "yes, it's short for Vincent. I think that's the main reason he hired me."

I couldn't help smiling as I shook the hand he held out. "I wouldn't be that rude."

Dirk snorted and Vince gave him a quizzical look. I just ignored him. After all, I'd already apologized, and he was the limo driver, not the master of the house. If anyone should be bowing and scraping, it was him.

"I'm sorry, you must be freezing," Vince said. "Please come in."

The heels of my boots echoed loudly as we walked down a long, cramped hallway that smelled just like the damp stone it was made of.

"Sorry about the side entry, but the front doors are heavy as hell and tend to sag, so they're hard to open. We usually only use them if we need to get something big into the building."

"It was no problem. These boots were made for walking."

"Is that a threat?"

I laughed. "Not at all."

"Good. I don't think they'd get you very far anyway. Thunderstorms are just off to the north and the forecast calls for several inches of ice and snow later tonight."

"Well I'm glad we made it here in time. I really don't care that much for either storms or cold weather."

"You probably won't care for it much here then. It's supposed to be unusually cold this winter."

"Lovely."

We emerged into a dark room with high, shadowed ceilings and bare stone walls and floors, one narrow window, and a stark rustic bench for furniture. Judging from the direction we'd taken, it must be one of the towers.

Either the window was very grimy or the storm had already closed in, because it looked threateningly dark outside for late afternoon.

"Just leave Dr. McBride's luggage by the bench, Dirk. Mrs. Petters has fresh coffee and pastries for you in the kitchen," Vince told him. When I pulled out my wallet, he added, "Thank you, Rachel, but that's not necessary. Dr. Kilmartin's already taken care of it."

"Oh. Well then." I put my wallet back into my bag and said

goodbye to Dirk after he deposited my stuff. Vince helped me out of my coat, and I set it on the bench along with my computer bag and purse.

"I know you're probably tired and anxious to get settled in your room," he said apologetically, "but Dr. Kilmartin requested that I take you directly to him when you arrived."

Nerves seized me again, but I smiled valiantly. "That's fine. I'm kind of anxious to see him again too. I'm dying of curiosity about this project."

Vince walked over to a wide door and pushed a button beside it. Only when it opened did I realize what it was.

"Call me crazy, but an elevator is probably the last thing I expected to find in a castle. Not that I'm complaining," I added. It boded well for the castle's plumbing.

"Dr. Kilmartin had it installed several years ago. There's another one in the southwest tower, and yet another in the labs." He ushered me inside and pushed the button for the second floor. The elevator hummed loudly before taking off so smoothly I could hardly tell it was moving. When the door opened, Colin was waiting on the other side.

"I'll escort her from here," he said.

Vince gave a nod and then turned to me. "Enjoy the rest of your evening, Rachel."

"Thanks, you too."

Colin led me away by the elbow, leaving Vince standing beside the elevator watching us.

"Hello again, Rachel," Colin said, a ghost of a smile curving his lips. "Did you have a pleasant trip?"

"It was fine. Until London, anyway. The hotel was nice, but I white-knuckled most of the flight today because we were skirting the same front that grounded last night's connection." *Shut up! You're rambling!* I took a deep breath. "But now that I'm on solid ground, I'm great."

"Good. Julian's impatient to see you."

Colin seemed tired and tense, and a little pallid, which was an unusual look for him. Though we'd never had that kind of relationship, I had to squash the urge to scold him for not taking care of himself. He was still gorgeous, don't get me wrong—taller than me by a couple of inches and very trim, with thick brown hair and heavy-lidded blue eyes that usually danced with amusement or sparked with temper. But the light in his eyes was dampened now, and his typical boyish grin was missing. It made me even more nervous.

My heartbeat galloped irregularly as he led me down a long carpeted hallway. This one had smooth plaster walls and smelled like apple cider. About halfway down the hall, he opened a door and ushered me into a warm, spacious living/dining area that smelled even better. Three places were set at the end of a large formal dining table and a covered soup tureen sat between them.

"Sit down." He gestured toward the seating area by the fireplace, where a subdued fire burned. "I'll go get Julian."

After he disappeared through another door, I sank down at the end of a plush leather sofa, swallowing against the butterflies trying to fight their way out of my throat. Lightning flashed repeatedly, and I noticed rain was sheeting down the high mullioned window. I didn't hear thunder, though—the only sounds in the room were a faint hissing from the fire and the ticking of a large, ornate grandfather clock. The thick stone walls must really provide an excellent sound barrier.

Flanking the fireplace were two built-in bookshelves bursting with paperbacks and a few framed photographs. When two minutes dragged into five, I gave in to my curiosity and got up for a closer look. The books ranged from legal thrillers to medical thrillers, but that wasn't what interested me.

Julian was in one of the photos. He stood with his arm around the shoulders of a younger, less intense version of himself. His brother? I seemed to recall hearing he had one at university in England at some point during my residency. Two of the other photos were of the same young man, one a posed football picture and the other a casual shot of him on a boat, grinning from ear to ear. The last was probably a formal portrait of Julian's parents—the resemblance between all the males was unmistakable.

Feeling like I was invading his privacy, I turned away. But before I could return to my seat, the door opened and Julian appeared.

In the space of a heartbeat, his larger-than-life presence occupied every corner of my mind. Though he'd hardly changed at all, there was something very different about him. Time had deepened the grooves in his boldly chiseled face and he wore dark-rimmed glasses, which made his gray eyes seem larger and more intense. His dark-blond hair was longer, his forehead perhaps a bit higher than I remembered. And he was dressed in a heather-blue turtleneck sweater and time-worn Levi's that clung lovingly to his tall, raw-boned physique.

It dawned on me that I'd never seen him without a lab coat.

I was in Dr. Julian Kilmartin's *home*.

The unexpected intimacy left me breathless as he paused just inside the door to inspect me—or that was how it felt, anyway. Suddenly I was acutely conscious of how long it had been since I'd looked in the mirror. Dammit, I should have said I needed to go to the bathroom. I hardly ever wore makeup and I'd caught myself rubbing my itchy eyes more than once during the drive. And it felt like half my hair had escaped from its ponytail. Why hadn't I used something sturdier than a scarf to tie it back?

Then Julian's lips curved in a smile, something else I'd never seen him wearing. It left me completely discombobulated as he walked toward me.

Taking my hands, he murmured, "Dr. McBride."

"Dr. Kilmartin." While my mouth replied automatically, the rest of me screamed with awareness that he was *touching* me.

In the two years we'd worked in the same hospital, he'd *never* touched me, never even brushed my arm in passing.

He gave a warm squeeze. "Thank you for coming."

Like I could refuse.

It didn't dawn on me until he laughed that I'd said that out loud.

"I'm glad to hear it," he said. Letting go of one of my hands, he gestured toward the table. Colin was already there, pulling out a chair. "Dinner generally isn't served until seven, but knowing you'd be exhausted after two days of travel, I moved it up a bit. Won't you join us?"

"Thank you, that would be wonderful."

"After you, then."

His hand on the small of my back, he guided me to the chair Colin had pulled out. Wow, they really went in for the courtly manners around here. I couldn't remember the last time anyone had escorted me to the table or pulled out my chair for me.

While Colin took the seat across from me, Julian sat down a bit gingerly at the head of the table.

Years of conditioning made me ask, "Are you all right?"

"Yes, yes." He waved me off as he leaned back. "Just overdid my last workout."

"Good for you," I said, unfolding the maroon napkin and laying it across my lap. "I can't remember the last time I worked out."

"You'll have to start. Being in peak physical condition is especially important for surgeons. Colin will show you the facilities tomorrow and Hans will help you set up a balanced but challenging exercise regimen."

"Of course, Sir," Colin said with a nod.

My hackles rose slightly, but I reminded myself who he was. The great Dr. Julian Kilmartin was no doubt used to ordering his minions around all day long. I'd have to either choose my battles or be assimilated.

I picked up my glass of water and took a long drink. Tepid and metallic, not my favorite combination. They didn't do ice in drinks over here, did they?

A tall, lovely blonde woman in a gray maid's uniform appeared at Julian's side bearing a wine bottle wrapped in a white cloth. Her name tag said *Lili*.

"May I serve you, Dr. Kilmartin?" she asked in thickly accented English.

"Thank you, Lili."

She showed him the label and then poured a sample into his stem glass, waiting for his nod of approval before filling all our glasses. Once she left, he took a long sip of the white wine and I followed suit. I wasn't normally a wine fan but this was delicious—sweet and fruity.

Colin took a long drink from his glass, and the sight of his very masculine throat muscles working made me breathless.

Tearing my gaze away, I turned to Julian. "So tell me about this surgery on the thirty-first."

He shook his head. "Grisly subjects are best saved until after we've finished eating, my dear. I'd rather hear about your adventures. Colin tells me you went on holiday recently?"

A quick glance at Colin showed nothing but polite interest. "Yes, I took a dive trip to the Turks and Caicos."

"I've never been, but I've seen photographs. It looks lovely."

"Lovely doesn't even begin to describe it," I told him, warming quickly to the subject. "The islands themselves aren't much to write home about, but the beaches are just beautiful. And the diving... Oh my God, it's absolutely amazing. It would take years to explore all the hundreds of miles of reefs. Between diving and snorkeling, I spent so much time in the water, my fingers and toes were wrinkled the whole week I was there."

He glanced at the hand holding my wineglass. "You have

lovely fingers."

A little disconcerted, I took another sip before saying, "Thank you."

"I've heard the people there are lovely too," he said casually, watching my face.

Suddenly it grew a little difficult to breathe evenly, and despite my efforts to contain it, heat spread up my neck. It was ridiculous—the man was just making polite conversation and I was reacting like he'd just asked to see a video of my fling with one of the hotel bartenders.

"Definitely," I stated emphatically. "The service at my hotel was outstanding, and everyone seemed like they were genuinely friendly and interested in you, rather than just schmoozing for a tip. I plan to go back every year, if I can find the time."

"Always nice to find friendly staff when you're on holiday," he observed. "I never cared much for being underwater myself. Something about the sensory deprivation, I think—being unable to hear or see properly, unable to smell anything."

"Unable to breathe," Colin added, rolling the stem of his wineglass between his long fingers.

"That would be a bit of a downer too, yes," Julian replied dryly.

"Which is why we wear scuba gear, Colin," I said with exaggerated patience, as if speaking to a backward schoolboy. Falling back into this kind of interaction with him was entirely too easy.

His grin widened. "Is that so."

Lili returned with a loaf of bread, apparently fresh from the oven. As she sliced off several fragrant pieces and laid them on our bread plates, my stomach growled loudly.

Julian just laughed when I slapped my hand over it. "For God's sake, girl, this is clearly no time to stand on ceremony. Eat."

"Sorry," I murmured as I tore off a piece of the bread and

buttered it, now ten shades of red. "I didn't have any lunch."

"Why not?" he asked with narrowed eyes.

My heart skipped a beat at his tone. Surely he wasn't really annoyed that I hadn't eaten? "I'm not the best flyer and there was quite a bit of turbulence."

"Ah. You're forgiven then."

I smiled. "Well that's a relief."

"Don't let it happen again, though," he added. "I'll expect you to eat nutritious meals at regular intervals."

My eyes widened. "I didn't realize my eating habits were subject to your approval."

In the middle of buttering his own bread, Colin paused to stare at me like I'd just spewed a stream of profanities.

Julian's eyes narrowed again. "You didn't, eh?"

Unnerved, I set down my bread without taking a bite. So much for choosing my battles. I was missing something here, but God only knew what. Once again, we seemed to be playing a game and I was the only player who didn't know the rules.

It occurred to me that I really knew very little about Julian Kilmartin. Long-standing hero worship aside, he was a stranger to me.

When both of them continued to study me as if trying to identify some new species, I grew uncomfortable. "What?"

"You didn't read your contracts, did you, Rachel?"

Julian's rumbling drawl sent a shiver of awareness up my spine, and I could have sworn I heard a silent "you naughty girl" tacked on at the end. Good Lord, spending so much time on this side of the Atlantic had really stiffened his British accent. Five years ago I'd have found it thrilling, but right now it made him even more a stranger.

"Of course I did," I said dismissively. I'd skimmed the employment contract, anyway. The nondisclosure and personal conduct agreements, I'd signed with barely a glance. I would never betray any employer, much less Julian Kilmartin, and conducting myself professionally was a point of pride.

The fingertips of his right hand tapped on the table, rolling from pinkie to index finger in time with the ticking of the wall clock. Again. And again. And again.

"Hmmm, and now you're lying."

I bit my lips, feeling my pulse quicken and my bones go a little bit rubbery. How did he know? Had I agreed to something I shouldn't have? Even more alarming, why was I excited to be caught in a half truth?

I strove for calm. "What does it matter?"

"If you'd read your contracts, my dear," he said, his expression as keenly enigmatic as any Bond villain's, "you wouldn't have to ask that question."

The lights flickered, and I twitched nervously.

"Have no fear, my dear Rachel. We have extensive backup power systems if the winds become too strong to safely operate the turbine."

"I wasn't worried," I lied, "but thanks for the reassurance."

"Mr. Price emailed your contract copies last night. Did you download them?"

"Yes, but—"

"Good girl."

His praise set my teeth on edge. "I'm not a girl."

As if I hadn't spoken, he continued, "Your assignment for this evening then, Rachel, is to study your contracts, particularly your personal conduct agreement, and decide whether or not you wish to honor them. You're not legally bound to do so, and if you wish to leave, Dirk will return you to the airport as soon as the roads are passable. It's entirely up to you."

My breath jammed in my throat. He wanted me to *leave*?

"If, however, you decide to fulfill the terms of your

contracts, I'll quiz you over the content of your personal conduct agreement during breakfast tomorrow and for every question you answer incorrectly, there will be consequences you won't enjoy. I will also expect you to have written out one hundred times, 'I will never sign any document without reading every word first'. Handwriting, not typing. You'll find all the necessary writing supplies in your desk."

I gaped at him. "You're kidding, right?"

"Rachel, if you'd read your personal conduct agreement, you would know beyond a shadow of a doubt that I do not kid about personal assignments."

"Maybe you didn't get the memo, Dr. Kilmartin, but I'm not a medical student anymore. I'm not even a resident—I'm a licensed vascular surgeon. A vascular surgeon *you* hired," I added pointedly.

"I'm well aware of that."

"Then why are you treating me this way?" I demanded.

"Because you did a very foolish thing by signing those contracts without reading them!" he roared as he slammed his fist down on the table, rattling the china and silver.

Numb with shock, I couldn't move, couldn't even breathe.

Julian leaned back, his nostrils flaring as he visibly worked to put a leash on his temper.

"Now, Rachel," he growled without looking directly at me, "Colin will escort you to your room, where you will remain until he collects you for breakfast. I suggest you behave or there will be consequences."

Colin got up and came around behind me, and I felt the tug on my chair.

When I continued to stare at Julian, he picked up his spoon. "Good night, Rachel."

Then he started to eat.

Chapter Three

My room was exquisite. Unfortunately, I was too unsettled to appreciate it.

Colin had escorted me down the hall without a word, keeping a tight enough grip on my elbow to bruise my skin, but my mind was in such turmoil I hadn't protested. I'd felt chastened. Disappointed. Bewildered. Angry. And yet wildly alive and perversely thrilled. I was humiliated that Julian and Colin both knew I'd signed my contracts without reading them—what kind of idiot did that?—and yet even my humiliation excited me.

They shouldn't be able to do this to me. I was a grown woman, a surgeon, and Julian was my boss. Period.

And yet I'd allowed him to send me to my room like the girl he'd called me and let Colin shove me through the door, pull it shut and lock it from the outside, all without a peep.

I laid my forehead against the painted wood and groaned, thinking about the buttered bread I'd held in my hand not ten minutes ago. I was absolutely starving. Not only had I skipped lunch because of the turbulence, I'd hardly had a bite of breakfast because I was too excited to eat.

Suddenly I remembered the protein bar I'd tucked in my laptop case yesterday morning. That would tide me over until breakfast.

My guitar was propped in the corner, and my suitcases both lay on a padded chest at the foot of the heavy, ornate bed. I was relieved to see my computer case on the floor beside the lovely little antique writing desk.

Sitting down in the ladder-back chair, I pulled out my

laptop and plugged it in, then dug for the protein bar.

It wasn't there.

"Dammit," I muttered. I was sure I'd seen it in there at the airport. Maybe Dirk, annoyed with me and unaware Mrs. Petters had treats waiting for him, had lifted it.

Jerk.

Hungry, and suddenly depressed and exhausted, I pulled off my boots and made a beeline for the bed. I paused when I reached it, startled to realize the mattress was too tall to sit down on. The whole bed was huge, with a flat, sturdy canopy, a ruffled valance that ran all the way around the outside, a beautiful pink-flowered quilt and a half-dozen fluffy pillows.

There was no step that I could find, so I just sort of vaulted up onto the thing, landing on my backside among the pillows. Now I really felt like a little girl. Part of me wanted to have a good cry, while another wanted to stomp around the room and rage at Julian—and Colin too, since he was the one who'd lured me here. The rest just wanted answers.

Which I'd probably have if I got my butt up and read the contracts.

But for the moment, I couldn't be bothered to do anything except lie here with my arms flung wide and my palms curled up loosely, staring at the heavy canopy slats above as I reflected on the novelty of feeling punished.

I was being punished by Julian Kilmartin.

Not in any way I'd ever imagined, of course, and certainly not in a fun way, but the awareness of it still sent a shiver of exhilaration through me. I'd never been punished before, at least not that I remembered. I was the good girl, the quiet girl, the one my parents didn't have to worry about, except that maybe I'd go blind from too much reading and studying.

It distressed me to have made Julian so angry, and yet, looking back, there was something inexplicably satisfying about it. Was I a fool to believe there might be a sexual element to his domineering behavior? Or was I just projecting my long-denied desires onto him?

Was I unconsciously trying to provoke him into fulfilling my sexual fantasies?

The idea made me cringe. I wasn't cut out to manipulate people and couldn't imagine how others did it on a regular basis. Manipulation took too much thought, too much energy. I preferred the straightforward approach to most things in life—if you wanted something, you had to ask for it and take the chance of being denied.

But what I wanted from Julian, and even from Colin, wasn't something I would ever be able to ask for. Not because I feared being denied—God knew, Colin would have been all over any request I made when we were together—but because I feared...

What? What was it I feared so deeply? I'd agonized over it for years and was still no closer to an answer. But it occurred to me that if all this self-examination was any indication, being sent to your room really was an effective punishment.

Eventually I noticed some kind of ridged black tracks running along the inside of all four canopy rails, with three steel rings plugged in along each side and two along the head and foot. What in the world were they for? Maybe Julian had discarded some kind of full-length drapes that came with the bed, although the tracks didn't look very conducive to sliding.

I must have fallen asleep pondering their purpose because when I opened my eyes, the room was pitch-black. The clock on the nightstand said it was nearly seven o'clock, but I had no idea when I'd arrived at Bangenschloss—my Circadian rhythms were off because of all the time changes over the last couple of days.

Yawning, I sat up and fumbled with the bedside lamp until

41

I found the switch. Then I slid down off the tall bed and refreshed my laptop connections. I felt the need to connect with Bree—not to tell her what was going on, of course. The last thing I needed to hear was "I told you so". I just wanted to hear her voice, to establish a link with the real world.

I was pleased to see a strong Wi-Fi signal labeled *KBTI*. Unfortunately, it was a secure connection and I didn't have the password. I was batting a thousand today.

Fortunately, there was more than one way to skin a cat. I found my purse and dug out my cell phone. But when I turned it on, there was no reception.

Great. Was it the storm, or was there never any reception out here? Surely it was the storm—Julian had enough money to build his own network of cell towers.

I sighed my disgust. Was anything going to go my way on this trip?

The KBTI folder on my desktop seemed to flash my name, but feeling rebellious after my nap, I studiously ignored it. Just because I was grounded to my room didn't mean I had to do what Julian said. There was no need to read the contracts if I was going to bail on them anyway, which I very might if he continued to treat me like this. And I sure as hell wasn't going to write out any lines. The man had been king of his own castle for far too long if he thought being my boss gave him the right to treat me like an errant vassal.

Bursting with angry energy now, I explored my room. I was momentarily distracted when I realized the fireplace was a very realistic-looking gas log and flipped on the wall switch. Flames danced to life, instantly making the room even cozier. The overstuffed chair and ottoman now looked incredibly inviting, and I could see myself spending hours there reading—if I were going to stay, that is.

Through one of the two doors opposite the bed, I found a luxurious en-suite bath. Besides the deep whirlpool tub, which was surrounded by white candles and jars of bath salts, there was a huge shower with multiple heads, and a bidet as well as a toilet. The pink marble tile was even warm under my feet. In short, it was a hedonist's dream, and I was sorely tempted to stay on at Bangenschloss just so I had time to enjoy it all.

The other door was a huge walk-in closet, and I was surprised to find it already filled with clothing—women's clothing, most of it ranging from slinky to downright indecent. The bar on the left side bulged with daringly low-cut dresses, diaphanous robes and nightgowns, and what looked like a million slutty Halloween costumes. A closet organizing system on the other two walls held shelf after shelf of outrageous do-me heels and drawers filled with thin silk sheaths and scarves, corsets, garters, thongs and hosiery.

"What the hell?" Grinding my teeth, I slammed the door. Whose was all this? Or did I want to know?

The nightstand drawers held even wilder surprises. The top one was fully stocked with a variety of condoms and personal lubricants, and the bottom was bursting with a shocking array of sex toys, all still in their packages.

Who in the hell usually stayed in this room anyway—the castle call girl?

Actually, that wouldn't surprise me at all. Julian was a rich man, and just because he'd never been associated with a woman in public didn't mean he had no sex drive. He probably wouldn't think twice about installing a paid sex minion or two in his private palace. For all I knew, prostitution was legal in this country.

That settled it. Romantic dream bath or no, I was not staying here one minute longer than I had to.

Knowing that playing along might be the fastest way to get out of here, I sat back down at the desk and opened the file with my contracts in it. I opened the employment contract first and took my laptop over to the bed so I could relax. It was such dry reading I barely managed to get through it without nodding off. Then I opened the personal conduct agreement.

Section One: Dual nature of Employee's roles. Rachel Anne McBride, hereinafter referred to as Employee, shall act in two separate and distinct capacities for the duration of her employment at Kilmartin BioTech Industries. Employee's role as a vascular surgeon is defined in the concurrent employment contract between Kilmartin BioTech Industries and Employee. Employee's role, rights and responsibilities as sexual submissive to Julian Xavier Kilmartin, hereinafter referred to as Employer, are defined below.

The paragraph was so full of legal jargon, I almost skimmed right over the words *sexual submissive.*

Almost.

I sat straight up, my eyes as wide as saucers. "Oh my fucking God!"

Thirteen sections later, I was still whispering the same words. Well, at least now I knew what the rings in the canopy were for.

And all that stuff in the closet and nightstand? Yeah. It was for me.

Me! I could hardly get my mind around it. Not only did Julian still want me as a woman, he wanted me in ways even I'd never fantasized about—shocking, perverted, *thrilling* ways that would probably have Bree hyperventilating before she called in the cavalry to rescue me.

God, was there really a surgery on the thirty-first, or had that all been a ruse to get me here?

Surely not. The employment contract with KBTI had been mind-numbingly legitimate.

My heart was still pounding a mile a minute. If I had a brain in my head, I'd leave my bags packed and stay in my room until the roads were passable, and then drive away and never look back. Why in God's name hadn't Colin warned me about this?

And speaking of Colin, where did he fit into the picture? I knew he had to.

I'm not going to ask, he'd said.

God, those words had teased me mercilessly for the last three days, and now I knew exactly what they meant. He hadn't warned me because it was all spelled out in black and white, right here in the employee conduct agreement—I would submit to anyone Julian wanted me to. If I chose to abide by the terms of the agreement, Colin wasn't going to give me a choice, any more than Julian was.

I flopped back against the pillows as the realization raised gooseflesh all over me and twisted my low belly into knots of anxious desire. During the two months we'd slept together, Colin had asked several times if he could tie me to the bed and I was too conflicted to let him. What would happen once he had me completely helpless—everything I wanted, or maybe things I didn't want but he thought I did because I'd allowed him to put me in that position? And why did both possibilities turn me on? Why did I feel like he could make me want things I shouldn't?

It wasn't that I didn't trust Colin, exactly. I'd certainly trusted him enough to have anal sex with him, and that had been huge for me. I blushed even now to remember those raw, edgy sessions. Colin Carter had a dirty, dirty mouth and he wasn't afraid to use it for anything. I'd never looked at my bed—or my body—quite the same way afterward.

But that was back before I really knew anything about BDSM, and when he talked about tying me up, I'd had the feeling he was operating on some sort of hidden agenda. It had made me extremely wary. If tying me up wasn't his end goal, what was?

I was too frightened—of both him and myself—to ask.

Unfortunately, once he put the idea of bondage in my head, I couldn't stop thinking about it. I'd *never* stopped thinking about it, no matter how desperately I wished that I could at times.

Had hooking me up with Julian been Colin's hidden agenda all along? My mind boggled at the idea. He hadn't seemed that selfless back then, but maybe I hadn't known him as well as I thought I did.

A knock on the door jarred me out of my sightless contemplation of the canopy.

Sliding off the bed, I tiptoed over and said, "Yes?"

"Dinner for you, Dr. McBride," Lili said.

Yes!

"I don't have a key for the door," I told her.

"I vill take care of it."

The lock clicked and then Lili backed her way into the room with a tea cart.

"Where would you like this, please, Dr. McBride?"

I looked around and pointed to the desk chair. "There would be fine."

"Very good." She parked the cart beside the desk and lifted the ceramic cover off the small bowl, leaving the plates covered. It was the cream soup, and it still smelled divine. "May I bring you something else to drink?"

There was nothing but a glass of water on the cart.

"More wine?" I ventured.

Her expression fell. "I am so sorry, but your limit is one glass per meal."

"But I only had a sip," I protested. And what was this "my limit" crap? Did that mean other people—like Julian and Colin—had different limits? I added it to my list of items to discuss with my so-called *Master*.

"I am sorry," Lili repeated.

"I guess the water will do then. Thank you."

She curtsied quickly—curtsied!—and then backed out of the room, closing the door behind her. I waited for the click of the key turning in the lock but it never came.

Really? She wasn't going to lock me in again?

After a tense couple of minutes, I turned the doorknob very slowly and pulled the door open without a sound. Someone had been busy with the WD-40. Every door in my parents' house creaked as though it were a house of horrors.

Poking my head out just far enough to see, I checked both directions. No one. Everything was quiet, and the brass wall sconces had been dimmed. Now was my chance...

To do what?

Indecision and nerves seized me. It wasn't like I was going to get away from Julian and Colin altogether, even if I wanted to. I was trapped at Bangenschloss for the moment, and the only thing I was likely to find on an unauthorized foray into the castle was more trouble. My inner good girl, whom I tended to heed religiously, told me to stay in my room—I'd been grounded in no uncertain terms and she didn't want to discover the consequences of violating that order any more than I did.

But my inner bad girl, who'd been ruthlessly locked down for way too long, was wildly curious and anxious to push the envelope.

The envelope is fine where it is!

Maybe Lili left the door open for a reason. Go for it!

If she did, it's probably a test that I don't want to fail.

Come on, nothing ventured, nothing gained.

Nothing ventured, nothing punished!

Nothing punished, nothing learned. Do you want to live in the dark forever, Rachel?

Well that settled it. Something had clicked in my head when I read that slave contract Julian called a personal conduct agreement, something like a light switch being thrown, only the thing that lit up was me. Suddenly I felt like I had years ago whenever Julian's stern gaze focused on me, a feeling I'd feared I might never experience again—breathless, panicky and poised to flee, but vibrantly, achingly alive.

Was this a test Julian had set up for me? I didn't know and I was terrified of getting caught, but I couldn't *not* test the limits. I needed to know how this kind of relationship really worked and if I was strong enough to deal with it.

My gurgling stomach reminded me of the meal awaiting me on the cart, and I gazed at it longingly for a moment before steeling myself to go hungry a little longer. Lili might be back to lock the door any minute—I had to seize this chance while it was available.

Taking a deep breath, I slipped into the dim corridor, leaving my door slightly ajar in case I needed to beat a hasty retreat. Adrenaline made my hands shake and my heart pound in my throat. Where in the hell was I going? To my right, seemingly an eternity away, was the tower with the elevator I'd come up in. Across from my room was a closed door. To my left, two more closed doors on the same side as mine before the corridor made an abrupt right turn I couldn't see around. What was down there?

Decision made, I alternately crept and made panicked leaps down the corridor, flattening myself inside doorframes when I heard any sort of noise—as if my protruding boobs wouldn't give me away.

Or my noisy stomach. I gave it a reproving pat and whispered, "Hush, you."

From my vantage point in the final doorframe on the left, I craned my neck to peer down the adjoining corridor but saw nothing. I heard something, though—several somethings that sent ice water trickling down my spine.

I listened as if my life depended on it.

Which it very well might, if what I heard was any

indication—guttural male cries, low-pitched chuckles and the murmur of male voices. They were all muted by an electronic hum that made the door under my right hand vibrate slightly. And there was a persistent crackling and snapping that sounded like radio static.

Or something more sinister.

Every muscle in my body tensed for flight. It took several deep breaths and a searing lecture on the evils of cowardice from my inner bad girl before I was calm enough to forge ahead.

Another glance back the way I'd come and then I darted onto uncharted carpet. It was a relatively short corridor with only two doors, one on my left, which I flattened myself into right away, and one in the terminal wall.

Terminal. I swallowed hard at the irony. Unlike all the other doors, which were traditional six-panel models painted pristine white, this one was round on top, made of lightly stained wood planks and held together by heavy black hardware—two flat metal pieces that formed a reinforcing X were riveted to the door just below the curve, and two more pieces anchored it across the top and bottom. The handle was nothing more than a thick leather strap doubled over and bolted to the wood.

The primitive door was open. Not much—only enough to see a sliver of darkness and almost continuous flashes of watery light—but it was open.

I bit my knuckle. Nothing said "Go away!" like a big black X on the door.

But it was *open.* An open door was an invitation...right?

The temptation to creep closer and try to *see* something clashed fiercely with the desire to scurry back to my room and reassess my priorities.

The sounds were more distinct now, and I swallowed hard when I recognized the distinctive buzz and snap of some kind of powerful electrical device discharging. It was a relief to realize the human sounds seemed unrelated to the snaps and flashes of light. During one of my ER rotations, I'd seen an electrical burn from electrostimulation gone wrong and I never wanted to see it again, much less experience it for myself.

But those throaty, masculine chuckles and amused murmurs were definitely a reaction to pained grunts and groans. Someone was being tortured in there. And someone else was enjoying it.

A sharp yelp made me gasp, and I slapped one trembling hand over my mouth while the other flattened on my stomach. That could be *me* in there, being tortured for someone else's amusement.

Okay, maybe I should have taken this a little slower. My heart was about to batter its way right out of my rib cage, and I couldn't tell if it was from excitement or terror.

Time to get my ass back to my room. I didn't have to travel the entire road to self-discovery in a single day.

Before I could flee, a loud, stuttering groan rang out, followed by, "Jesus, *please*, Sir! *Ah!* Motherfucker! Fuckfuck*FUUUUCK*!"

My eyes widened. That was Colin.

"Oh my God," I whispered against my bloodless fingers. They were torturing Colin? He was a *bottom*?

I took a shaky step toward the door, and then another. What was happening to him?

Was it something that would happen to me if I stuck around?

Did I want to find out?

A heartbeat later, the choice was no longer mine. My wrists were seized from behind and I was hauled against a hard masculine body with my arms crossed over my chest. I was too breathless with terror to even squeak when he put his mouth against my ear.

"*Gotcha*, Dr. McBride!"

Chapter Four

I stomped hard on his instep, but it was a useless tactic when he wore boots and I didn't—my heel hurt and he probably didn't even feel it.

Filing away that bit of wisdom for future use, I twisted in his arms. "Let go of me!"

"That wasn't very nice, slave."

I knew that voice, and I gasped as a burst of adrenaline-fueled arousal streaked down between my legs. Vincent Price had just called me "slave".

Oh shit, I was really doing this.

"Vince, please—"

"Quiet, slave!" he barked, lifting me up and carrying me toward the terminal chamber of torture. "And that's Master Vincent to you right now."

I struggled against his hold, trying to make him drop me, but it was useless. His arms were like iron.

Jesus, this was the single hottest thing that had ever happened to me with my clothes on.

Everything inside me went weak with lust when he kicked the door open with his big black combat boot and marched into the shadows.

"Dr. Kilmartin!" he called as his grip loosened and I slid to the cold floor.

The room was completely dark, but in the corner off to my right I could see another open door illuminated by the flashing light. The electrical discharges were obviously happening in there.

Fight-or-flight kicked in suddenly and I dove for the exit, only to be yanked back against Vince's chest.

"Oh no you don't." He kicked the door shut. "You're a naughty little slave girl, aren't you?"

I giggled hysterically. *Giggled.*

"You think this is funny, slave?"

Julian's stern voice pierced the darkness around me like a velvet-coated blade and it happened instantly—I began collapsing in on myself like the dying star of my imagination.

"No, Sir."

It was scary how readily that word sprang to my lips. I hadn't even thought of the agreement when it slipped out.

"You always did call me that, didn't you, Rachel?" he said in a contemplative tone as he strolled into the dark room. "When all the other nervous new residents called me Doctor and bluffed their way through our interactions, you called me Sir and didn't meet my eyes unless you absolutely had to. It made me want to chase you through the hospital, drag you down screaming and fuck you like a goddam feral animal while they all looked on in horrified fascination."

My eyes slid to half-mast as I sagged boneless in Vince's— Master Vincent's—arms. My clit tingled like it had been stroked. "God, Sir, I wish you had."

"Believe me, little slave, I've wished the same too often for my own sanity."

Fluorescent ceiling lights flickered on, illuminating a scene nowhere near as terrifying as I'd envisioned. In fact, the large rectangular room looked like a medical exam room—in a dungeon. The walls and floor were the same gray limestone as the castle's exterior, only a lot cleaner, and the room smelled as though someone had used an ozone air purifier in it recently.

I relaxed a little. The castle infirmary, I could deal with.

But where was Colin?

Julian was dressed as I always remembered him, as if he'd just been pulled away from the lab—blue scrubs, sneakers and a lab coat. And he carried a clipboard.

Now I was totally lost.

When he stopped in front of me, Vince released me.

"Why aren't you in your room, Dr. McBride?" Julian demanded.

I met his penetrating stare with a challenge of my own. "Where's Colin?"

"I would be more concerned about your own circumstances at the moment, my dear." His dire tone gave everything south of my navel hot, wet clenches of dread. "Did you read your personal conduct agreement?"

Swallowing, I nodded. "Yes, Sir."

"Do you accept the terms of the agreements you've already signed?"

Sanity reared its ugly head and I hesitated for a moment before asking, "Would you mind if I had a word with Colin before I answer that?"

He stared at me for a long moment. "You're sure you want to see him?"

Disconcerted by the implication that I might not like what I saw and afraid to imagine what that might be, I hesitated again. Suddenly the presence of an infirmary seemed overtly threatening.

I licked my dry lips. "Of course."

"You don't sound too sure," he observed, running a finger along my jaw and making me shiver with awareness.

"I am!"

He chuckled darkly. "Dear Rachel, that vivid imagination is going to be your one-way ticket into more delightfully frightening and nasty scenarios than you can conceive."

Fizzing with excitement and nerves, I stared after him as he turned back to the door.

"Come along, if you're brave enough. Colin's in here."

As I followed him into the mostly dark room, I couldn't help gasping at the first, most obvious thing—two Tesla coils, probably three feet tall, occupied a huge stone shelf built high into the far wall, sending out frantic purplish arcs of electricity in every direction. Well that explained the ozone smell. When I realized the arcs didn't reach past the edge of the shelf, I relaxed just a little bit again.

Until I got a look at the rest of the scene revealed by the flickering light.

"Oh boy, you really go all out for Halloween, don't you?" I said loudly, staring around me with wide eyes.

His reply was typical Julian Kilmartin. "Why do anything halfway? Atmosphere is everything, after all."

Much larger than the infirmary, the room was like a set from an old-time horror movie, filled with all the stuff you'd expect to see in a mad scientist's laboratory. Below the Tesla shelf, a long lab table was covered with an intricate maze of copper pipe, rubber tubing, Bunsen burners, racks of test tubes and half-filled beakers bubbling neon-green, as if the mad scientist had been called away midexperiment. Shelves of books and brown chemical bottles filled the wall to the left of me, and similar shelves on the right were packed with jars of preserved animals, human hands, brains and other organs—even a few heads—all subtly lit from below.

In the middle of it all was a very naked Colin, his elegant body stretched out almost upright on an inclined table, his head lolling off to one side as though he were asleep. Black cuffs secured his spread ankles to the footrest, and similar cuffs on his wrists were attached to the upper corners by red ropes.

At his side was a rolling cart with an open laptop facing away from me. The shelf below held some sort of e-stim unit, and I covered my mouth with both hands when I realized it was

hand and a teeny-tiny violet wand in the other."

Smiling reluctantly, I said, "That would have been a shock for his mother."

"Literally," he said with a grin of his own. "But probably not. His parents were kinky too."

My eyes bugged. "Really?"

Colin nodded. "A lot of brilliant people are kinky. Look at me. And you," he added.

"I'm not *kinky*," I said quickly. "I'm just..."

"A subbie little surgeon-girl who desperately needs to get her freak on with big, scary Dr. Kilmartin. And me. And whoever else Julian feels like subjecting you to." When I opened my mouth, he said, "Don't deny it, Rachel. I could see right through you five years ago and I can see through you now. You're here—not just in Julian's castle but in his dungeon. That makes you at least as kinky as the rest of us, and I'm going to enjoy the hell out of watching you finally give in to it."

The bottom fell out of my stomach. "Colin..."

"What, slave girl?"

I hesitated and then laid my hand on his bare chest, right over his heart. "You accused me once of being with you because of Julian."

"Christ, you're touching me," he groaned.

"Sorry, but I need to say this and I can't do it and not touch you."

"Then hurry up and spit it out."

"I wasn't with you because of Julian," I said quickly. "You were fascinating in your own right. I just wanted you to know that."

Colin's lips crooked. "Same goes. But can you take your hand off me now, before I come on your skirt?"

I jumped back and then scowled when he laughed. "You're not even hard."

"I don't have to be, little innocent. *Sir!*"

His shout made me jump again.

"Yes, Colin?" Julian appeared in the doorway, with Dirk and Vince right behind him.

"I think your new slave should be punished for thinking she wasn't safe with you, Sir."

Outraged, I slapped his ribs. "I didn't say that, you ass!"

Julian's eyes narrowed dangerously. "What *did* you say then, slave?"

"I just wanted to make sure that I *was* safe. I think you'd have done the same in my position."

"You do, eh?"

"I certainly do."

"So you accept Colin's word that I'm not some axe-wielding maniac?"

"Of course!"

"And you accept the terms of all the agreements you signed, including the personal conduct agreement."

I swallowed hard. "Yes, Sir."

"Then you should be properly attired."

I glanced down at the outfit I'd arrived in. "Obviously I didn't get the memo about lab costumes. And I'm pretty sure I didn't see one in my new *wardrobe*," I added with a cross look.

"That's because you're a *slave*," he growled. "If you've read your personal conduct agreement, you'll know slaves go naked in the dungeon unless I specify something for you to wear."

Oh hell. I'd conveniently forgotten that little detail.

"You may fold your clothing and give it to Master Vincent for safekeeping. Once you're properly attired, Master Dirk will restrain you so you may observe Colin's forfeit until it's time to address *your* behavior."

Staring into his uncompromising eyes, I pressed my cold,

damp palms against my skirt, completely at war with myself.

"Forfeit for what?" I asked, stalling for time.

"He lost a bet with me," Julian replied with finality. "Now, if you're having trouble following directions, slave, I'm sure Master Vincent and Master Dirk will be happy to assist you out of your clothes—although bear in mind that there may not be much left to fold when they're done. I'd do it myself, but then the fun would be over entirely too soon."

I closed my eyes, sucking in an unsteady breath. Oh God, why did the idea of being forced to do things turn me on so much?

"Rachel, I realize this is all new to you. Open your eyes and tell me your safe words."

Safe words. Right. I'd done this much once before. "Yellow and red."

"You know what they mean?"

Another shuddery breath. "Yes, Sir."

"All right then," he said. "Unless one of us hears a safe word, you'd best be undressed in ten seconds or Master Vincent and Master Dirk *will* strip you completely naked, no matter how much you scream and cry and fight. Understood?"

Relaxing even as my choices were taken away, I said, "Yes, Sir."

His arched brow sent a tremor of adrenaline through me and, operating on instinct, I slowly reached for the top button of my black cardigan...and just fiddled with it.

Part of me—surely not the good girl?—screamed at me to hurry up and get undressed before I got into trouble. The bad girl just smiled, knowing I was in trouble no matter what I did.

Julian's lips curled. "Gentlemen, I believe my little cock tease needs a helping hand...or four."

Chapter Five

It was almost a letdown when Dirk turned on his heel and disappeared through the infirmary door.

But I held my breath as Vince prowled toward me with the unblinking intensity of a predator. "Thank you, slave, for failing to cooperate," he purred. "I do enjoy helping strip a reluctant little sub."

When he moved behind me, I let out the breath I'd been holding. Then I jumped when he gave the scarf holding back my hair a sharp tug.

"Such pretty dark hair," he said, winding the navy and hunter-green silk around his hand as he came back into view.

Dirk reappeared all too soon, flipping a switch by the door as he walked by. Light fixtures on the back wall flared to life—two heavy wrought-iron sconces with flame-shaped incandescent bulbs. Between them, four chains were bolted to the stone, two long ones up high and two short ones at ankle height. An adjustable black cuff dangled at the end of each.

I put my hands behind me and glanced around for another avenue of escape. There actually was another door cut into the corner, directly in line with the one we'd entered through, but the next room was completely dark. God only knew what might await me that way. A way out, possibly—it seemed like we must have doubled back when we came through the infirmary, so the door across from my room could be in there. But I wasn't really that anxious to get away.

Yet.

"Are you wearing anything of personal value?" Dirk asked.

"No." He raised his brow and just stood there until I added,

"Sir?"

"Excellent." When he nodded at Vince, they grabbed my arms and propelled me backward to the wall, completely unaffected by my instinctive struggles. The instant I was spread-eagled in the nicely padded cuffs, something in me…settled. My pulse throbbed slowly, and my chest rose and fell visibly as my breathing deepened. Whatever happened next was no longer up to me. It was scary, but at the same time a relief. This was rather what I'd hoped to feel during my one aborted foray into the world of BDSM two years ago, only more so.

While I pondered the feeling, Julian set the clipboard on the lab table and touched something behind Colin that lowered his arms to his sides but didn't release him. Colin rolled his shoulders and flexed his arms in a mesmerizing display of lean muscle.

I forgot all about everything but Dirk when he held up a scalpel with an evil smile.

The settled feeling vanished like it had never been. "Julian?" I said nervously, unable to take my eyes off the gleaming surgical instrument.

"You asked for this, slave, remember?"

With the cold stone wall behind me and the scalpel in front of me, I drew in another breath and held it, cringing back as Dirk reached out and neatly sliced the top button off my sweater, and then the next one down. Both landed with small *tic* sounds on the cold stone floor.

I finally started breathing again—panting, actually—when he lowered the scalpel to the button between my breasts. Against all reason, they swelled anxiously, my nipples prickling and my clit throbbing a drumbeat of fierce arousal.

"Little adrenaline junkie," Dirk murmured as he flicked the button off.

A puff of laughter escaped me. "Hardly. This is the craziest thing I've ever done."

"And you're wildly turned on, aren't you? I'm a surgeon too, you know. Cardiothoracic. You have to be at least a bit of an adrenaline junkie to become a surgeon, I think." *Tic!* Another button landed on the floor.

I stared into his dark eyes, completely confused, and he smiled. "Did you know your irises have almost disappeared, little horny slave?"

Tic, tic, tic...

"Why?" I finally managed to croak.

"Why the deception?" When I nodded, he said, "Because I wanted to see the real Rachel McBride. People tend to be more open around lowly staff. Imagine my dismay when you insulted Julian's fine home before you'd even set foot inside."

Heat crept into my cheeks but I couldn't think of anything to say in my defense. Colin, I'd noticed, was watching Dirk's progress avidly, and he mouthed "bad girl" at me before grinning from ear to ear.

I stuck my tongue out at him.

Then Dirk used the scalpel to spread open my sweater, revealing the wrinkled white blouse underneath.

"You dress like a schoolgirl," he said severely. "And this afternoon you acted like a schoolgirl, saying the first thing that came to your mind, without thought for your generous host. You should be disciplined like a schoolgirl, don't you think, slave?"

Was there a right answer to that?

"Feel free to discipline her in any way you see fit for her poor manners, Dirk."

I bit my lip, cursing the arousal that slithered through my abdomen and down between my thighs.

"Thank you, Julian, I shall do that when I believe she is in the proper headspace to benefit from it."

"Excellent."

Dirk pulled my blouse from my skirt and made much better time slicing away its buttons. When he reached my ecru cami, he immediately slid the scalpel underneath and sliced it right down the front. The soft buzz of the fabric parting set my clit on fire.

"Now we're getting somewhere." He pulled the sides of my clothes apart. "Such fine, big *Titten* you hide behind all that ugly material!"

I let my head fall back against the wall, breathing heavily. Why, why, *why* did this turn me on so freaking much? I should hate the things Dirk said to me, about me. I should hate feeling like a sex object—or more to the point, a collection of sex objects.

"I told you," Colin said, his heavy eyes fixed on the *Titten* in question. His cock, which had been flaccid when I arrived, now stood at stiff attention, booby-trap apparatus and all.

"Colin!" I cried. Was there anything he *hadn't* shared about me?

His eyes didn't move, but he licked his lips. "What?"

Dirk distracted me by taking the handle of the scalpel between his teeth and yanking my bra cups down under my breasts.

I groaned, unnerved and yet unbelievably aroused to be so crudely exposed to the eyes of these men, three of whom I'd never slept with and two of whom I'd never met before today. My nipples were already tight, hard peaks begging for attention—which Dirk provided without hesitation, once he'd taken the scalpel in hand again, leaning over to tease them with his hot tongue.

Whimpering, desperately craving more, I pushed forward helplessly and he chuckled. "Your pretty little slut is dripping in her schoolgirl tights, Julian. I can smell it."

Slut. For just an instant I tensed, but arousal triumphed.

"Please."

"No manners, no patience and probably no control over her orgasm," he said scornfully. I was just starting to feel like the worst slave ever when he added, "You have years of intensive training ahead, you lucky bastard."

"One can only hope," Julian replied with a grim smile as he walked closer. Gesturing at my chest, he said, "I want this all off."

At once, Dirk sliced everything above my waist, including my bra, into ribbons.

"Was that really necessary?" I complained as he pulled the pieces off me.

"No, you mouthy little slut, but it was certainly fun," he said with a smile.

Again the word *slut* buffeted me, whipping up my emotions like a high wind on water. I bit my tongue. *I'm not a slut.*

Then Julian touched me for the first time. He laid the fingertips of his long, narrow right hand on my collarbone, letting them rest there for a moment before ghosting them up over my throat and chin to explore the contours of my lips.

Then he laid both hands on my waist. "Kiss me, Rachel."

All the breath rushed out of me and my heart thumped crazily while I stared at him as if I'd never seen him before. Which I hadn't, at least not from this close and not in any circumstances where I felt free to study him. His face was much larger than I'd imagined, his bold nose longer, his chiseled lips fuller and the cleft in his stubborn chin deeper. It was a distinguished face. A heroic face.

A face I had permission to kiss.

Before he had a chance to change his mind, I stood on my toes and pressed my hungry mouth to his. My eyes closed and my mind emptied of everything but tactile awareness of Julian—his soft lips, his smooth-shaven chin nudging mine, his quick breaths gusting against my cheek...

Julian. He was real to me now, in every way.

I don't know why I was startled when his lips parted and the kiss turned sexual. His tongue made an arrogant foray into my mouth, sparking fires much farther south in my anatomy, and I groaned with excitement. Before I could respond in kind, he captured the edge of my bottom lip between his teeth, holding it as if declaring ownership.

Everything in me stilled, and I stood there acquiescent, breathing in the clean, masculine scent of him and starkly aware that his claim encompassed far more than that tender bit of skin.

Then my stomach growled and he released my lip abruptly as his grip on my waist tightened.

"Did you eat your dinner before you escaped?" he demanded.

"Um...no?"

His eyes narrowed to slits. "What am I going to do with you, slave? You neglected to read your contracts, you insulted my castle, you left your room without permission, you refused to undress and now I find out you didn't eat the meal I provided for you?"

"I'm s—"

"The list of your transgressions grows rather alarming, doesn't it, slave?" When I nodded miserably, he said, "Real punishment, unfortunately for us both, will have to wait until tomorrow night since I committed to showing you only pleasure this evening."

I didn't see anything unfortunate about it but thought it best to keep that to myself.

"You hang there and be quiet until I come up with some sort of correction that's appropriate for the offense. Now get her stripped," he barked at Dirk, stepping away from me. "We have unfinished business with Colin."

Thirty seconds later, I was completely naked, all my clothes in shreds on the floor in front of me.

"Now, where were we?" Julian said, all business again as he reached behind Colin's table.

Colin sighed when his arms were pulled up again. "As if you'd forget, Sir."

"Did you just roll your eyes at me, Colin?"

"No, Sir!"

"Are you contradicting me now?"

Colin sighed again. "No, Sir."

"I have two disobedient slaves desperately in need of correction, Dirk."

"Indeed you do."

"I'd planned to let him fuck her tonight after all," Julian said, "but if I do, I'll be rewarding someone's misbehavior."

"*Sir!*" Colin whined. *Whined.*

"Dirk, if you please."

Dirk walked over to the shelves on the right. Opening a case I hadn't noticed before, he picked up something that looked kind of like an electric carving knife with a comb instead of blades and plugged it into a wall outlet. When he twisted the knob on the bottom, the comb began to glow neon pink.

Oh hell, a violet wand. I'd never seen one, but I knew enough about them to go tense all over. I hated static shocks from the laundry—the violet wand was bound to be a hell of a lot worse than that.

"Hello again, Colin." Dirk swept the comb slowly up the side of Colin's abdomen, skirting the light brown arrow of his chest hair. I couldn't tell if it was touching him or not, but small pink sparks arced from comb teeth into his skin, and Colin and I both gasped.

"Are you sure that's safe?" I asked tremulously.

Julian glared at me. "Was I unclear when I told you to be quiet, slave?"

"No, but—"

"Do you honestly believe I would endanger the health of anyone in my care?"

"Not deliberately, no."

"You think I'm incompetent then," he said stiffly.

My eyes widened in alarm. "Of course not, Sir!"

"There's no *of course* about it, slave—either you trust me or you don't. Or perhaps you're back to thinking I'm a maniac?"

I bit my lip. "I'm sorry, Sir. Of course I don't think that. I'm just... I don't want anything bad to happen to Colin."

"Why thank you, Rachel."

"However big an ass he is," I added meanly, unwilling to let Colin make too much of my concern.

He just grinned.

"Your next assignment, slave—and those are beginning to pile up already too, aren't they?—will be to write a one-thousand-word research paper on the violet wand, due at breakfast one week from today."

I sighed. "Yes, Sir. I assume I'll be given the code for Internet access?"

"Of course. But for now, just to set your mind at ease, the wand doesn't send current through the body, just across the skin. Done right, it's not the least bit dangerous."

Done right. Key words there. How would I know if it was done right?

"Dirk," Julian said in a silky tone, "perhaps the little slave would feel better about the wand if she experienced it for herself."

Dirk turned immediately, switching off the wand. "It would be my pleasure."

Chapter Six

He returned to the case and switched out the glass-comb head for a slender one with a flattened ball on the end. "The mushroom probe, I think, for her first time, *ja*?"

Probe? No. No probing.

"That's what I would start with," Julian said agreeably.

Appalled, I shrank into the wall. "That's okay, I'm sure Colin's fine. He's prob—probably used to it."

"He is," Julian acknowledged. "In fact, not to put too fine a point on it, he's addicted to it, aren't you, fuckhole mine?"

"Yes, Sir, I am."

Already overwhelmed with questions, I filed away the *fuckhole* reference and stared at Colin in the flickering dark. "Really? You enjoy it that much?"

"Rachel, if I didn't, he wouldn't do it. Much," he added with a grin.

I glared at him. "Not helping."

Fully expecting Dirk to start probing sensitive areas, I cringed when he came close, but he drew the probe down my inner forearm, barely touching my skin. The effervescent sensation raised the hairs on my arms and made me shiver. It was like really dry champagne on my tongue, disappearing before I could even swallow.

"There was no spark," I said inanely.

"There won't be on a low setting," Dirk said, "especially when the electrode is touching your skin. More power and a little distance would give you more bite." He ran it slowly over my arms, my neck, my cheek... All I felt was the pleasant effervescent tingling.

"Oh, Sir," Colin groaned. Julian was typing something into the laptop, which was also connected to the e-stim unit, and I watched, mesmerized, as Colin stiffened and began to writhe gently, his cock bobbing.

"There, that should keep him occupied while I help introduce my new slave to the pleasures of the wand," Julian said, meandering toward me. "The e-stim unit has a microphone picking up the ambient sounds in the room— voices, the discharges from the coils—and he feels them in the output level. Louder sounds mean higher intensity for my fuckhole, *don't they, Colin?*"

He shouted the last three words, and Colin went up on his toes.

"Yes, Sir," he said through clenched teeth.

All three of the sadists in the room chuckled. I could hardly stop staring at Colin's penis. What was happening to it? What did it feel like?

Julian took the wand and twisted the knob on the base. When he held the electrode close to my navel, a spark made me yelp and suck in my stomach. He zapped me again, this time on the underside of my breast. I gasped and thought about calling "yellow", but thinking was all I did.

When he brought the wand close to my other breast, I cringed as far away as the chains would let me, but Julian just grinned and followed. The spark hit my bunched-up nipple and seemed to zap straight down to my clit.

"Yellow," I squeaked.

Frowning, he drew back. "Why did you use your safe word, Rachel?"

"Because I'm...scared, Sir."

He cocked a brow. "Do you honestly believe that I'll really hurt you?"

"Well, no. But, Sir—"

"I can plainly see your sweet little shaved pussy raining cream down your thighs, slave. You're completely turned on by this."

Exactly. That was what scared me.

"Don't safe-word again unless you're genuinely frightened or in pain, or you'll suffer consequences you won't enjoy. Are we clear on that, slave?"

"Yes, Sir."

He leaned toward Dirk and murmured something too low for me to hear. Dirk took the wand, and when he returned with some kind of cord plugged into it where the electrode had been, Julian stripped off his lab coat, leaving his long, pale arms bare. Then he tucked the metal tube at the end of the cord into the waistband of his pants.

When he nodded, Dirk turned the wand back on and stood there holding it.

Julian reached out and trailed the fingers of one hand ever so lightly down my ribs, and I inhaled sharply as tickly shocks of sensation zapped me. Holy Christ, he'd electrified himself.

He did it over and over, painting my ribs, my abdomen, the insides of my arms and my armpits with continuous streams of little shocks while I gasped and giggled, jerking in my bonds.

"Hold still, slave, or I'll have to tighten your restraints."

"I'm trying, Sir," I defended. When he just looked at me, I steeled myself. "Okay, holding still."

"I think you'll enjoy this," Julian said. Then he brushed my stiff nipples with his index fingers.

I jerked hard. "Oh my God."

The streams of hot, tingly sensation were unbelievable, drawing the mysterious connection between my nipples and my clit tighter and tighter.

He pulled his fingers bare millimeters away and the shocks became more intense as he traced them in tiny circles. It felt

intensely pleasurable, is the perfect pitch I'll strive for each time we play, but to find it I'll have to cross it a little and then back into it. And as with the guitar, your tolerances will have to be constantly fine-tuned. They aren't uniform over your entire body, nor are they static, if you'll forgive the pun. Like guitar strings, your limits will stretch over time and be affected by a host of other influences, such as your skin condition, general health and mood. The settings that are too high tonight might feel blissful tomorrow and not be high enough the next day.

"Establishing your tolerances will be a constant challenge for both of us, and we have to be able to trust each other—you'll have to trust me to back off when it becomes too much, and I'll have to trust you to safe-word if I'm not backing off enough. Do you understand?"

"Yes," I said warily.

"Now, for your pretty wet cunt, I intend to start again at the wand's lowest setting and work my way up to that perfect pitch. Do you think you can let me do that?"

As he spoke, I'd relaxed a bit. But that didn't mean I was ready to keep going.

"What is it that's worrying you, really?" he asked, watching me closely.

"I...I just..." I shook my head. "I don't know. I feel like I'm about to jump off a cliff and I don't know what's at the bottom, or even if there is one. What if I just keep falling?"

Julian leaned forward and wrapped his arms around me, holding me close with one hand at the small of my back and rubbing the other in comforting circles over my butt. Resting his chin between my breasts, he looked up at me, his eyes luminous in the flickering light.

"Darling Rachel, *I'm* at the bottom," he said. "I've waited seven incredibly long, difficult years for the opportunity to catch you when you let go, and I think you've been waiting for it too. But you have to let go first. You have to give yourself to me and trust me not to let you fall too far."

"But how will you know? We haven't discussed my hard limits, or soft limits, or anything else," I protested.

His stare intensified. "Can you trust me, little slave, just for tonight, to be watching and listening for what you need? Can you accept without proof that I'll know your limits and respect them, even if I push them a bit?"

That was asking a lot and I wasn't at all sure that I could give it to him, but I wanted to try.

I nodded. "Okay, I think I'm ready."

"Then grasp the chains as instructed and don't let go."

He nodded at Dirk and I watched, tense with anticipation and dread, as his finger hovered over my mons and then drew close enough to deliver a snapping shock. I gasped and twisted at the sharp tingling, but Julian persisted, skimming his finger all over my pubic mound and down the creases of my thighs. It tickled and stung and drove me wild with need, and just when I least expected it, Julian leaned down and started teasing between my arousal-slick nether lips with his electrified tongue.

I squealed, panting and gasping, squeezing my eyes shut as I writhed in my bonds, but he never let me get away for more than a heartbeat.

"Take it up," he murmured.

When I realized what he meant, I opened my eyes. "No!"

It was too late. Sharper shocks seared my inner labia and clit as his tongue moved restlessly up and down, and I screamed with fear and frantic arousal. My chest heaved while strange, painful twitches pulled me tighter and tighter. Then my legs began to shake and I went up onto my toes.

"Oh Christ, I'm going to come!"

Hot fingers pushed up into me as Julian's tongue finally made full, lavish contact with my clit.

The orgasm streaked through me like an electrified blade,

tearing me open, making me gush sensation with every hard contraction. I thought I screamed but the only thing I heard was the pounding in my ears and a choked gurgling as the upheaval in my body went on and on. When it began to wane, I felt links of cool chain slipping slowly through my hands and then I hung free, floating away on clouds of emptiness. Not the bad kind of emptiness, but the good kind, where there was no emotional clutter, no conflict, no pressure, no indecision.

Was this what heaven was like?

A hand cupped my head and I opened my eyes. Julian was leaning into me, his face against my ear. "I desperately need to fuck you, my beautiful slave, and Colin and I are both disease-free."

"I'm on the pill, so please fuck me, Sir," I mumbled immediately.

He backed away far enough to free himself, dragged me up the wall by my butt and then set me on the head of his hard cock. I instinctively wrapped my legs around his waist, moaning at the thick, delicious intrusion as I sank onto him. And sank. And sank.

My eyes flew open and I stiffened my legs, trying to resist the downward pull. He was *huge*, shoving into every crevice and making my already tender opening sting. "Oh my God, Julian, stop!"

Breathing hard into my neck, he paused. "Safe word?"

I thought for a second. "Yellow."

He shuddered. "All right."

As he hovered there, leaving me teetering on the edge of pain, the edge retreated a bit and I began to relax my legs, but he held me up.

"I think it's okay now, Sir," I whispered.

Instead of letting me sink, he thrust up a bit and then groaned. "Still okay?"

"Yes, Sir."

"Thank God. Dirk, get behind her."

I blinked in confusion when Julian pulled me away from the wall so Dirk could slip in behind me.

Still breathing harshly, he explained, "This could get rough. I don't want your back bruised by the wall."

How thoughtful. "Thank you, Sir."

"Don't thank me yet."

I realized what he meant almost at once. Julian gave me no further quarter, squeezing my butt cheeks almost painfully as he fucked me deep and hard. It didn't exactly hurt, but the sensation of his big cock bottoming out in me sparked an internal ache that made me moan and squirm. Then Dirk's hands found their way to my breasts and squeezed roughly, and I finally noticed the hard ridge against my lower back. The realization that I was smashed between two fully clothed, fully aroused male bodies sent my mind drifting off on heavenly currents again.

Julian paused long enough to heft me up a little higher and I opened my eyes. Over his shoulder, I could see Colin staring at us with hungry, tortured eyes, and I wished it was him behind me, pushing his stiff cock into me.

Then Dirk began tweaking my nipples, pulling on them, twisting them to the point of pain, and I gasped as heat splashed down into my already aching pussy.

Julian groaned, increasing the pace of his pounding. "You feel so good," he gasped. "So clean."

The odd comment caught my attention. Okay, clean was good.

Dirk forced one hand downward between Julian and me, and then his fingertips made contact with my clit, rubbing hard, sure circles on it.

"Come on your Master's cock, naughty little cunt," he ordered.

Almost against my will, I obeyed, throwing my head back

against his shoulder and howling as I came again.

Julian's groans grew choked, his pace blistering as he forced me back into Dirk.

Dirk didn't let up on my clit. "Again," he barked, pinching my nipple ruthlessly.

With Julian's cock swelling and throbbing inside my poor, swollen pussy, his broken cries in my ear, I half screamed and half sobbed as I came one more time.

I had no idea how much time had passed when I finally floated up to awareness curled up on Julian's lap. We were still in the mad scientist's lab. Someone must have brought in a chair.

"Are you cold?" Julian asked. When I shook my head, snuggling into his warmth and savoring the strokes of his hand over my back, Vince brought me a bottle of clear Gatorade from a small refrigerator under the lab table, which I hadn't noticed because it was black like the cabinets.

"Drink it all," Julian ordered. "And be careful to moisturize your skin every day. I enjoy electrical play and indulge myself quite often, but it tends to be very drying."

He turned me on his lap until my back was against him and I fully faced Colin. Then he held out his hand so that Dirk could squeeze a large blob of aloe gel into his palm. While I drank, he rubbed the gel into my torso with both hands, lingering over my still-sensitive nipples. The scent of ozone wafted from my warming skin.

Vince took the empty bottle as soon as I'd drained it, and then Julian curved my hands around the seat of the chair.

"Don't let go," he ordered, pulling my thighs apart until my toes touched the floor on either side of us. When I squirmed, suddenly feeling too exposed, he said, "Leave them that way. He enjoys the view."

As his hands resumed their slow exploration of my tender breasts, weighing and squeezing, he nuzzled my neck and ear.

"You smell exactly as I always imagined you would," he murmured.

My breath caught at one sharp pinch. "Like ozone?"

"Mmm-hmm. Ozone and hyacinth and hot, sticky cunt."

An odd confusion of embarrassment, excitement and intense pleasure prickled its way up my chest and neck. "I always wondered how you tasted," I confessed.

He rumbled his pleasure. "Believe me, little slave, I want you to find out. But not tonight."

Julian reached down and, over Colin's growl of protest, turned one of the knobs on the e-stim unit. I stared in unconcealed fascination as Colin's cock bobbed and twitched, and his stomach and thigh muscles repeatedly tensed and released.

In return, Colin's eyes traced laser-hot tracks from my face to the wide-open split of my legs, leaving me as hot and throbbing as if he'd actually touched me.

"You keep your pussy bare now," he grunted. "I like it. I *want* it. I want it, I want it, I *want* it, Sir, *please.*"

"I know you do, but you'll be no use to Rachel in that condition," Julian said. He held out his right hand for more aloe gel and immediately lavished it on the swollen, tingling folds of my pussy, massaging my inner lips and clit with unmistakable intent.

I groaned. "Not again, Sir, please."

"Oh, I think yes, slave."

With his other hand, he adjusted the knobs again before returning to tweak my nipples.

Colin whined deeply, panting, writhing, all but dancing in his bonds. His cock looked incredibly swollen, like an overstuffed sausage about to burst its casing as it moved up and down in long sweeping bobs that seemed almost deliberate. From this height, I could finally see a pink gel ring squeezing the base of his cock and scrotum.

Julian's fingers slid over me harder, faster, deeper, and it dawned on me that he intended to make us both come at the same time. Arousal seared me like the lightning still crackling from the Tesla coils, making me tense and arch.

"Ah fuck, *pleeeeeease...*" Colin cried.

Julian tweaked another knob and Colin whimpered, and then let loose a series of hoarse shouts as semen trickled from his cock in long, hard contractions.

The sight was enough to pull me over the edge along with him. Even as I imagined the taste and regretted the waste of his come, I was seized by orgasmic contractions that left me breathless. Julian didn't let up on me until Colin hung motionless in his restraints, seemingly dead to the world.

Chapter Seven

I knelt on my bed, rubbing more moisturizer into Colin's torso and arms as I watched him drift in a light sleep. I thought I'd never in my life witnessed anything so unbelievably sexy as his reluctant orgasm at Julian's hands—except without the hands, or stimulation of any kind besides the electrodes on him and inside him.

Then I'd witnessed the aftermath and been utterly blown away.

Sitting in a comfortable chair Dirk brought me from another room, I'd watched with fascination as Julian removed some kind of ring from just below the head of Colin's penis and carefully extracted a long, slim electrode from his urethra. Colin had jumped and whimpered when Julian reached under his scrotum and slowly pulled out a massive metal butt plug electrode.

"Wow," I'd mouthed. And, "Ow." The thought of it made my cheeks clench together even now. There'd better not be anything like that in store for me.

Vince, whom I'd lost track of at some point, appeared with a pair of sweats and helped a groggy-looking Colin step into them. Then he'd handed him a bottle of water and nudged him toward Julian's outstretched arms.

Looking at me with a strange combination of wicked mischief and self-consciousness, Colin had cracked open the water as he settled onto the lap I'd occupied only moments before and let Julian perform the same moisturizing ritual he'd performed on me. He had the water gone in no time flat and let the bottle drop to the floor as he relaxed into Julian's hands.

It was indescribably beautiful to watch. Julian kept his nose against Colin's neck and jaw as he worked, as if he couldn't bear to be denied the scent of his skin. Half-naked, Colin looked small sprawled out on top of Julian's fully clothed body. Seeing their faces side by side, he looked younger and softer too. They were almost a study in opposites—and they clearly loved and trusted each other deeply. Why had it never occurred to me five years ago that they might be lovers?

Because I would have been devastated, that's why. I'd be devastated right now if I hadn't been exactly where Colin was just a few minutes earlier, if Julian hadn't played with me as though I were every bit as much his toy. I reminded myself sternly that they'd been together for years, while I'd been here less than a day—it would be foolish to believe what I'd experienced with Julian was the same kind of love.

But my unruly heart couldn't help hoping it might be someday.

Julian slid one of his big hands into the front of Colin's sweats and massaged his genitals, pulling rumbling groans from deep inside him. Colin didn't open his eyes, but simply undulated in time with the bold strokes.

Then Julian pressed Colin's chin toward him and claimed his mouth in a blunt declaration of carnal ownership.

That's when I'd started to feel the resurgence of tingly arousal.

As if he had some kind of hotline to my hormones, Julian grinned at me when he gave Colin a final lick and pulled away. "I think you'd better take Rachel to bed now, Colin. She looks lonely."

"Yes, Sir," Colin replied in a drowsy tone. A chuckling Dirk had helped him off Julian's lap, and he and Vince had half carried him to my room while I gave Julian the soft kiss good night he'd asked for with a crooking finger and a pucker.

Then I'd wandered to my room, completely bemused and

only vaguely aware that I was totally naked.

Colin finally opened his eyes and smiled. "Rachel."

I smiled back. "Colin."

He sighed and cupped my cheek. "Jesus, I've missed you so much."

I blinked. "Really?"

"Really."

He pulled me down and gave me the long, leisurely tongue kiss I'd dreamed about long after he vanished from my life. Colin kissed like he had all the time in the world for it, like kissing was all there was, and I'd adored it. He was such a bad boy and yet such an attentive kisser. Maybe that's why so many women were attracted to bad boys—they were the only ones who really knew how to kiss.

And Colin *was* a bad boy, at least in my mind, and I'd thought so long before we were lovers. He'd acted like he was exempt from the rules that governed the rest of us, always so full of pent-up energy he seemed like a bomb about to go off. He was constantly cutting in line at the cafeteria, not paying for fruit he grabbed on his way out, showing up late for rotations and usually looking as though he'd just come off a hard night's drinking, telling his patients and their families to ignore visitation hours, bringing in fast food for diet-restricted patients...

He got away with it all because he was so brilliant and charming and Dr. Kilmartin's prize resident. His brazenness pissed me off on an almost hourly basis, but I just bit my tongue and waited for him to finally get what was coming to him.

Then one day he'd turned those devastating blue eyes on me and asked me out. Taking my wide-eyed shock as acceptance, he'd dragged me to his beat-up old Camaro, picked up a pizza he'd already ordered at a drive-through window, rolled two stop signs on the way to my apartment and gotten me under him in my bed, graying out from multiple orgasms, that very evening.

Bad, bad boy, Colin Carter was.

As if to prove it, he pushed his sweats down and kicked them off without breaking lip contact. He pulled me over him with a sigh and I spread my thighs around his hips, rocking eagerly as the kiss heated up.

Breaking away, he breathed, "Ride me, Rachel."

I sat up. "Really?"

"Why do you keep asking that?" he asked. "Of course, really."

"Well you never let me be on top when we were together before."

"I was always too impatient," he said with a sleepy-eyed smile, molding my breasts with his hands. "That's why Julian turned my gonads inside out earlier, so I could take my time and do more then bend you over the bed and fuck you brainless."

Hot lust erupted in my belly. "I never minded."

"And I loved that about you, trust me," he murmured. "Now back up and get on my cock, slave. I feel like letting you do all the work for a change."

I complied without hesitation and nearly cried with happiness as my swollen, tender opening spread to accept his lovely cock. "Oh God!"

His stomach jumped with a low laugh. "No, it's just me. Are you all right?" he asked, searching my face avidly. "Is this too much tonight?"

"Mmm, no, I'm good. It feels...really good." But I appreciated his asking. There was a time he wouldn't have.

He stroked my nipples with his thumbs. "You missed me too, didn't you, Rachel?"

Looking down at him through my lashes, I said, "Maybe."

"Admit it or I'll get on top and make you."

"Okay, I missed you." I let my hands slide up his furry chest. "A lot."

Tears spurted down my cheeks before I even knew they were coming. Horrified, I tried to turn away, but his hold on my breasts tightened and I gasped as the tears ran faster. "I'm sorry, I don't know why I'm crying."

Colin slid a hand up behind my neck and pulled me down, hugging me. "Shh, it's okay. It's normal to experience sub drop after an intense scene, and it was your first time. I'd be surprised if you didn't drop at least a little. Just relax and let me hold you."

"Okay," I choked.

I lay there, breathing deeply and dripping tears on his shoulder for a long while, comforted by his hand sweeping slowly over my back. Why wasn't he this nice five years ago? On second thought, it was probably a good thing he wasn't, otherwise I'd have been completely in love with him, instead of just a little bit in love with and a lot wary of him. That would have made his vanishing act hurt a lot more.

Of course, if he'd been nicer, he might not have pulled the vanishing act in the first place.

I sighed, licking a tear off his skin. Then I noticed that his erection, still firmly buried inside me, hadn't flagged in the least and giggled.

"What?" he demanded suspiciously.

I giggled again. "You're—" yet another giggle erupted, "—you're still *hard*!"

He chuckled. "Well yeah. I'm not done yet."

"Aren't a woman's tears supposed to be the biggest boner-killer ever?"

"Only if a guy's a pussy," he snorted. "Trust me, it would take a lot more than a little salt water to kill this boner. So are you going to ride me or do I get to be on top now?"

I pushed up immediately. "I'm riding."

"Then get busy, slave."

Colin let me ride him to the breathless end, but true to form, he managed to get a finger deep into my butt with just the secretions from my body. I think it was still there when I fell asleep.

The next morning I woke before sunrise without a trace of new-place disorientation. Colin was still sawing logs behind me, and I snuggled back into his fragrant warmth, wide-eyed with wonder.

Last night had *happened*. After all these years of waiting and wishing, I'd been thoroughly mastered by the larger-than-life man of my dreams, and then crawled into bed with the only other man who'd ever really meant anything to me. And the two of them were engaged in their own D/s relationship.

It was like a neon triangle that had only been lit on two sides and the third had finally flared to life last night, creating a radiantly complete shape.

What kind of triangle it was, I couldn't say. Ideally it would be an equilateral, with three equal sides, but at the moment it felt more scalene, with the longest, brightest line connecting Julian and Colin, and the shortest and most tentative connection between Julian and me.

This line between Colin and me, though—it just felt right, as if we'd only been apart for days instead of years. As if we'd always been together and always would be.

It occurred to me that I still loved Colin, and more than just a little. I *loved* him. Madly.

My feelings about Julian were less clear, which made me almost glad he hadn't joined us in bed last night. But I was *so* glad I'd waited to experience dominance and submission with him first. He was everything I'd ever hoped for, times a thousand.

It scared me now to remember how close I'd come to giving my submission to someone else.

Almost two years ago, when the need to know had grown too difficult to ignore, I'd begun researching and exploring the lifestyle online and met Master Rod in a BDSM chat room. He was just the right mix of inquisitive, funny, protective and masterful, and when we started Skyping—without video at first—I'd discovered he had a British accent, which I'd received as almost a sign from God. He was as close as I was going to get to Julian without actually having Julian.

Then we'd added video, and the long brown hair trailing around his shoulders had kind of spoiled the effect. I'd told myself to snap out of it—he wasn't Julian and it wouldn't be fair to either of us to pretend he was. I'd gradually succumbed to his encouragement and begun doing things—sexual things, out of sight of the webcam—that would have curled my mother's hair, and when we finally agreed to meet, I thought I was ready. I met him at the airport when he flew in from a business meeting in New York and was giddy with excitement and nerves when he took me out for a very nice dinner.

Then he took me to a private BDSM club, where he had some kind of reciprocal membership with a London club. He offered to show me around, let me watch others scening on the main floor, but I was too impatient. I'd watched plenty of scenes online—now I wanted to be the one scening.

Sensitive to my newness, he'd taken me to a private room—private being a relative term, since there was no door. Once there, he'd shown me a flogger and described what he intended to do, then told me to undress. As I did, an overpowering sense of wrongness had gripped me. I told myself it was just cold feet, like those most every bride got right before she married her Mr. Right, and forced myself to let him cuff me to a cross, facing him.

When he straightened, he took one look at my face and

said, "You don't have to do this, little Rae. I won't be angry."

I'd burst into tears and he immediately unhooked me, dragging me to an easy chair on the dark periphery of the main room and holding me while I sobbed out my longing for a man who didn't even know I was alive and never would. I apologized profusely, feeling like a complete idiot, but he just shushed me, rubbing my back and saying he felt privileged to have met me, that he was envious and that any Dom would be thrilled to hold the heart of such a devoted sub. His presence was so strong and comforting, it didn't even dawn on me until we stood up to leave that I was stark naked in a semipublic place.

When the taxi dropped me off at my apartment, he'd walked me to the door and told me not to give up on my dreams, that life had a way of giving us what we wanted when we least expected it.

But keeping the faith had seemed impossible—not to mention pointless—and after that night I'd basically given up on my need for submission, just packed it away like a bride who was left at the altar packs away her wedding dress.

Since then, my world had been a little bit grayer, a little bit more stressful.

But the minute I opened my door to Colin, color had begun to bleed back in, and now the world seemed positively vibrant. I was so happy I wanted to hop out of bed naked, break out my guitar and dash off a silly little love song about it.

It was too cold for that, so I just lay there in the waxing dawn and basked in the feeling of being in Colin's arms again.

When he woke with an impressive erection, I turned around before he could slide it into the nearest available opening and put my hand on his chest. "So what was the bet?"

Tucking his arm under his head, he gave me a heavy-lidded look. "What bet?"

"Last night. Julian said you were paying some kind of forfeit because you'd lost a bet."

"Oh, that bet. Before you arrived, I bet that you'd read your contracts word for word before signing them and knew what you were getting into. He bet you hadn't." He cupped my face, stroking my lips with his thumb as he eyed me with a rueful grin. "You picked a hell of a time to start breaking the rules, Rachel McBride."

"I'm sorry. And the forfeit?"

"He got to fuck you first, and I got to come down my leg when all I wanted was to come in you."

Wow, I'd never been the stakes in a bet before—at least not that I knew of. "What if you won?"

"He'd have fucked you first and I wouldn't have had to come down my leg before I came in you."

"So Julian wouldn't have had to pay any kind of forfeit?"

Colin smiled. "Nope. Besides, he hoped he was wrong, so either way he'd come out the winner."

"That hardly seems fair."

"He's the Dom, Rachel."

The words thrilled me, especially knowing Julian was the Dom of both of us.

"Let me make it up to you." Pushing him to his back, I threw back the covers, intent on relearning all the intimate things I'd once known about his body. I started licking and sucking at his earlobes and worked my way down his neck to his cute little nipples.

By the time I reached his eager cock, he was already groaning, so I grasped the root and sucked the head into my mouth, swirling my tongue around it sensuously.

He hissed with pleasure. "God yes! I've missed that."

Almost teary-eyed, I pulled off him and whispered, "Me too."

I started to go back down and paused, tipping my head to the side. It looked like he had a tattoo around his cock, just

"Yes, Sir," I said hurriedly. "Thank you very much, Sir. I'm starving."

"Because you didn't eat the dinner I provided for you last night," he reminded me with another frown. "I'm still thinking on a punishment for that one, though I suppose going hungry qualifies as its own punishment. Don't do it again."

"Yes, Sir."

Lili placed a plate of scrambled eggs, bacon and wheat toast in front of me and I thanked her before tucking into them.

"So, do you have questions this morning, Rachel?" Julian asked as he spread jam on his toast.

God, where to start? "Colin said I had to ask you about the tattoo on his penis."

"I knew she'd go right for that one," Colin murmured before sipping his coffee.

Julian sighed. "That's a rather distressing story that begins the day of Colin's thoughtless words to you five years ago, when he goaded you about your attraction to me."

I listened with wide eyes and a full mouth as he continued, "We hadn't become lovers yet, but he was living in my house and I'd been playing my sadistic little games with him for more than a year. I'd just received some shocking news and was already planning on taking him further, being a little more brutal with him, than I ever had before. Which wasn't a prudent call on my part, I know, but he'd been begging for it for weeks so why not satisfy us both?"

Breathless and nerve wracked, I gulped down the last of my eggs.

"I was even planning on fucking him, though I'd intended to save that until his residency ended. I'd wanted to make it a special occasion we'd both remember fondly. But I needed him that night, and the occasion was momentous enough to warrant a change of plans. Do you know what happened, Rachel, when Colin came home and confessed what he'd said to you, that he'd hurt you?"

I shook my head, almost afraid to hear.

"I beat him within an inch of safe-wording and then made him my sweet, dirty fuckhole. I rode his beautiful, hellishly striped and bruised virgin ass until he screamed himself hoarse. Isn't that right, fuckhole mine?"

"Yes, Sir," Colin said. "Thank you, Sir."

"Don't ever thank me for that, Colin," Julian said sharply. "I wasn't proud of myself afterward, and I still regret that our formal relationship started with violence, not to mention such a lack of control and rational thought on my part. If I'd realized you were provoking me out of jealousy—"

Colin's eyes widened. "Sir, I—"

"Don't bother denying it or I'll have you caned again for lying. I played right into your hands and if I hadn't been so wrecked, I might have realized it."

"Yes, Sir."

"Before I tell Rachel the rest of the story, why don't you show her your other stamp of ownership."

Colin slid me a sideways look and then rose from his chair to stand beside me, facing away. My gaze was just wandering down his long, finely muscled back, clearly outlined beneath his bright-blue polo, when I heard the clink of his belt buckle and the buzz of his zipper.

When he dropped trou, I dropped jaw. He was wearing low-rise, white-trimmed, bright-blue underwear that left most of his spectacular buttocks bare.

Even more shocking, there was actually a tattooed stamp, probably five inches in diameter, spanning the lower part of both cheeks. It was made of two concentric circles with block lettering in between—on the left side it said *PROPERTY OF JXK*, and on the right was a date very near the last time I'd seen Colin.

How had I missed that in all our nude capering? I touched

the date with an awed fingertip.

"The morning after I claimed his ass, I took him to a friend of mine and had those stamps tattooed on him to remind him whom the various parts of his body belong to," Julian said with a compelling look. "He hasn't fucked anyone with that cock, in any orifice, since the last time he was with you."

My mouth worked for a second before I said, "Not even oral?"

"Not even oral."

"Good God, why not?"

Julian shrugged. "I'm a possessive man, and once I claimed him, he was never going to be allowed to fuck anyone but you anyway. I don't bottom. Ever," he added darkly. "I would have used my mouth on him, but I thought making him save his cock for you was a punishment that fit his crime."

God, that was...harsh. No wonder Colin had whined last night at the thought of not having me.

"But...*why*? We were just sleeping together."

"Rachel, you were mine for the taking from the moment we met—"

Flushing, I crossed my arms. "Excuse me, conceited much?"

"Please have the courtesy to let me finish."

When I narrowed my eyes and held my tongue, he continued, "If you're honest, you'll admit the attraction between us was instantaneous and entirely mutual."

"All right, yes," I admitted grudgingly. "It was mutual." Which made me feel only slightly better about having been so transparent.

"Thank you for your candor. So while you were clearly meant to be mine, I was a fellow and you were a resident, so any sexual relationship between us was forbidden. I could probably have gotten away with a very discreet D/s relationship like I had with Colin, but at that point in time you were too...unformed for me to feel comfortable taking advantage of our attraction."

"Unformed!" This tale just got worse and worse.

"Rachel, your residency was just beginning to shape you into the surgeon you would become, and you needed to complete it without my influence."

"That's a bunch of crap. You had nothing to do with my residency."

"Not directly, no, but I was in a position of authority at the hospital and you were very susceptible to my dominance. I couldn't chance that you might one day view yourself as some sort of Galatea to my Pygmalion."

I was floored. "Wow, you didn't think much of me, did you?"

"Don't put words in my mouth, Rachel Anne," he said calmly. "I actually thought quite highly of you—it was you who lacked confidence in yourself."

I stilled. "So?"

"So you also suffered from an overabundance of empathy with your patients and had difficulty compartmentalizing. Isn't that true?"

"Yes..." I said slowly. "At first."

"Do you think it would have been any easier for you to leave your submission to me at home than it was to leave your patients and their difficulties at the hospital?"

"I don't know." Then I thought about my gut reaction to the sight of him. "Probably not."

"I don't believe I could have left my dominance at home either, Rachel. Self-confidence and the ability to compartmentalize are vital assets for every surgeon. Without them, you burn out much too quickly, and it would have gone against every dominant instinct I had to stand back and watch that happen to you. Interference from me would only have reinforced your self-doubt, but if I'd claimed you as my submissive, I don't think I could have helped myself. Then you might have forever wondered if I were responsible for your success."

"So you gave me up for my own good," I said sourly.

"I didn't give you up. I merely bided my time. My intent was to remain on the fringes of your daily life and let Colin indulge in a little domination play with you until you were ready to be claimed, but...life had other plans."

I sighed. "You realize this whole thing is incredibly Machiavellian."

He smiled. "I'll take that as a compliment."

"Permission to sit back down, Sir?" Colin said.

Julian shifted in his chair. "First show her what belongs to me."

Sighing, Colin bent over and reached back to pull his cheeks apart. His anus was perfectly centered in the circle.

"It looks even better with my cock buried to the root in it," Julian observed. "What do you think, Rachel?"

Clearing my throat, I said, "Not long on subtlety, is it?"

"It's not supposed to be."

I squirmed in my seat, alarmed to find myself aroused again. What would it feel like to be owned so completely, and to have that ownership so proudly and explicitly proclaimed to anyone who got too close? Would I ever find out?

It was a shock to realize I was a bit jealous of Colin again. I'd always sworn I would never get a tattoo, especially after they became so trendy, but my mind immediately went to work on how an artist could possibly center one around my vagina. There was some incredibly sensitive flesh there—although there was plenty of fat too, which should make it marginally less painful. As an added bonus, my family would never have to know I had it.

Colin sighed. "Am I done here, Sir?"

"You are, but come here."

Colin tucked in his shirt and zipped up as he rounded the end of the table and then dropped easily to his knees beside Julian's chair, resting his hands on his thighs. "Yes, Sir?"

Plunging his hand into Colin's thick hair, Julian stroked his head repeatedly and watched as Colin let his head fall back with a contented moan. "Were you embarrassed to show Rachel your stamp, my darling fuckhole?"

"No, Sir. It amused me and turned me on. I mean, how often can you get away with mooning a beautiful girl, up close and personal, at the breakfast table?"

"You amuse me," Julian murmured with a smile. "Turn me on too."

"Thank you, Sir."

With his free hand, Julian took off his glasses and tossed them on the table. Then he pulled Colin forward by the neck and kissed him like he was the next breakfast course and he just couldn't get enough.

My eyes prickled and I wondered if there would ever come a time when I wouldn't find the spectacle of their kissing heartbreakingly lovely—or when I wouldn't be even a little bit jealous.

When he finally pulled away, Colin swayed before opening his eyes.

"And now," Julian said, "I suppose you'd both better finish your breakfasts so that Rachel can get her lines out of the way. We have much to accomplish today."

At nine fifteen, I walked down the hall between them, trying to shake the cramp out of my right hand. I couldn't remember the last time I'd handwritten much more than notes on a chart.

"So tell me about this surgery we're preparing for," I said as we stepped into the elevator. "Is it related to your Bain's research?"

"It is. Let's get your key to the labs and then I'll give you the full tour and explain everything as we go." He let his eyes wander down over my body—which was clad in my own conservative gray slacks and a black sweater set, thank you very much—and then raised them to mine again. "You look very competent this morning, Dr. McBride."

Uncertain what he was trying to say, I simply replied, "Thank you."

We rode down to the next level and entered a corridor that was more reminiscent of a hospital. Our first stop was a large, unlocked linen closet, where Colin picked up a lab coat for me to put on. He and Julian were both already wearing lab coats they'd pulled from his coat closet.

The next stop was a security-protected door, where Colin held up some kind of card to the scanner. When the lock released, he held the door open for me.

"We'll need to get your access set up first," he said. He hit a button on what looked like a laminating machine, and when a card similar to his popped out, he held it up in front of my face. "Lick this."

I gasped and my hands flew up to my cheeks. It was a close-up of me from last night. For God's sake, I looked like some strung-out, low-rent streetwalker—neck and shoulders bare, dark-brown hair a rat's nest, blue eyes glazed and unfocused, mascara smudged, lips wet, parted and swollen...

How in the *hell* had they managed this?

"That's your employee ID," Julian said behind me. "Lick it, please, before the biocoating sets up."

That was my *employee ID*? I spun around and gaped at him. "Absolutely not! There's no—"

Without warning, my hair was seized and twisted hard

enough to make me yelp. When my hands flew up to claw at whatever had me, the ID card was shoved far enough into my open mouth to make me gag and dragged right back out before my teeth could snap down on the evil fingers guiding it.

"Thank you," Colin said cheerfully as he released me.

Stumbling away, I put my back to the wall and stared at him while he leaned against the counter, waving the card in the air and grinning at me like an eight-year-old who'd just pulled the ponytail of a little girl he liked.

Why in God's name had I thought I loved him?

"Gorgeous picture," he said in an admiring tone. "You look like you just had your face fucked and are begging for more."

"What the hell was that?" I demanded. My scalp stung as though it had been swarmed by killer bees—and my clit was throbbing madly, dammit.

"That, Dr. McBride, was just a taste of what you will feel when you fail to follow my instructions in a timely manner," Julian said. "Normally I'll keep our professional and personal relationships completely separate, but since we're alone and time was of the essence, I felt it best to act decisively. I've been very lenient with you so far, but you need to realize there's a limit to what I'll tolerate. Now, come with me."

When he turned and walked out, I glared at Colin. "You didn't have to pull that hard, you asshat!"

"No, but I'll bet my next paycheck it made you wet," he said with a grin. When I couldn't answer, he held out the ID card. "Keep this with you at all times."

I eyed it with loathing. "I'm not using that."

Colin looked like he was fighting a laugh. "Relax, Rachel— Julian and I are the only ones with access to the identification systems. Nobody else will see it." He tucked the card into the pocket of my lab coat. "Now go, before you get yourself into more trouble."

When we caught up to Julian, he was holding open a door

labeled *Surgical Suite.* I followed him down yet another corridor and into the largest scrub room I'd ever seen. There were enough sinks for a dozen doctors to scrub in at once.

I corralled my slack jaw long enough to say, "You really don't do anything halfway, do you?"

He shrugged. "What would be the point?"

From there, we went directly into an OR that made the scrub room look small by comparison. In addition to the operating table, the room had seven remote monitoring stations, all numbered and connected by a complex, multicolored system of arrowed lines taped to the floor. Several of the lines ran into yet another OR that was just as large and complex. It almost looked like they were choreographing two different operations.

I was totally lost. "What sort of procedure will we be performing here?"

"Reciprocal transplant surgeries," Julian said. "There will be a total of seventy-six personnel in and out the operating rooms during the procedures, so we needed a well-defined system to manage them all. We've already been doing partial walk-throughs with the various teams, but now that you're here, we'll begin full walk-throughs followed by practice runs on cadavers."

"*Reciprocal* transplant surgeries?" I gaped at him. "They're going to trade organs?"

Julian shook his head. "We're going to perform the first human-head transplants."

Chapter Nine

He said it so casually, I thought he was joking. But neither he nor Colin cracked a smile.

"That's impossible."

"Nothing is impossible. If it can be dreamed, it can be done."

"But...*why*? Why would you even want to attempt something like that? Why would anyone agree to be the subject of such an experiment?"

Julian began ticking off points on his fingers. "We have a patient in the final stages of Bain's atrophy, we have a revolutionary new procedure that could give him a chance at life, and we have a viable donor. Why wouldn't we want to attempt it?"

My head was spinning. "You do realize this would require a *living* donor."

He lifted his brows. "It wouldn't make much sense to transplant the head to a dead body, would it?"

"You said *reciprocal*—that means the donor would receive the patient's dying body. You can't do that, Julian. Even if he survived the procedure, the donor would eventually die of the disease currently killing the recipient."

"The donor would be allowed to expire on the table."

I gaped at him. "Do the words 'First do no harm' ring any bells for you, *Doctor*? What you're suggesting is not only highly unethical, it's illegal as hell! You can't sacrifice one person's life to save another. *Life* being a relative term," I added acidly. "Even if you could somehow keep the recipient's vital organs functioning, he'd be completely paralyzed *forever*. What kind of life would that be? How would it be any better than suffering from Bain's?"

"The experiment is fully sanctioned by the Montanevan government. And you can't kill a dead man. The donor will have been officially declared dead before the procedure commences."

Horror crept through me, and I put my hands on my head. "Oh my God, you're serious. I just gave up a prestigious fellowship at a highly respected medical practice and flew halfway around the world for a fucking *Frankenstein experiment*?"

Colin winced. "Rachel, don't—"

I squeaked when Julian's fingers clamped on my jaw.

"Watch your mouth, Dr. McBride," he snarled in my face, his eyes glinting with fury. "If you wish to voice an opinion about my project, you may do so respectfully or not at all."

Prying at his fingers, I tried to lean away but he cupped the back of my head with his other hand.

"Let go of me!" I gasped.

"Not until you're ready to listen," he said implacably.

"I've heard everything I need to. I'm leaving, Julian. I categorically refuse to be a part of this experiment."

"You're not leaving until you've heard me out."

I sent Colin a beseeching look. "Colin, help me."

He shook his head. "I'm sorry, Rachel, but he's right. There are things you need to know before you run away."

Feeling betrayed, I said, "Fine, I'll listen but only if you take your hands off me."

Julian's jaw tensed and he looked like he might refuse, but finally his hold eased and I slid out of his grasp. I immediately walked as far away from him as I could get and still be in the same room.

Leaning back against the wall to support my shaking legs, I

crossed my arms. "I'm listening."

He sighed and forked his hands through his hair. "I apologize. I should have thought of a better way to present all this information."

"Trust me, there's no good way to present something like this, Julian," I told him flatly. "Just get on with it."

After sending me a stern look, he sighed again. "All right, let me begin by making it clear that the donor *will* die whether he participates in our experiment or not. That is not in doubt. It is an absolute certainty."

"How do you know?"

"He's scheduled to die by lethal injection at 10:00 p.m. on the day of the procedure, and there will be no last-minute clemency."

"Oh my God. Why?"

"He raped and murdered six teenage boys, one of them Prime Minister Lucescu's grandson."

My mouth worked soundlessly.

"The condemned prisoner's name is Augustine Pohlson, and he is the last of only four prisoners ever to occupy Montaneva's death row. Right now the death penalty is available only for the aggravated murder of children, but on November first, it will be abolished for all offenses so that Montaneva can join the EU."

"I'm...speechless," I finally managed. "How did you manage to arrange this?"

"Dragos Lucescu is a personal friend of mine."

Of course he was.

"And the prisoner has consented to the donation?"

"He has," Julian said with a sharp nod.

"Just like that," I said skeptically.

Colin's jaw tensed. "He made numerous demands, all of which will have been met before his execution."

"Such as?"

"There's a confidentiality agreement in place, which has been approved by the donor's legal counsel," Julian said, clearly warning Colin with both look and tone not to break it.

"Wow. That's..." I shook my head. "It would be strange enough to have to adjust to living with someone else's body, but a serial killer's?"

"Beggars can't be choosers," Julian said flatly. "The fact is, Pohlson is going to die, and not only do we know the exact time, place and manner of his death and have access to his body within minutes of cardiac arrest, but his age, size, body type and skin tone are fairly consistent with the recipient's. We'll never have a better opportunity. Why should we let his perfectly healthy body rot in the ground when it can be used to save not just the recipient, but the lives of many innocent people?"

The words made sense but something in me still balked.

"Think about it, Rachel," Colin urged. "A body is just like a gun, or a hammer, or even a shoestring—any of them can be used for good or evil. Pohlson's body was just one of his tools. The true evil resides in his brain, which will be well and truly dead once his head is severed from its blood supply."

I shook my head. "I know you're right, but I still don't know if I'd choose that life over death."

"Fortunately, you don't have to," Julian replied. "Obviously the reciprocal procedure will be considerably less involved since it's only for aesthetic purposes. We just need to provide an intact and reasonably normal-looking corpse for the grieving family to bury."

My stomach turned. "Why the whole head? If you've developed that kind of capability, why not just the brain?"

"Mainly because the recipient will wish to carry on with his own life. That would be very difficult to do wearing Augustine Pohlson's face."

"How can you possibly expect him to carry on with his life?"

I asked. "Even assuming you've discovered how to regenerate nerve axons, there's no way to fully reconnect the central nervous system once it's severed. It's just too mind-bogglingly complex and too little understood."

Julian smiled. "As a matter of fact, we *have* discovered how to regenerate nerve axons. We've already treated the patient with stem cells harvested from his own bone marrow, which were nourished with a targeted blend of bioengineered materials. The effects, unfortunately, were only temporary, but they've given us enough time to reach this milestone. After the spinal cord is microsurgically reattached, the attachment site will be treated with similarly nourished stem cells obtained from stored cord blood."

I stared at him, wide-eyed. "The recipient's parents banked his cord blood? He must be pretty young."

"Too young to die of Bain's, I promise you."

"All right, I'll accept that you're able to regenerate nerves, but properly reconnecting the entire central nervous system? No way. It just can't be done."

His smile this time was cunning. "Would you care to bet on that?"

"Thanks, but no," I said with a wary glance at Colin, who just grinned.

"All right, then. Come." Julian took my hand, his eyes alight with excitement. "I want to show you something."

The castle was much larger than it looked from the front. Once we reached the first floor, it took several minutes to walk from the northwest tower to the south wing. Before we entered the lab, I heard the yipping and whining of dogs and braced myself for all kinds of grotesque animal head transplants gone wrong.

Fortunately, all I saw was a variety of very normal dogs in

large kennels. Most of them went wild with excitement at the sight of us, jumping and pacing and barking, begging for attention.

A dark-haired man poked his head around another door and then walked in. "Colin, Dr. Kilmartin," he said enthusiastically, wiping his hands on his coveralls before offering one to Julian. "Sorry about the racket, but they're going crazy being cooped up inside and I haven't exercised them all yet."

"Not a problem, Michael," Julian said as they shook hands. "I just wanted Dr. McBride to meet our friends here."

Colin squatted by a kennel housing two very similar black toy poodles. "Victor and Hugo, meet Dr. Rachel McBride. Rachel, Victor and Hugo."

Sending him a quizzical glance, I squatted too, and reached through the chain-link door with my fingers. "Nice to meet you," I said as they both licked at me.

"Victor and Hugo were our first successful reciprocal transplant subjects two years ago," Julian said.

My eyes widened and I stared hard at their necks. I couldn't see a thing. "That can't be."

"Ah, but it is. Look at Hugo's neck. Feel it."

Colin opened the small trap door at the bottom and reached in for one of the dogs. Taking the wriggling, wagging little body, I managed to secure him in the crook of my arm long enough to get an up-close look at his neck.

"Oh my God," I breathed, tracing the barely visible scar all the way around with my fingers. "You actually did it?"

"We did. His head was originally on Victor's body and vice versa."

"I can't believe it. They're both..."

"Perfectly functional in every way," Julian finished with a satisfied smile. "In fact, both have sired a litter of puppies since the surgery."

My mind reeled as I stroked the dog's head. "But how?"

"We devised a chemical process called neurocode marking," Colin explained. "New axons tend to follow previously traced pathways, and by chemically marking them in both bodies prior to surgery, we can dictate which neural pathways the regenerated axons should follow—kind of like laying down a highly individualized trail of breadcrumbs for each of them."

I looked around. All the kennels contained pairs of almost identical dogs. "So all of these were reciprocal transplants?"

Julian nodded. "All eight pairs, yes."

"And how many more were unsuccessful?"

"At least that many," he said flatly. "But none after Victor and Hugo. None after we finally hit upon the proper neurochemical compound."

"And you believe you can achieve this same level of function in human subjects?"

"I know we can," he said. "Everything the donor body was able to accomplish, the recipient should be able to accomplish. With the exception, of course, of occupations that require a great deal of knowledge and training, such as musician, artist or surgeon. The donor body will lack muscle memory, and probably the fine motor skills, for pursuits like neurosurgery, but it's a small price to pay for an otherwise full life."

While Colin returned the dog to the kennel, Julian reached out to help me up.

I shook my head in wonder. "If this operation is successful, do you realize what it could mean?"

"Besides an untimely end to wheelchair manufacturers?"

"Julian, how can you joke about this?"

"I'm not joking. The neurocoding process alone could save thousands of people from wheelchairs every year."

"*If* it's successful."

"It will be."

I sighed. "All right, you've convinced me to stay. *But*," I added, "it's all got to be strictly by the book and documented every step of the way. You're skating on some very thin ice here, both morally and ethically, and it won't take much for everyone involved to fall through."

"I promise you, Rachel, I've documented everything thoroughly. When we get back to the—" Julian pulled his phone out of his jeans pocket and glanced at it. "Excuse me, but I really must take this. Colin, why don't you show Rachel to the exercise facilities and have Hans prepare a training schedule for her. We can resume our tour after lunch."

Bangenschloss was bursting at the seams with sadists.

Hans, it turned out, was a buff, blond sadist of the personal trainer variety who didn't let the fact that I'd just flown in the previous day stand in the way of his plan for salvaging my pathetic physique. When Colin made it clear we had nowhere to be until lunch at one o'clock, Hans ordered me to the locker room to change into my workout clothes. I was simultaneously thrilled and terrified to inform him I hadn't brought any.

Then I was simultaneously irked and relieved to be informed my locker was stocked with everything I needed for an effective workout, including cross-training shoes.

Apparently shirts didn't number among the things I needed for my workout to be effective. I slunk out of the locker room feeling conspicuously naked in black spandex pants and a white sports bra. Colin had changed too, but he got to wear loose shorts and a wife-beater.

Grinning like the rat he was, he went straight to the treadmill and started at a slow jog.

Hans went straight for my vital statistics, humming and clucking and generally looking very concerned as he jotted down measurements for my height, weight, thighs, hips and waist.

When he got to my bust, I was surprised and a little unnerved to see an appreciative smile curving his lips. "*Reichliche Titten*," he murmured, as the backs of his fingers brushed over them. "I cannot wait to see them freed of such confinement."

I rolled my eyes. "You wouldn't happen to be related to Dirk, would you?"

His smile widened. "*Ja*. He is my brother."

Great. Did that mean there was a chance he'd actually see my breasts freed of their confinement?

The idea was less intimidating than intriguing, which disturbed me a bit. One day into the lifestyle and I was already shedding inhibitions at an alarming rate.

After Hans wrote down the measurements, he pulled out calipers and began assessing my body fat, which almost made me want to go back to bust measuring. That, at least, had made him smile.

"Soft," he pronounced, with a scowl, "which is splendid *für irhe Titten*, but not so much *für ihre Arme*. We will fix."

"Don't go overboard on the arms yet," said Colin, who'd already moved on to the strength-training machines. "She has to be able to operate for at least the next couple of weeks."

"*Ja, ja*," Hans muttered with a roll of his hazel eyes.

He put me on the treadmill for a ten-minute "warm-up" that left me gasping for air and then proceeded to torture me with circuit training, alternating between sets on the leg, ab and back machines and short bursts on the treadmill. Then I went head-to-head with the BOSU ball, but by that time my leg muscles were already trembling too much to maintain balance and the ball kicked my butt.

"Pussy," Hans snorted, squatting beside me when I flopped out on my back.

"Is that a request?" I joked, still gasping for breath.

"Is that an offer?" he countered, laying his big hand between my legs without waiting for confirmation.

I rolled away, jackknifing to a sitting position. "I was kidding!"

He shrugged and stood up. "If you've been properly introduced to Dirk, you should know better than to tease a German."

"He's right." Colin pulled me to my feet and handed me a small towel. "Germans are pretty hardcore."

Still eyeing Hans with distrust, I said, "I'll keep that in mind."

To my dismay, they both followed me into the locker room and proceeded to strip out of their workout clothes, which took only seconds.

"Unless you want to meet Julian for lunch smelling like that," Colin said, "I'd suggest you get naked and get in the shower, Rachel." He started toward me. "Or do you need help again?"

I could only stand there with my heart pounding in my throat while he dug his fingers under the sweat-soaked band of my bra and pulled it off over my head. Then I grabbed his naked shoulders when he squatted to yank off my shoes and socks, and then stripped down my pants and panties with one sharp tug.

And just like that, I was naked with two naked men, one of them a veritable stranger. Again.

"Pretty," Hans said with an appreciative tug at his erect cock. "Very pretty."

I winced when Colin pulled the band out of my hair and took several strands with it.

"Shower," he said, nudging me forward. "Now."

Giving Hans a wide berth, I darted into the next tiled room, which was equipped with several showerheads along one wall and corresponding sinks and mirrors on the opposite wall. At the far end of the room were two doors, one wood and the other glass, which I assumed led to a sauna and steam room.

And in the middle of the floor was a gigantic sunken hot tub filled with steaming, roiling water. The sight of it made me groan with longing. I loved hot-tubbing after a workout, especially when I could do it sans swimsuit. There was nothing like the feel of all those hot currents and bubbles rushing over my naked skin.

"No time today," Colin said repressively, shoving me toward a showerhead and turning it on. The water was freezing and I jumped back with an outraged gasp.

"You jerk!" Just to show him, I jumped into the hot tub and sat down. The water was just this side of boiling, making my chilled skin prickle.

Standing at the edge of the tub, he put his hands on his hips and sighed, while I grinned up at him. "Rachel, get out of there—now. We're going to be late."

"I'm just waiting until the shower warms up," I said, swirling my hands through the chlorinated water. My bad girl was really having fun now.

"Okay, but don't say I didn't warn you."

By the time my good girl pressed the panic button, big hands were already dragging me out of the tub by my underarms and plopping my butt on the cool tiled edge.

Oh shit, Julian must have been in the steam room. He was naked but for the towel barely hanging on to his hips, and his hair and skin were dripping.

"What did he tell you, Rachel?" he demanded with a grim look.

Oh shit. Oh shit. "To get in the shower," I said meekly.

"To get in the shower, *what*, Rachel?"

"To get in the shower, Sir," I said even more meekly.

"Why did he tell you that, Rachel?"

I swallowed. "Because he didn't want us to be late for lunch, Sir."

"Correct. I'm a very busy man and we still have entirely too much to accomplish today—indeed, every day for the next two weeks. But you apparently don't give a damn about anyone's timetable but your own, do you, Rachel?"

My eyes filled with tears. God, this was awful. This was why I'd never misbehaved, even as a child. I just couldn't deal with disappointing someone I loved. Even my bad girl was miserable and apprehensive.

"I do care, Sir," I gulped. "I'm so sorry."

Julian laid a hand on my head. "I'm glad to hear it, but that doesn't excuse your selfishness and disobedience."

The tears got away then, sliding down my cheeks and dripping on my thighs as I bent my head in shame.

He sat down beside me on the edge of the tub. "Come," he said, urging me toward him with a hand around my shoulders. "You'll feel better after this is finished."

I felt better already as I leaned into him, comforted by the tender touch. But then I realized he was pulling me facedown over his lap and my stomach contracted violently.

"No, Sir!" I tried to back away but he forced me down onto my elbows with a hand in the middle of my back. Immediately I laid the side of my face against the cold tile and reached back to cover my defenseless butt, kicking wildly, trying to squirm back into the water. "No, Sir, please! I'm sorry! I won't do it again."

"Colin, Hans, if you please," he said.

Colin knelt in front of me and pulled my arms forward, pinning my wrists to the tile over my head, while Hans knelt behind me and held my ankles against his hairy thighs. But I continued to struggle, sobbing openly now.

"Have you never received a spanking before, Rachel?" Julian asked quietly, smoothing his hand over my buttocks in a gentle motion.

"No, Sir," I choked out.

"Oh my." He sighed. "Then you're long overdue, my little slave. Now tell me your safe words."

I choked back my sobs and took a deep breath. How could I have forgotten about my safe words? I could be out of this just by opening my mouth.

"Red and yellow," I finally replied.

"You're welcome to use them at any time, but I want you to think about something before you do. How will you feel if you leave this room knowing you refused to accept the consequences of your actions? How will you feel if you leave this room knowing you disappointed both Colin and me and didn't even try to make amends?"

Another sob built in my chest but I held it back. God, he was right—I was utterly miserable and would continue to be miserable until I'd done whatever was necessary to earn his forgiveness, and Colin's.

Resigned to my fate, I sighed, relaxing just a teeny bit.

"I will give you spankings that will make you feel very, very good, Rachel," he said, smoothing his hand over my butt again, relaxing me even more. "This won't be one of them."

Chapter Ten

Before I could prepare myself, he slapped my right cheek hard enough to make me arch and cry out. Tears spurted again down my face, dripping onto the tile, but I bit my lips and braced myself for the next one. It wasn't long in coming and, son of a bitch, it hurt! I'd expected him to go for the other side, but he hit the exact same spot, and it burned like he'd pressed a hot iron to it.

"Relax, Rachel," Colin said softly. "It hurts less if you don't resist the pain."

I sniffled and tried to do as he said, letting my hot forehead rest on the tile. I held it there, biting my lip while Julian delivered eight more slaps to the same spot. By the time he finished, I was sobbing and writhing, desperate to get away. Then he started all over on the left side, and by the time he'd hit me another ten times, I was yelling with each one.

"Do you feel better yet, Rachel?" he asked, rubbing both flaming cheeks with his flaming hand.

I could only sob, leaking hot tears all over the tile. I'd never felt so fucking miserable in my entire life. I was cold, except for where my body rested on Julian's—and my inflamed butt, of course—and I wanted nothing more than to be held and forgiven.

Julian hit me on the right again, lower, closer to my thigh, and I screeched with dread.

"No more, please!"

They came faster this time, the rhythmic slaps echoing in the locker room while I just laid there and sobbed.

When he stopped to rub me again, I prayed it was really

over this time. His palm felt like sandpaper on my skin.

"There," he said, "now you have permission to go in the hot tub, Rachel. In fact, I insist on it."

Hans let go of my ankles, but Colin didn't let go of my wrists when Julian pushed me off his lap into the tub. I gasped as the hot water seared my chilled skin again. An instant later, I screamed. My white-hot butt felt like it was being boiled in acid. Writhing and moaning, I begged Colin to let me out as I tried to climb up onto the ledge and out of the tub, but Hans jumped in behind me and held my hips under the water.

I collapsed onto my forearms, sobbing wretchedly into the tile.

"Have you had enough of the hot tub yet, Rachel?" Julian asked.

"Yes, Sir. Please forgive me. Please. I never wanted to disappoint you, Sir, and I'm so sorry I did."

"All right," he said, stroking the damp, tangled hair away from my cheek. "You've been punished. I hate that I had to be so harsh with you, but you must learn when it's appropriate to be bratty and when it's not. Once you make amends for your actions, you'll be completely forgiven."

Hope exploded in my chest and I raised my head to look at him with swollen eyes. "Anything, Sir."

"Good." He tugged the towel aside, revealing his stirring cock, and my eyes widened. He was uncut. I hadn't seen all that many uncircumcised penises, and I'd certainly never touched one intimately. Or tasted one. I wanted to, badly. Right this minute. I longed to shower all my love and penitence on it and worship it with my tongue.

Mesmerized, I barely noticed when Colin let go and Hans scooted me sideways until Julian's fascinating cock was right in front of my face. Gasping at the implication, I looked up and saw Julian's brows rise expectantly.

Sucking his cock was how I had to make amends? Oh

jackpot!

I attacked, sucking him into my watering mouth, swirling my tongue around the head and trying to slide the tip inside that entrancing rim of flesh. It disappeared almost immediately as his cock expanded.

When I whimpered my disappointment, Julian groaned, burying his hand in my hair. "If you're a very good girl, Rachel, I'll let you play with it after I come sometime."

Marginally consoled, I wrapped my hands behind his butt and went to work, sucking, swirling and bobbing, determined to give him the best blowjob ever. He swelled to proportions I'd never had in my mouth before, making me realize just why taking him last night had been so difficult. He had to have at least two inches on Colin, and probably four on Tris, the guy I'd hooked up with during my dive trip.

Julian's hand began to exert downward pressure, making me take more of him, but when he hit the back of my throat, I gagged and tried to pull away. He was having none of that, though—he let me back off an inch but that was it.

"I told you, Sir, she's a come slut but she can't deep throat."

I growled. Damn Colin! Enjoying oral sex did not make me a come slut. Or did it? I really loved it when he came in my mouth, and I desperately wanted Julian to.

"We'll have to fill that deficit in her education, stat," Julian murmured. "Why don't you show her how it's done, Colin?"

"Yes, Sir," Colin said with genuine enthusiasm.

If it were for any other reason, I would have been loath to give up my prize. But when Colin splashed in beside me and knelt on the ledge beside Julian's legs, I backed away at once, already sweating with lustful anticipation. I wanted to see Julian and Colin together more than I wanted anything else in the world at that moment.

Julian leaned back on his hands, making his cock stand

even taller. Colin didn't hesitate—he bent over with his hands clasped behind his back and slowly took it all the way down to the root. He didn't even twitch when Julian reached up and pressed his head down even farther.

Julian held him there for a few seconds that must have seemed like years to Colin and then said, "Swallow."

Colin obeyed, and I watched with wide eyes as the muscles of his throat worked around the thick column of flesh.

"Again."

When Colin did it again, I swallowed too and whimpered with envy and dismay. I'd never be able to do that. How in the hell was he not fighting and gagging and gasping for air?

"All it takes is a little training and self-discipline, Rachel," Julian said, smiling at my expression.

Dread seized me. It would take a lot more than *a little* to make me capable of that.

Just when I was beginning to worry about the oxygen supply to Colin's brain, Julian slid his hand down to Colin's neck and squeezed. "Excellent, my boy, but why don't you let Rachel do what she can now."

If I'd been in Colin's position, I would have jerked away, coughing and sputtering and possibly vomiting in the hot tub, but he rose as casually as if he'd been breathing through Julian's urethra. I bristled when he sat beside Julian and gave me a wickedly self-satisfied smile. He'd always wanted me to do this and it looked like he was going to get his way.

When Julian crooked a finger at me, I leaned forward and applied myself to the task with slightly less enthusiasm. He immediately began guiding my head with both hands, using me, rudely masturbating himself with my mouth, and all I could do was try to maintain some sort of suction and not seize up when he hit the back of my throat.

He swelled even more and forced out, "Swallow it, Rachel, because come is all you're getting for lunch."

And then his hands forced me down, down, making me thrash and gag as his semen spurted into the back of my throat. Between the spasms, I managed to recover enough to swallow around the thick head a couple of times, and then swirled it with my tongue when his hold on me eased.

"Very nice, little slave," he said softly, patting me on the head before he stood up on the ledge and wrapped the towel around his hips again.

His praise brought tears of joy and gratitude to my eyes. I'd made amends and I was forgiven.

Then Colin slid into his place, wearing a huge grin. "You'd better hurry, Rachel. That ass is going to need some ice soon."

Great. Now that he'd mentioned it, I remembered how much it hurt and heaved an exaggerated sigh. "I don't know why I like you when you're so mean to me."

"Suck, slave. I need to shower."

I obeyed, pleased to know he wasn't going to turn the tables on me this time and deprive me of his orgasm. By the time he came, naturally going deep enough to gag me repeatedly, my jaw ached and my throat was sore.

When he stood up, I put one foot up on the ledge and tried to climb out.

"Whoa, where do you think you're going?" he asked.

"To shower?" I said with wide eyes.

He shook his head. "You don't have time to shower. You're not done yet."

Oh hell. I settled back into the tub just in time for Hans to sit down in front of me.

"Hello, Rachel," he said cheerfully, wagging his erection at me. "This is my cock and he's very pleased to meet you."

I scowled, but my heart blipped with deviant excitement.

"Really?" I asked Julian, who was watching while he soaped his body with leisurely strokes.

"Do you feel better now, Rachel?" he asked with an indulgent smile.

"Much," I said in a heartfelt tone.

"Then you'll feel even better after you're done with Hans. Now get busy, slave. We have work to do."

Fighting a smile, I got to work.

During lunch, I sat on two ice packs and watched—wet, smelly and unkempt—as Julian and Colin ate slices of fresh, hot bread and bowls of fragrant stew. Intermittent growls from my stomach made them both smile, and though I tried to pout, I was too bizarrely happy to do anything but smile back at them. Bree would blow an artery if she could see me right now.

Afterward we went back and finished our tour of the hospital floor, including the medical labs, nursing stations and several state-of-the-art intensive care rooms. Then we stopped at the office with the printer and Colin handed me a red three-ring binder so heavy I almost dropped it.

"Here's a little light reading for you, otherwise known as the Operation FrankenDom playbook," he said. "Learn it. You may be called upon to assist another surgeon, if necessary."

I grinned. "Is it really..."

Operation FrankenDom was indeed printed in big black letters on the cover. The subtitle underneath was Vascular Surgery.

And underneath that, McBride of FrankenDom.

"You're insane," I told Julian. "You know that, right?"

"The proper term is mad," he corrected. "Mad scientists only become insane when they lose their sense of humor."

"I suppose your title is Igor?" I asked Colin.

He grimaced. "No, which is why I'm careful to keep my playbook hidden away in my room."

When I stared at him questioningly, Julian said, "Can't you guess? He's *FrankenDom's Fuckhole*."

I cleared my throat. "Um, yeah, I'd keep that hidden in my room too."

From there, we went back to the operating rooms and they walked me through the basics of the procedure.

"You'll work with Dr. Lang on severing the patient's blood supply while another team of vascular surgeons severs the donor's," Julian explained. "Then you'll both accompany the patient's head to the other OR and reestablish the blood supply, reinforcing the common carotid and jugular veins with bio-absorbable mesh stents."

"I assume they'll both be hypothermic?" I asked. Reducing the body's core temperature by a significant amount would slow the metabolism, allowing the patient's brain to survive longer without oxygen.

"Yes, they will," he said with an approving look. "With you and Dr. Lang working on both sides of the patient at once, you'll have sufficient time to connect all the major arteries before brain damage occurs. It should go without saying that the cardiovascular system will be the last severed and the first restored in both subjects, and you'll be suturing faster than you've ever sutured in your life. Once the integrity of the patient's vascular system has been verified, a state-of-the-art heart-lung machine will rewarm the patient while the spinal cord is fused. This will, of course, be the most time-consuming portion of the procedure. Afterward, the skull will be temporarily attached to the spine while muscles and ligaments are reattached."

"That sounds like a very long day."

"We estimate the entire process will last at least thirty hours, assuming there are no complications."

"It could be months after that before you have any idea whether or not the procedure was successful," I pointed out.

"That's the nature of the beast, Rachel. Much of scientific research, and even medicine, is a waiting game."

"I know." I sighed. "So who's the first patient?"

"He prefers to remain anonymous, for obvious reasons."

I stiffened. "Julian, I don't operate on anyone without knowing who they are. For obvious reasons," I added tartly.

His eyes narrowed. "Sarcasm ill becomes you, Doctor."

"Sarcasm is a body's natural defense against stupidity, *Doctor*," I fired back.

"Indeed," he replied stiffly.

Too late, I realized just what I'd said, and to whom.

"I'm sorry, Sir," I said at once, trembling with dismay. "I didn't mean that at all. I was channeling my sister Bree. She says that all the time, and it just popped out. That's no excuse, I know, and I'm appalled that I said it to you, of all people. Please forgive me."

When he said nothing, I took a deep breath and went on, "You need to understand, Sir, that I *cannot* go into this operation blindly. It already stretches the limits of our credibility as scientists, and if it fails, we could be all crucified by the media, and shunned by every medical and scientific community in the world. We could lose our licenses to practice medicine in the US. We could be sued for wrongful death. And no matter what assurances the Montanevan government has given you, we could even go to prison. I refuse to risk my career and my reputation without knowing exactly what I'm signing up for. Hell, for all I know, it's the president of the US and if he dies, I'll be arrested for assassinating him."

Julian sighed. "Rachel, I promise you, it's not the president. He doesn't have Bain's—although the vice president's father does, and we may eventually be called upon to perform the same procedure on him."

Turning, I headed straight for the door. "Sorry, Sir, but I'm gone."

"Stop."

I spun on my heel. "What?"

"You will not reveal this to anyone, Rachel. He couldn't live with the details of his transplant being leaked to the public."

"I signed the confidentiality agreement and I'll honor it. He has nothing to fear from me."

Julian sighed again. "Very well. The patient is my brother, Jordan."

"Oh...God," I said faintly. That handsome, smiling, active young man in the photographs was in the final stages of Bain's atrophy? "I'm so sorry, Sir."

Julian scrubbed his hands over his face. "That was the bad news I received the day Colin came home and said he'd upset you. I think I went a little mad that day."

"I'm sure."

"I hadn't really begun to make headway into Bain's yet, had barely conceived this half-baked germ of an idea about how to tackle it, and suddenly I was fighting for my brother's life. That's why I took Colin and disappeared. I didn't want to abandon you, but the clock was ticking and I had to focus every ounce of energy and every brain cell I had on finding a cure."

"I understand," I said softly.

"So you'll stay? You'll still participate in the surgery?"

Sighing, I nodded. How could I refuse? "Of course I will."

He hesitated and then said, "Thank you. I am forever in your debt."

That evening, Julian was called away, so Colin had our dinner and ice packs delivered to my bedroom while I showered. Then I lay naked on my stomach, with the ice packs draped over my rear end, and let him sit on the cedar chest and feed me bites of roasted lamb, herbed potatoes and baby carrots, between sips of red wine.

"So tell me about you and Julian," I invited.

"What would you like to know?"

"Everything. But that's probably a lot to cover in one evening, so why don't you start with how you got into a D/s relationship with him. Were you already into that?"

He grinned as he finished chewing a bite of his own meal. "A little, but from the other side, which you probably already guessed."

"I was actually really surprised to find you bottoming for Julian," I said, grabbing my wine glass off the rolling cart. "You seem like a total top to me."

"I *am* a total top to you."

I rolled my eyes. "You know what I mean."

He sat there quietly for a while, eating and thinking. Then he finally poked a bite of potato into my mouth and said, "I was a top, but I wasn't in any way worthy of the title Dom. I just liked the thrill of topping, the risky edge to it. I didn't care about the girls I tied up or what they got out of the experience, besides an orgasm or two."

I nodded thoughtfully. That fit with what I'd seen of him for the first of those two years.

"Actually, I wasn't just an asshole with women. My father died when I was a baby, and my mother spoiled me pretty badly all my life. I graduated high school at sixteen, finished medical school at twenty-three, and by the time I met Julian, I thought I was God's gift to neurology. I had the brains and the hands to become a world-class surgeon and I knew it. But I was also impulsive, insensitive and hardheaded, and while Julian saw incredible potential in me, he also saw incredible potential for disaster.

"When he expressed interest in mentoring me, he made it clear that he was doing it out of sheer terror for my future patients, and at first I was offended enough to walk away. But he kept challenging me, saying I couldn't take what he'd dish out, and when he finally said it in front of another resident, I said, 'Fuck that. You're on, old man'."

Smothering a laugh, I said, "I'll bet he took that well."

Colin chuckled too. "Yeah, he dressed me down like a drill sergeant, spitting on my face while he yelled at me right there in the hall. I took it just to show him I could, but I was supremely pissed and spent the next few weeks spewing attitude in private and in public. One day I told him I was leaving before the end of my shift because I had a girl to tie up, and he laughed so hard he was doubled over when he said, 'You think you're a *Dom*? That poor girl'."

"Ouch."

"Mm-hmm. I kind of lost it then. I threw a punch and missed, and before I knew it, he had me on the floor with my arm twisted behind my back and his knee in my kidney. He pulled my head up by my hair and informed me that no Dom was allowed to dish out anything he couldn't take. 'How much can you take, Dr. Carter?' he asked me. 'I'm guessing precious little'."

Enthralled, I said, "Oh boy."

"Yup. I couldn't let that challenge go unanswered, so I agreed to go with him to a real dungeon and prove myself. I wasn't as confident as I acted, though, and when the dungeon turned out to be in his basement, I almost backed out. Kind of like you today, I'd never really been disciplined. My middle school principal had given me a few fairly public swats with a board of education, but those were meant to hurt my pride more than my ass and I'd laughed myself silly afterward. Julian was going to test my pain tolerance in a very isolated place, and I was suddenly very afraid he'd prove I had none—and then just keep going. It was a shock to feel that...vulnerable."

"Oh, Colin," I sighed. Such a bad boy.

"Did you get enough?" he asked, gesturing at the plates.

When I nodded, he pushed the cart away and stood up. Plucking the ice packs and towel from my rear, he dropped them on the cart and traced a sore spot with his finger. "He got you pretty good, didn't he, Miss Tenderbottom? You've got some bruising."

I tried to get a look at it but my neck didn't twist that far. "Really?"

"No, I just said that to make you say *really.*"

Blowing him a raspberry, I slid off the bed and went to look in the mirror. Wow, there really were some mottled marks all over both cheeks. I couldn't decide how I felt about them.

"What's the matter?" Colin asked, rubbing my butt and watching his hand in the mirror.

"Is it bad that I'm kind of excited he left marks?"

"Not at all. It's pretty normal, actually—just don't try to manipulate him into leaving more or he'll figure out some other punishment you'll hate a lot more."

I shuddered. "No thanks. I hated that one enough already."

After he pushed the cart out into the hall, he ducked into the bathroom and I heard the echo of urine splashing in the toilet.

"Hurry up and get back to the story," I said loudly. "The suspense is killing me."

"You'll live."

By the time he came back, I'd gotten under the covers, and he stripped and climbed in with me, pulling me against his chest.

"So where was I again?" he teased.

"About to back out of a well-deserved beating from Julian."

"Ah, right. So anyway, I almost backed out again when he said subs had to be naked. But I forced myself to peel anyway, and when he stood there and looked me over, I was..." He shook his head and sighed. "It was a really ugly shock to get a hard-on for him. I'd never even thought about being attracted to a guy, but when he looked at me with those scorn-filled eyes, the damn thing refused to go down. I wasn't even thinking about sex—in fact, I was pretty damn scared, but that only made me harder."

Breathing a little rapidly from the excitement of the past, I slid my hand under the covers and found Colin's cock well on its way to excited in the present. Exploring him eagerly, I asked, "How did Julian react?"

Colin rubbed circles on my shoulder with his palm and spread his thighs wider in invitation. "He smiled and said, 'Now that's what I like to see, a sub impatient for his beating'. I started to deny it, but then I realized I'd be admitting I was hard for something else. I knew then I was in deep, deep trouble. I was an infant compared to him, ignorant as hell and totally defenseless. I didn't move a muscle when he walked in a circle around me and pronounced me a very pretty boy. When I didn't answer, he said, 'The proper response to a compliment from your Dom is *Thank you, Sir*', so I said it without even hesitating. That's when I knew my life of doing whatever I wanted and acting however I pleased was over."

"Wow," I breathed, circling the base of his balls with my thumb and forefinger and tugging. "So did he beat you?"

"Mmmmm. Yes, he did, but lightly enough that it was more of an insult. When he released me from the cross, I told him I could take more than that and he said, 'Perhaps. We'll see next time'. I wanted to tell him there damn well wouldn't be a next time, but of course there was, and by the time it happened, I was desperate for it. When I tried to manipulate him into punishing me by acting out, he just ignored me. Only when I behaved in a way that pleased him did he let me show him what I could take. Except that last day with you," he added with a sigh. "That was the first and only time he ever hurt me in anger, and the last time he ever beat me with anything but the flat of his hand."

I instinctively soothed him with my fingers. "I'm sorry. Do you miss it?"

"He's so shockingly creative, I don't usually have time to miss it," Colin said dryly. "Rachel..."

He sounded so serious, I looked up to find him looking down at me. "What is it?"

"I wasn't just jealous of Julian. I was jealous because you were just as into him as he was into you. You went all subbie and hot the very first time you saw him, and I know because I was standing right there watching your face. You never reacted to me like that—I wasn't even a blip on your radar, except as an annoyance. Unless I was acting like an assmunch, you didn't even notice I was alive."

Dumbfounded, I blinked at him. "Colin...that's not true."

"Yes, it is. You two had this primal, instant connection, and I wanted you both, but you couldn't stand me and he couldn't be bothered to fuck me. Sometimes I thought maybe it was all a big mind fuck, that you were both just playing with me until you could have each other."

"No, no!" I wrapped my arms around him. "That wasn't it at all!"

"I figured that out later, but that's what I was afraid of, why I goaded you and why I pushed him. I wanted to make *something* happen because I couldn't stand the waiting and not knowing. And I got what I wanted—for just that one night, Julian didn't hold anything back, and though I was a blubbering mess by the time he finished with me, I loved every minute of it. The next morning, he explained to me, with his icy control very much back in place, exactly how badly I'd screwed myself, and him...and you."

"Oh, Colin, I'm so sorry!"

"Don't be. I'm not—not now, anyway. That day, the date on my stamp, was the day I grew up, the day I learned there are some people you'll sacrifice anything for, *everything* for. Julian

128

didn't make me choose between going with him and staying with you. Instead he told me I was going to help him save his brother, but he put your name on my dick and told me if you couldn't have it, no one could. I was...relieved. I wanted to be reserved for you. It made getting you back my destiny, one of the goals I was working for every single day."

I sighed against his chest. "I wish I'd been in on that goal."

"I know. I'm sorry."

He kissed me then, one of those long, drugging Colin kisses, and before I knew it, I was sprawled out on top of him, breathing heavily while he explored my sore cheeks with his hands. In love and in lust, I pushed up and back, but before I could impale myself on him, he caught my hips.

"We don't have permission," he said with a wry quirk of his lips.

"Aw!" I whined as I flopped back down on his chest. "You could have told me that sooner. Why?"

"He says we both need rest, but I'm pretty sure it's because he can't be here to play with us."

"Hmph. That's not fair. You both got to come at noon."

"And you got to suck the come out of three cocks at noon," he pointed out. "Hans said to tell you he can't wait for your next workout, by the way."

Snorting with reluctant laughter, I thumped him with my fist. "Shut up and go to sleep."

"I would but there's a body on top of me and someone forgot to turn off the light."

When I slid off him to reach for the lamp, he cuddled up behind me. "Good night, my little come slut."

I smiled in the dark. "Good night, Colin."

Chapter Eleven

Although I'd gone to sleep at barely nine o'clock the evening before, I woke up late and had to rush to make it to breakfast on time. I didn't quite make it because my legs were so stiff and sore from the day before I could barely walk, let alone run.

Julian scowled at me when I limped in. "What time is breakfast served, Rachel?"

"Eight o'clock, Sir, but—" I bit my tongue, refusing to look at Colin. It would have been *nice* if he'd woken me before he left this morning, but it wasn't his responsibility.

"But what, slave?"

"Nothing, Sir. It's my fault. It won't happen again."

"Glad to hear it. Now sit down and eat, quickly. Normally I'd make you skip the meal but you missed a meal yesterday so I'll have to think of some other punishment."

Sighing with both relief and resignation, I took my seat. "Yes, Sir."

But things went downhill from there. I'd just taken the first bite of my oatmeal when Julian said, "I assume your workout ran late?"

I closed my eyes. *Oh crap.* "No, Sir. I actually didn't make it to my workout."

"And why not?" he drawled.

"I forgot all about it, Sir. I don't usually work out in the morning." Or anytime.

I braved a glance at him and then wished I hadn't. He looked annoyed.

"Rachel, I reminded you right before you went to sleep,"

Colin said gently.

Gasping, I cried, "You did not!"

He shook his head, giving me a pitying look. "Rachel, did I or did I not say right before you turned out the light that Hans was looking forward to your next workout?"

"Colin! That wasn't a *reminder*. You were tea—"

"It sounds like a reminder to me," Julian said. "I realize that you don't enjoy working out, Rachel, but it's not acceptable for you to just not show up. I'm surprised Hans didn't call to tell me you'd wasted an hour of his time this morning."

"But, Sir—"

"Silence!"

Bristling with annoyance, I shut my mouth.

"Now, you'll finish your breakfast and go directly to the exercise facilities for your session with Hans. When you're done, you'll shower and meet us in the operating room. You will not go anywhere near the hot tub—understood?"

Groaning inwardly, I nodded. I wouldn't even *look* at the hot tub, no matter how badly I needed a good, long soak.

It took me forever to limp down to the exercise room, and Hans lectured me for being late, for missing my first solo appointment, for not stretching before bed and when I got up, and for being generally lazy and out of shape. As if that weren't torture enough, he worked me harder than he had the day before, shouting at me in German half the time when I couldn't keep up the pace he demanded or lift as much weight as he thought I should be able to. When my triceps turned to burning noodles and he sneered at me because I couldn't do one more rep, I finally snapped.

"Colin told you to take it easy on my arms, you prick!"

"I am taking it easy, you little wienie," he scoffed.

"Fine. I'm a wienie. A *done* wienie," I added, stomping off to the locker room.

At my locker, I stripped as quickly as I could, groaning at the soreness in my legs and abs. I'd absolutely kill for five minutes in the hot tub, but I would have to settle for a hot shower.

I looked around for the towels and finally saw a pile of them on a table between the steam and sauna doors. After I turned on one of the showerheads to let the water warm up, I picked my way gingerly across the cool tile and grabbed two towels off the table.

When I turned around, I ran into Hans and stumbled.

"Whoa!" He tried to catch me, but instead he bumped me right into the hot tub.

As I went under, my mind went ten different directions at once. Julian was going to kill me. Was there any way I could keep him from finding out? Forget it, the guilt would eat me alive. I had to tell him. How long could I possibly stay in here and still consider it an accident? God, it felt so good! My butt still burned more than the rest of me in the hot water, and even that felt good. Colin was going to laugh his ass off when he heard. I still hated Hans. Just two more seconds...

There was a splash beside me and Hans pulled me up. "Rachel, I'm so sorry! Are you hurt?"

"Oh crap!" I gasped, struggling onto the ledge. I climbed out gracelessly, not caring if he was getting a shot of me from a lewdly unflattering angle.

He vaulted out of the tub, still fully clothed, and took me by the arms. "Are you all right?"

"I'm fine, really," I assured him. "I just need to shower and get out of here, okay?"

"If you're sure..." he said, his face still a study in caring concern.

"Absolutely. But thank you."

"All right." He wandered over to a locker and started undressing.

Oh God, was I ever going to get used to this?

Once I made my way to the OR—right on schedule, thankfully—the rest of the day passed relatively uneventfully. Though, as I expected, the fact that I'd been in the hot tub, however unintentionally, weighed on my mind. I'd tried to scrub the chlorine odor from my hair and skin, but I could still smell it. Could anyone else, or was it like Poe's *Tell-Tale Heart*—my guilt manifesting itself in an olfactory hallucination?

I should have just confessed right away and gotten it over with, but there never seemed to be a good time. We spent the remainder of the morning doing another quick walk-through of my part of the operation, and then after a rushed lunch of ham sandwiches and hot chocolate, Julian took me to the library, which was on the third floor. High-ceilinged and well-lit by numerous mullioned windows and bright chandeliers, it was easily the largest library I'd ever seen outside of a university.

There, lounging in easy chairs, or poring over medical tomes on the large wooden library tables, were at least two dozen people who turned out to be specialists typical of transplant teams. Besides the obvious neurosurgeons and vascular surgeons, there were anesthesiologists, cardiologists, radiologists, hepatologists, nephrologists, orthopedic surgeons, pathologists...

None of them wore any identification, and I assumed they had the same kind of nameless, genetic-based identification I did. It didn't escape my notice that hardly any of them were women, but that wasn't an unusual statistic in the medical community and especially in surgery.

I was pleased to finally meet Dr. Lang, who would be operating opposite me during the procedure. Probably in his midfifties, he was lean and well groomed, and on the short side for a man—just about my height, actually, which meant I wouldn't have to stand on a platform to operate.

Julian explained that the remaining members of the transplant team were arriving that evening, so we could begin full walk-throughs the next day. Practice runs on cadavers would commence five days later.

That's when I started getting butterflies. Good God, we were going to cut off two men's heads and try to reattach them to each other's bodies. Sometimes it sneaked up and jumped out at me from behind the mental door I'd closed on it.

Dinner was a quiet affair, mostly because I was quiet. Did I really carry the conversation that much, or were Julian and Colin quieter than usual too? They both seemed to be watching me, but there could be a hundred reasons for that.

Like plans for the evening, I hoped. I was feeling tense and a little anxious, and I wouldn't mind having that taken away for a while.

"So how was your workout this morning, Rachel?" Colin asked.

I froze, my appetite for the delicious broiled salmon suddenly deserting me. "Painful," I answered honestly.

He laughed. "Well, I hope you stayed away from the hot tub."

My breath congealed in my throat as I looked at him, and his smile faded. "Rachel? Please tell me you didn't..."

"Rachel Anne, look at me," Julian said.

Biting my lips, I obeyed, and he sighed, looking very disappointed in me.

"You disobeyed me, didn't you? Why?"

Tears prickled in my eyes and I blinked them back. I absolutely hated having to defend myself, and I hated even more having to start my defense with "It wasn't my fault".

"It was an accident, Sir," I said instead. "I went to get a towel and bumped into Hans when I turned around."

He watched my face for a long moment before saying, "If it

was an accident, why didn't you tell me about it right away?"

I wanted to hit myself then. *Why* hadn't I? I'd thought about it. I'd intended to.

"Because I didn't want to see that look on your face," I admitted.

"What look is that?"

"Disappointment, Sir."

Still watching me closely, he said, "I believe, little slave, that I'm being manipulated."

My eyes widened. "No, Sir, I—"

"Bite your tongue." He glared at me. "Now. Put it out and bite the tip so that you don't interrupt me again."

Feeling like an idiot and a wienie and a martyr, I complied.

"Better. As I was saying, Rachel Anne, I believe you're trying to manipulate me the way Colin did five years ago, and I'm not falling for it again. I won't have either of you topping me from the bottom, do you understand? If you wish to be punished, you should have the courage to ask for it and let me decide whether or not to administer such punishment. Do you understand?" he repeated insistently.

"But, Sir—"

"Did I give you permission to speak?" he barked.

I bit my tongue and shook my head.

"No, I didn't give you permission to speak, or no, you don't understand?" he demanded in a frustrated tone. "Which is it?"

After staring at him for a second, I held up one finger.

"I didn't give you permission to speak?"

I shook my head.

"So you understand my position on being topped from the bottom?"

I nodded grudgingly. Dammit, that wasn't what I'd been doing, but he wouldn't give me the chance to explain myself.

He heaved an exasperated sigh and shoved his hands through his hair. "Fine. Then you'll understand why you won't be punished tonight. You're clearly not in the proper headspace to benefit from it."

Perversely, I felt a pinch of disappointment—although that *really* wasn't what I'd been trying to do.

"Right now I want you to go to your room and write out two hundred times 'I will not top from the bottom'. When you've finished your lines, you can give them to Lili and then we might as well get the rest of your employment paperwork taken care of since it appears we won't be doing anything fun again this evening."

My stomach dropped and I suddenly felt like crying.

"Yes, Sir," I whispered. I'd been half-afraid of and half anticipating what might happen tonight in Julian's dungeon, and now, thanks to my cowardice, nothing would.

Julian pulled away from the table and walked out without another word. Colin got up too, leaving me to face the rest of my cold dinner alone.

"Good job, Rachel," he murmured with a grin as he walked by.

I couldn't even muster the defiance to flip him off.

Lili was nowhere to be seen when I got back to my room, but when I finished my lines and opened the door, she was waiting for me in her plain gray uniform and flats, her blonde hair once again done up in a prim bun. She wore no makeup that I could detect, but she was still a knockout.

In her hand was a silver tray with a lid.

"Good evening, Doctor," she said, pushing into my room and setting the tray on my desk. Then she held out her hand. "Your lines?"

turned on by his cool detachment. My heart thudded heavily, right in time with my clit, and my nipples prickled against my bra cups.

"All right, Rachel, you know the drill," he said, opening a cabinet door and pulling out a disposable gown and drape. "The opening goes in front. You can leave your socks on but everything else needs to come off. I'll be back in just a minute."

I stared after him as he walked out the rounded door. Really? He was going to perform a gynecological exam? And a *rectal inspection?*

Feeling vulnerable, and yet undeniably aroused, I took off my clothes and tossed them over the back of a chair without folding them, leaving my socks on. I grabbed a tissue from the box on the counter and quickly wiped away the evidence of my excitement, silently cursing Colin and his unholy detachment. Then I put on the short gown and sat back down on the flat table with the paper drape tucked securely around my butt and thighs.

Just like at my own gynecologist's office, it seemed like forever before he returned, and this time he wasn't alone. Julian strolled in behind him, also dressed in a lab coat. They'd both put on blue surgical masks.

Without greeting me, Julian picked up my chart and looked it over.

"Go ahead and lie back," Colin said, unfolding the stirrups from their hiding place.

Everything in me balked. And clenched hotly.

He frowned a little. "Is everything okay, Rachel?"

My hands tightened on the front of my paper gown as I stared at him. Did he really think this was...normal?

Or could this possibly be some kind of kinky medical scene?

"We don't have all night, Dr. McBride," Julian said briskly. "The sooner you lie down, the sooner we can all get out of here."

Feeling stupid and a little deflated, I obeyed, trying not to stiffen when Colin picked up my legs and guided them into the widely spread stirrups. Dammit, scening would have been so much more fun than a pelvic exam. This just made my already sore adductors burn.

He pulled the drape up over my knees, but my bare crotch was now completely exposed to anyone who walked in the door. Wasn't there supposed to be a female nurse present for this kind of exam?

The idea made me roll my eyes at myself. *Really? After everything you've agreed to since you got here, why in God's name would they think you required the presence of a nurse?*

I heard the creak of a gooseneck lamp being adjusted and then bright, warm light flooded my exposed privates.

"All right, Rachel," Julian said from behind the drape, "I need you to scoot your bottom down a little more, right over the edge of the table."

Even as I obeyed, I was thinking, *This man licked you down there with his electrified tongue!* and trying not to respond physically to the memory.

"Very good," he said. "Now, I'm going to take care of the pelvic while Colin does the breast exam."

His masked face a study in professionalism, Colin lifted my right arm up over my head, then peeled back the gown and began palpating my breast with his cool fingers. Excitement streaked down my belly and I clenched involuntarily, struggling to control my breathing.

There was a chuckle from behind the drape. "Somebody seems to have a gyno fetish. I'll have to remember that."

I was so embarrassed I couldn't even tell him it wasn't true. Arousal was a living, writhing thing in my hollow belly.

Colin continued his exam as if Julian hadn't spoken, but he gave me a scolding look as he moved around to my left side. Swallowing my humiliation, I closed my eyes and prayed for it to be over quickly.

"Cool touch," Julian warned an instant before his gloved fingers parted my labia. I felt the speculum slide into me and crank open. Oh God, I was so wet he didn't even need any lube.

"I'll be right back," he said, walking out of the room and leaving the cool metal speculum just hanging there against my butt cheeks, which were warm from the bright light. As promised, he came right back.

"I hope you don't mind, Rachel," he said, "but I've invited a few other doctors to observe our rectal inspection procedures."

My jaw dropped. *A few other doctors?*

Before I could protest, three more men wearing white lab coats and surgical masks crowded into the room. Dirk was at the head of the line. The second looked vaguely familiar, but he wasn't anyone I'd seen here before. The third might be Hans, but he wasn't a doctor—was he?

"Seriously?" I breathed, closing my eyes and turning my hot face away. Oh God, *were* we scening? Was this all just a big mind fuck?

"How are her breasts?" Julian inquired.

Pulling my arm down to my side and mercifully covering me again, Colin said, "I think they're missing something."

My eyes popped open again. "They're *breasts.* What could they possibly be missing?"

"I'll show you in just a minute," he said.

Without warning, the speculum slid from me and I quivered in reaction. Then Julian's gloved fingers slid inside.

"Some pressure here," he said, pressing the fingers of his other hand down on my abdomen as he probed deeply inside me.

I arched up with a groan and was instantly appalled by my fierce reaction. "Oh God!"

Colin reached down under the edge of the table and took

my wrist. Before I realized what was happening, he'd fastened a cuff around it while Dirk stepped up and cuffed the other wrist. My arms were bound to the table.

I just about hyperventilated. "Oh crap, we *are* scening, aren't we?"

"You're just figuring that out, slave girl?" Colin asked as he and Dirk cuffed my ankles and hooked them to the stirrups. "We've been fucking with your head all day. You didn't really think Hans pushing you into the hot tub was an accident, did you?"

"What!" Julian's probing intensified, became something very close to slow thrusting, and I groaned again. "Why didn't you tell me?"

"Because you enjoyed not knowing so very much more, my kinky little slut," Julian said in a silky tone.

"I'm not a slut," I told him, breathing loudly as I stared at the fluorescent fixture overhead.

Colin peeled back both sides of my gown and ripped away the drape, leaving my restrained body completely exposed. "Yet you didn't say no, didn't use your safe word, when all those doctors crowded into the room to stare at your open cunt. And I believe you sucked off three of the men in this room in the space of about fifteen minutes yesterday. Swallowed every drop of their come too."

"That makes her a slut in my book," Dirk said severely.

"I should say so," Hans agreed.

"I hate you all."

"If that's what you need to believe," Colin said. "But you really ought to loosen up a little, Rachel—learn to enjoy being a slut. And being in trouble, for that matter. Otherwise life's no fun at all."

Tugging down his mask, he gave me an evil smile and reached for the instrument tray, which I couldn't see.

"This might pinch a bit." He leaned down and sucked my

forty-five-degree angle or more. Suddenly I was staring directly at the bulge in his slacks.

He unzipped and pulled his stiff cock out through the fly. "Open your mouth for me, come slut."

I obeyed with heavy eyes, more than ready for another mouthful of him. When he pushed the head between my parted lips, I moaned and went straight to work, sucking and licking. God, would I ever get over how much I'd missed his musky, masculine body?

Tears burned my nose and I sniffled, blinking.

"Rachel, are you okay?" he asked, pulling back.

I sucked hard, refusing to let him go, and he groaned. "God, that's good. Yeah, like that. Now let's go deeper." He rubbed his hand gently over my throat. "This table is perfect for deep-throating."

When I whimpered my alarm, he said, "I know you think you can't do it, but the only way to learn is to keep trying. This table creates a straighter shot down your throat, so I want you to relax your mouth and throat and let me in. Don't try to suck or swallow—let me do the work. Your job is to just keep breathing through your nose, take a deep breath when I tell you to and resist your gag reflex as long as you can. I promise I won't let anything happen to you."

Taking a deep breath to relax, I nodded and slid my tongue around his coronal ridge.

"That feels really good, little slut, but no tongue either. Try to keep it out of the way. Now relax."

I sighed and obeyed, letting my eyes slide shut again. Leaving his fingers on my throat, he started moving in and out slowly, sliding against my tongue and the roof of my mouth, edging deeper with every thrust. I floated on the feeling of being used and bound, helpless to protect myself against whatever he decided to do. When he nudged between my tonsils and withdrew, we both shuddered but I managed not to gag at all.

He stayed at that depth for a minute, sliding in and out, letting me get used to the feel of my throat being blocked.

"Now take a deep breath."

When I did, he slid in and kept sliding until the fabric of his slacks pushed against my nose and chin—and stayed there. Instinctively I started counting as I tried to keep my throat relaxed. *One, two, three, four, five, six, seven, eight, nine...*

I jerked against the wrist cuffs when my throat and stomach convulsed, and Colin pulled back immediately. Not out, just back far enough for me to gag loudly and catch my breath around his penis. Tears dripped from the corners of my eyes, and my nose felt full but it couldn't drip upside down.

"That was awesome, sweet come slut. Thank you."

"Yay," I cheered weakly around the obstruction in my mouth.

"Let's try it again. Take a couple of breaths... Now here it comes."

He pushed in again, deeper, and stayed there. I kept my eyes squeezed tightly shut against the crotch of his slacks. My throat wanted to squeeze again but I managed to count to fifteen before I panicked.

Once again, Colin drew back at once, but this time he pulled out all the way, rubbing my throat as I gagged and coughed and cried. "Beautiful," he said, leaning down to kiss me again.

"I need to blow my nose," I gasped.

Strangely, blowing into the tissue he held was the most embarrassing event of the evening for me.

"You're being such a good little slut, I think you've earned your rectal inspection," Julian said.

I shook my head to clear it. "That's a reward?"

"You doubt me?"

"Uh...no, Sir."

"I have it on good authority you enjoy this very much, cheeky little slut."

Uh-oh.

I felt gloved hands on my butt cheeks and thumbs pulling them apart. And then a tongue in a place only one man's had been.

"Nooooo," I wailed.

"Why not?" Julian breathed against my butt. "Didn't Colin come in this tight little hole yesterday morning?"

Masculine groans reminded me of all the doctors observing, and a hot flush swept over my entire body. Now they all knew I let Colin do that to me.

I was so lost in deviant excitement, I couldn't answer.

Colin tapped my cheek with his fingers. "Back to work, slave. I plan to come so far down that throat you'll never even taste it."

Julian's tongue penetrated deeply and I moaned as I opened to accept Colin's cock. This time he pushed deep right away and backed out, paused and then pushed deep, never staying deep long enough to gag me. The longer he did that, the closer together the strokes got, and finally it dawned on me that he was fucking my throat.

Absorbed in what was happening in my mouth, I lost track of Julian until he stood up and unzipped his pants. My pulse hammered suddenly, but before I could think, he leaned between my obscenely restrained legs and pushed his penis into my tender pussy, not pausing until the fabric of his slacks and lab coat pressed against me. Like Colin, he'd just pulled his cock out through his fly instead of dropping his pants.

Why did that feel so much dirtier?

"Rachel, Rachel," he tutted as he rocked tightly against me, hot and hard inside me. "Your cunt is soaking my best trousers. I'm afraid I'll have to punish you for that, my dear. After I've come, you may clean everything off with your tongue.

Understood?"

Thrilled, I gurgled, but Colin went deep again and stayed this time, rocking against me as tightly as Julian was, blocking out the world with the crotch of his pants. Seconds later, my hard gagging triggered a harder orgasm and I floated away.

If I wasn't a slut before, I certainly was after tonight.

Chapter Twelve

My mother would be thrilled to know I settled into a healthy routine over the next two weeks. Three balanced meals a day. Exercise first thing every morning, followed by whatever personal assignments I'd earned the day before. Long afternoons spent reading the playbook, honing my speed-suturing skills, and participating in walk-throughs and practice surgeries with Colin and the other surgeons. And surprisingly early bedtimes, considering what we got up to most evenings.

Of course, she'd be less thrilled to know about that aspect of my routine, and the deep-throating lessons Julian and Colin managed to work into even the busiest day, but I think she'd admit it was a price worth paying for the benefits of a healthy routine.

What Julian did with the bulk of his afternoons wasn't clear, but every time I started to think too much about the radical nature of the upcoming procedure, he'd subject me to some kinky scene in the evening that undid me completely, leaving me drifting and free of worry, at least for a few hours. It was almost as if he had an inside track to my most deeply buried fantasies—in all our scenes, I was either being objectified or in some kind of trouble, or both.

I loved the classroom scenes in the library, where I received much more pleasurable bare-handed correction for a variety of behaviors that were either coerced or encouraged. One night Colin shoved my book off onto the floor and Julian, or rather Professor Kilmartin, made me stand up in my too-small schoolgirl costume and bend over, straight-legged, with my feet apart, to pick it up. Then he punished me for so proudly showing off my naked pussy.

On another occasion, Colin talked me into giving him a blowjob when Mr. Kilmartin left the room. When he returned and caught me on my knees under Colin's table, there was hell to pay, but the rush of misbehaving had already sucked me under before I ever bent over the teacher's desk.

One night when Julian was gone, Colin showed me the room beyond the mad scientist's lab—the punishment room. Although the name was scary as hell, it was really just a typical BDSM dungeon, an assessment that, when I thought about it later, seemed frightfully jaded. But to me, the room lacked imagination and individuality and...Julian. Colin told me that if I wanted to play with impact toys here, he'd be the one to top me. I got the feeling he wouldn't mind starting that night, but I wasn't ready for that yet and didn't know if I would ever be. I joked that I'd do it for him, expecting him to remind me who was the top, and I was surprised when he just said I'd need some training first.

Later in the first week, we played an adult combination of hide-and-seek and tag that proved I was indeed very much an adrenaline junkie, and that I hardly had any inhibitions left. Colin and I took turns hiding on our floor of the castle—naked, of course—while Julian, Dirk, Vince and Hans looked for us. Once we were spotted, we could run and try to hide again, but when we were caught—which we invariably were—the victor got to choose something from the punishment room or our own toy collections to "tag" us with. Being chased screaming through the castle was the most fun I'd ever had in my life, and it was even more fun after I accumulated a collar, a pair of alligator nipple clamps joined by a silver chain, and a chastity belt equipped with something that slid into my vagina and another something that snugged up firmly against my clit. I didn't get a good look at the somethings because Colin distracted me with languorous kisses, the louse. I really wished I'd spent more time exploring all the stuff hidden in my room so I'd know what was in there.

Though Colin was also tagged with nipple clamps, he

eventually acquired a few different and rather intimidating tags, including a set of painful-looking black ball-stretchers. He also got the huge silver butt plug I'd seen the first night and a ring around his cock, both of which were attached by wires to a black box on a belt around his waist. When Julian pulled something that looked like a key fob from his pocket and hit a button on it, Colin jumped and hissed, then growled at Julian. Grinning, Julian hit the button just to make Colin do it again.

"He doesn't like the training mode," Julian explained when I looked puzzled. Then his grin widened. "You won't either."

That gave me something to worry over the next couple of rounds. When Colin was caught the next time, Hans tagged him with a black leather hood with a penis-shaped gag in the mouth hole. Colin didn't look happy as it went on.

My eyes widened when I realized the only opening was under his nostrils. Colin was blind and possibly deaf with that thing on. "That's hardly fair!"

"That's what makes it fun, little slave," Julian informed me.

Needless to say, Colin came nowhere close to catching me all the way down the hall in the elevator tower, but Vince did. When he brought me back to the dungeon and put me in ankle cuffs hooked to an eighteen-inch-long bar, I didn't even bother whining. Instead, I watched as Julian changed the game, using just the remote in his hand to herd Colin around the room.

"That's just cruel," I scolded as they chuckled at Colin's jerks, gasps and growls.

Julian turned and looked at me. "Is that so?"

I could tell from his tone I was in trouble, and when he pulled another remote from his pocket I said, "Oh shit."

"Why aren't you running?" Julian asked, glancing at his watch. "Time's almost up."

"What!" Growling myself, I hobbled toward the door as fast as I could. A twisting sensation seized my abdomen as biting tingles hit my clit. Gasping, I stumbled to a halt and bent over, pressing my hands to the belt over my crotch. "Oh my God."

"Run, Rachel, run!" Julian urged.

I groaned. He had to be kidding. Straightening with difficulty, I made my way into the corridor. The tingles turned needle sharp and I yelped, grabbing for my crotch again.

"Wrong way, Rachel."

"Oh you bastard," I muttered.

Sharp needles turned to sharp knives and my mouth opened in a soundless scream as I hunched over. Then the sensation dialed back abruptly.

"What was that, slave?" Julian asked.

Taking a deep breath, I said, "Thank you for the correction, Sir."

"Much better. Now run."

I turned and went the opposite direction. The needles struck again. "Yeow!"

Grinding my teeth at their chuckles, I turned and opened my bedroom door. More needles. "Where the fuck do you want me to go?" I yelled.

Knives.

This time I fell to my knees with a shout. "I'm sorry, Sir! Please tell me what you want me to do."

The knives eased to needles. "I want you to follow where I lead you."

"Sir, is your middle name Obfuscation, by any chance?" I asked breathlessly.

Laughs erupted behind me and the sensation settled back into an almost pleasurable tightness and throbbing. "No, slave, but I might make use of that moniker at some point. Where are you supposed to go?"

What the hell? I'd tried to go both directions down the corridor and into my room. That only left one direction—back into the dungeon. Was I supposed to have run to him instead of away from him?

Pushing back up to my feet with my hands, I turned and hobbled back across the corridor, cringing as I crossed the threshold. When nothing happened, I continued toward Julian. Needles made me veer off to the right, where Colin now knelt on the stone floor, leaning forward on his hands and moving like he was fucking an invisible person. Someone had removed his hood and he was watching me with his mouth hanging open.

When the needles let up, I made my way to Colin and stopped in front of him. Needles made me move to his side and turn around. Pained pleasure made my knees buckle, and within seconds, I was in a posture identical to Colin's, thrusting my hips at nothing as orgasm bore down on me. Without touching either of us, without saying a word, he made Colin and me come together again while he and the others watched avidly.

I was surrounded by perverts, sadists and control freaks, and I loved it.

A couple of days later, we had another scene in the medical clinic that made the first one seem tame by comparison. I safeworded fairly quickly and made it clear that certain bodily functions always had been, and always would be, private.

Julian made it clear that he would never stop pushing that limit. When I demanded to know why, he said, "Because it's rooted in shame, and there's no place in our relationship for shame."

I knew then that limit was doomed, but I made up my mind to fight the good fight as long as I could. That night, as Colin and I cuddled in the dark, he warned me that if I stayed with them, I would eventually have no limits. Julian wouldn't allow any to stand.

For a second, I squirmed. "But why? Why can't he respect

that I have...well, limits?"

"He needs the control," Colin said softly. "There's too much in this world that's beyond his control, so he controls what he can."

I hesitated for just a second before asking, "Do you have any limits?"

"Not anymore. I'm his to do with whatever he pleases, and it's made me a better man—and, believe it or not, a better Dom—than I ever thought I could be. *I'm* his Galatea."

My heart thudded uncomfortably in my throat as tears welled in my eyes. I envied what they had. I wanted it. But I was afraid.

As if he could read my mind, Colin said, "Rachel, you're a doctor. You know all bodily processes are not only natural, but required. You wouldn't think twice about letting a nurse check your fluid output levels or bowel function after you had abdominal surgery, would you?"

"That's different—it's *necessary*. And I certainly wouldn't enjoy it."

I felt him shrug. "It's necessary for Julian too. And you don't have to enjoy it. That's a lot of what being a slave is about—doing things for your Master's pleasure rather than your own."

That comment was enough to keep my mind working overtime for days.

Unfortunately, there wasn't much else besides work to distract me. Every time I looked out the window and found the driveway plowed and the cobblestone walkways through the weed gardens scooped, I thought about going for a walk just to clear my head. Then I noticed the clear ice building up in the corners of the windows—on the *inside*—and decided I wasn't brave enough to face the cold.

One day when I looked out, I saw Julian pushing someone in a wheelchair down the walk, away from the castle. Though the man wore one of those Scandinavian hats with ear flaps, I could see a jaw and nose that were unmistakable.

Had his brother already arrived for the surgery? Would I get to meet him beforehand? I hoped so, especially since there was a good chance he might not survive long enough to meet me afterward.

That evening at dinner, I asked, "Was that your brother I saw you with this afternoon?"

Julian paused with his soup spoon at his lips, looking startled. "This afternoon?"

"Yes, outside on the walk. I saw you through the window and thought he looked a lot like you."

He glanced at Colin and then sipped the soup off the spoon before answering. "Yes, that was Jordan. He stopped for a short visit."

"Can I meet him?"

Julian shook his head. "I'm sorry, but he's already gone and won't be back until the day of the surgery."

"That's too bad. I would have loved to get to know him."

Looking annoyed, Julian said, "You can get to know him when he wakes up after the surgery. And he *will* wake up. Do not doubt it."

"I'm sure he will," I said quickly.

He stiffened. "Don't placate me with banality, Dr. McBride. *Believe* me. Have faith in me. I *will not* let my brother die, do you understand?"

"I do," I said with tears in my eyes. "I'm sorry, Sir. I do believe in you. I love you."

Julian wiped his mouth with his napkin before standing up. "I love you too, Rachel," he said quietly.

Then he left without finishing his dinner and we didn't see

him for the rest of the evening. I should have been happy that he loved me, but instead I worried. Why did his confession sound so...resigned? What was he doing? What was he thinking? I hated having to go to bed without at least our usual parting kiss.

"Do you think he's okay?" I asked when we got to my room.

Colin sighed as he pulled off his shirt. "He'll be fine. He's just got a lot on his mind and a lot to do between now and the surgery."

"I wish I hadn't upset him. That's the last thing he needs right now."

"You can't help how you feel, Rachel, and I think it's best to be honest about it. He'll get over it."

I hoped he was right, but I had a bad feeling about it.

Chapter Thirteen

October 31

The day of the execution, Julian had a few last-minute details to tie up in Montaneva's capital city before the surgery, so at one o'clock, he gave Colin and me each a casual kiss goodbye. We wouldn't see him again before the surgery—when he returned, he'd go directly to the surgical suite to oversee the patient prep.

Colin and I didn't talk about the surgery. Instead, we ate a light supper and basically meditated, working up that razor-sharp focus we'd need to successfully complete our tasks.

At nine o'clock, we went up to the surgical suite to check in. We needed to be waiting, ready to scrub in when all the surgeons operating ahead of us, a few of whom I still hadn't met, were done.

We were all tense, watching the clock, hating the fact that we were counting down the death of one man so that another could live.

When word came that the condemned had been declared dead, the clock started. By the time the donor arrived at Bangenschloss, he had already been anesthetized, prepped and marked, and was well on his way to being hypothermic.

The patient was reportedly prepped and cooling right on schedule as well.

Before I scrubbed in, I stretched and did deep-breathing exercises to make sure I was as sharp and limber as I could be. I didn't allow myself to consider anything but a positive outcome. After I scrubbed in, I stayed away from the observation window, concentrating only on the clinical procedure I was about to perform.

When Dr. Lang and I stepped up to the table, the only part of the patient visible between the drapes was his neck, which was a deep yellow from the iodine-impregnated incision drape. Everything but his blood supply had already been neatly severed. Having been informed in passing that everything had proceeded according to plan, I quickly applied two clamps to each vessel and sliced between them as Dr. Lang did the same on the other side.

I didn't watch the male nurse lift the patient's head, which was affixed to a halo and carefully strapped to a sterile board, but instead stalked immediately into the other operating room and assumed my position beside the headless body. The instant the draped head touched the table, Dr. Lang and I set to work. One by one, I inserted mesh stents, suturing the main arteries and veins on the patient's left side with a series of small pre-threaded needles and tying them off before moving on to the next one.

I was so focused on my own task that I had no idea how much time had passed or how Dr. Lang was progressing. When I finished, I looked up and found him suturing the last major vessel, the external jugular vein. He completed the task just seconds behind me.

With a short glance and nod at each other, we quickly released all the clamps.

"Start the machine," I ordered.

Immediately the heart-lung machine began pumping blood through the patient's system. After a quick check of the polypropylene sutures to make sure they were holding securely, we reconnected the smaller vessels and then stepped out of the way to make room for Julian and Colin and their equipment.

It was a shock to realize that our part was finished, and in just forty-two minutes. I'd done my best, and the patient's survival was out of my hands now.

Which meant I was free to pray and pace and chew my nails to bloody nubs.

For the rest of the afternoon and evening, all of us who'd already completed our parts of the surgery took turns standing at the observation window watching the other surgeons complete theirs. Colin and Julian stayed in the OR while the remaining surgeons carefully reattached the skull, stabilized the cervical spine and sutured muscles, stepping in once in a while to reattach more nerves.

I was so exhausted all I wanted to do was sleep, but I couldn't relax until they did. It would be days, perhaps even weeks or months, before we'd know anything about the outcome of today's procedure, but I wouldn't rest until I knew the patient's head was as completely attached to his body as we could get it.

Once the plastic surgeons had closed the main incision and sprayed on stem cells that would eventually render the scar barely visible, the operation was declared complete at twenty-seven hours, twelve minutes, and the patient was moved to the intensive-care-level recovery room.

We all cheered as the last four surgeons stripped off their gloves and gowns and walked out of the operating room. I flew into Julian's arms, vibrating with exhaustion and an excess of joy and fear and hope, and just hugged him while everyone else crowded around to congratulate the neurosurgical team.

When the noise finally died down and the crowd began to disperse, he stroked the back of my head.

"I love you so much," he said, kissing my ear. Then he hooked an arm around Colin's neck and pulled him into the embrace, planting a kiss on his temple. "I love you too, my dear. Thank you both, from the very bottom of my heart. You can't know what this means to me."

"Oh, I think we can, Sir," Colin said quietly, hugging both of us. "I'm proud of you, Rachel."

"Proud of me?" I asked incredulously, pulling back to stare at him. "All I did was hook up the pipes. You and Julian did all the truly amazing work."

"We got to work together," Julian said. "You went in there without us. Trust me, it makes a difference. So thank you again, Dr. McBride. I'm very proud to be working with you."

I flushed with pleasure and longed to kiss his wonderful, strong, tired face, but one of the other surgeons was waiting to speak to Julian so I simply murmured, "Thank you, Sir."

"I was going to say the very same thing, Dr. McBride," the surgeon hovering beside me said in a very British accent.

Looking up, I said, "Thank you, Doctor... Oh, uh..."

This time I flushed with embarrassment rather than pleasure. It was the voyeur doctor from that first night in the clinic, the one who'd looked vaguely familiar.

"Dr. McBride, you remember Dr. Thurlough, don't you?" Julian said. "Dr. Roderick Thurlough?"

Frowning, I stared up at the man. Where did I know him from?

"Perhaps this will help," he offered, pulling off his surgical cap and releasing his hair from the ponytail I hadn't noticed last night. Then he grinned. "Hello, Rae."

My eyes went wide. I'd only ever known one long-haired Englishman.

"Mas—" I looked around and lowered my voice on the off chance that at least one person in this crowd had no knowledge of Julian's other life. "Master Rod?"

"Lovely to see you again, my dear," he murmured. "Every delicious inch of you."

That didn't help the stinging in my cheeks. "The pleasure was all yours."

His eyebrow rose. "The way you carried on? I hardly think so."

I glanced around in consternation. Dammit, I'd asked for that one.

"What are you doing here?" I demanded.

"Performing orthopedic surgery on the patient."

"No, I mean…" I looked back and forth between him and Julian. Could this possibly be a coincidence? No—considering the pointed way Julian introduced him, he had to know that I'd been acquainted with Master Rod before last night.

Julian sighed. "Rachel, I'm your Dominant. Do you honestly believe I'd go off and leave you unprotected for the rest of your residency?"

"What are you talking about?"

"When I was forced to leave the US after my brother's diagnosis, I continued to monitor your progress and activities through a variety of resources. The only time I interfered was when you began exploring your kinks online."

My eyes widened in shock. "What!"

"Don't give me that look, Dr. McBride. Unprotected submissives can get in over their heads very quickly with the wrong Dom or sadist. Colin had opened your eyes to your need for sexual domination, and it was my responsibility to make sure your early experiences in the lifestyle were not only safe, sane and consensual, but positive and self-affirming. So I arranged for you to meet an appropriate Dom—a starter Dom, if you will."

"You set me up with Master Rod?" Aghast, I hissed, "Julian, I almost had sex with him!"

"Since I hadn't claimed you yet, I would have been pleased that you'd reached that level of self-awareness and found the confidence to pursue what you needed," he said.

"You must be joking."

"Rachel, you need the release of total submission. You've needed it for years, and that was the only way I could provide it at the time. However," he said, laying his hand on the back of

161

my neck, "I won't pretend I wasn't pleased when you stopped short of submitting to him in the flesh."

Wiped out both physically and emotionally, I couldn't even begin to formulate a reply to that. Good God, who *was* this man?

"I'm still envious of Julian, even if he is my employer," Master Rod said with a wry grin. "As I believe I told you, any Dom would be proud to hold the heart of such a devoted sub."

"Indeed," Julian said. He kissed my temple. "All right, Dr. McBride, I'm going to stay with Jordan in recovery for a while and make sure he's settling in. Why don't you and Colin go get some sleep. I'll be up later."

For the first time, Colin and I dropped into bed together and simply slept. I awoke sometime in the middle of the night to the feel of cool, familiar hands sliding over my spread thighs. *Julian.*

"Forgive me, my dear," he murmured, kneeling over me in the dark. "I need you too badly to wait another moment."

Still half-asleep and aware only of my endless love and yearning for him, I welcomed him, pulling at his shoulders as he set the head of his cock against my body's sleep-warmed opening. I wasn't the least bit aroused yet, and I gasped in discomfort when he pushed partway in.

He swore and then pulled out slowly. "I'm sorry, that was poorly done of me. I assumed you'd still be wet."

"We were too pooped to party," Colin mumbled from the pillow beside me.

Julian leaned over me, breathing roughly, his chest squashing my right breast as he fumbled in the side drawer. Apparently finding what he sought, he pushed away from me and I heard a snap and the unmistakable sound of flesh being lubed.

Then his fingers slid into me, spreading the slick moisture into every crevice. "Beautiful little cunt," Julian whispered. "So hot and tight and mine."

His crude praise incited a surge of my own natural lubricant and I reached for him again, suddenly unable to wait myself. He fell on me at once, sliding his forearms under my shoulders as he shoved deep, and then deeper. God, he was thick. I could feel every inch of him throbbing inside me—or was that me throbbing? The fit was so tight, it was hard to tell.

Julian kissed me then, a long, deep, inquisitive greeting that felt so long overdue, I nearly cried. When he rolled to his back, taking me up on top without breaking the kiss or slipping out, I gasped against his mouth. Both of his hands immediately roved down to my butt and his fingers zeroed in on the place where our bodies were joined.

"Mmmm," he hummed into my mouth.

I hummed back and kissed him hungrily, squeezing my internal muscles on his restless cock. God, I loved being on top for a change. I was vaguely conscious of Colin moving on the bed and the snap of the lube lid, but it didn't dawn on me what was about to happen until he spread my butt cheeks wider with one hand and slid the cold, slick fingers of the other into my anus.

Fear and excitement churned through me.

Raising my head, I said, "Um, Colin..."

"I told you we'd do this to you, Rachel," he said, thrusting inside me in a way that told me this was the only warm-up I was getting. "We're doing it now."

I swallowed hard, wishing the light were on so I could see, but kind of glad it wasn't so they couldn't see me. "Okay."

Julian groaned deeply. "That's my good little slut." Then he clamped his fingers on my cheeks and pulled them wide. "Now means *now*, Colin. In. I need to feel you."

There was no hesitation when Colin shifted and put his

cock against me. He forged deep on the first thrust and stretched out over me with a groan, pressing his lips against the top of my spine as he pressed me into Julian. Breathless, overfilled and insanely aroused, I felt his arms and Julian's come down by my sides. I reached down too, and found their hands linked.

A tidal wave of emotion rolled over me. Love. And fear. They loved each other so much. What did it mean to me? Why did I feel like they'd be together long after I moved on?

"Fuck me," I gasped, desperate to move away from this state of suspension. "Do it."

Colin started moving at once and Julian and I both groaned. It felt sooooo good.

Julian's thighs shifted behind me and his hands grabbed my butt again, holding me in place as he thrust up hard, making me cry out. He did it again and again, in a rhythm that seemed completely unrelated to Colin's. It was like they were both looking out for number one, like I was nothing more than an inanimate object for them both to get off in.

The idea drove me wild, as did the unpredictability of the stimulation. I couldn't slip into any sort of internal rhythm with them jarring me haphazardly. Thrilled and frustrated, I tried to move too, but Julian forced my hips down against him and fucked me harder, driving into me like he had only seconds to reach orgasm.

"Don't move," he gasped. "You take what we give you."

I raked my nails up his ribs. Hard.

"Fuck!" he shouted, bucking wildly and just about knocking Colin off. They both stopped moving as he grappled with my evading arms until he got ahold of my wrists. "Bratty little slut wants some pain with her pleasure, Colin."

Panting, Colin said, "I can do that, Sir."

Bracing himself away from my back, he grabbed a handful of my hair and pulled my head back hard enough to bring tears to my eyes. Then he held me there and started slapping the hell out of my right thigh and hip. Julian managed to snag my nipples between his thumbs and my wrist bones and I screamed when he pinched them brutally.

I was still keening when Colin let go and my head dropped onto Julian's shoulder. Colin began to slap my other thigh and hip, alternating randomly between the sides, and finally I burst into sobs. "Ow, ow, ow!"

He seized my hips and fucked me roughly.

"Don't come, little slut," Julian growled, pulling on my stinging nipples. "You do not have permission."

"Oh God," I choked. I couldn't come from this pain, but I might come from the excitement. "Please, oh God—"

His voice rose. "Don't you dare fucking come, Rachel Anne. You don't want to know what will happen to you if you do."

I whimpered, trying to stop it, trying to block out—

"I want to see what happens to you," Colin panted. "Come, Rachel." He wiggled a hand in between my belly and Julian's, and I gasped when I realized he was going for my clit.

"No! Colin, don't!"

"Rachel, if you come, I'm going to forget you ever had a safe word and fucking turn you inside out with pain and humiliation."

Colin found my clit and worked it in rough circles as he pounded into my aching butt. "Let's do it. Come on, Rachel, come so we can turn you into a real slave and do whatever the hell we want to you."

The chilling, tingling wave rose in my abdomen and I struggled wildly, keening, "No, no, no, no..."

"Mmmm, oh yeah, here she comes, Sir."

Julian gasped, letting go of my wrists to slap both my hips over and over. "Stop it, Rachel, now!"

I shook my head wildly. "No, no, no..."

The orgasm blew my head off and I sank straight to the bottom, where it was dark and warm and peaceful.

Chapter Fourteen

November 2

By the time I opened my eyes late the next morning, the peaceful feeling had vanished along with Julian, and the vague stirrings of foreboding had returned.

Colin was wrapped around me like a vine. He woke almost as soon as I did and rocked his morning erection against my bare butt.

"I love you, Rachel," he murmured in my ear.

Tears prickled the back of my nose. "I love you too."

With the arm under my head, he pulled my face around and kissed me. Tenderly. Almost solemnly. "Thank you," he finally said. "Let's go see how Jordan's doing."

My apprehension increased, but I shoved it down and got up immediately. There would be time enough to sort through my concerns after Jordan turned the corner.

When we went down to the medical floor, he was still holding his own but deeply sedated. Julian sat in a chair beside his bed, looking even more exhausted than he had the day before.

"I couldn't sleep, but I don't know what to do with myself," he said. "I love that the surgery is finished but I hate having nothing to do. It's all up to Jordan now, and I hate it."

Feeling protective, I sat down in his lap and wrapped my arms around him. "He's going to be fine, Julian."

He threaded his hand through my hair and kissed my

temple. "I know. It's just the waiting and wondering and worrying that drives me mad." Then he turned my face to his. "I love you very much, Rachel. Never doubt that. No matter what happens."

I looked into his eyes and was startled at the darkness in their depths. He'd never expressed the least doubt before this moment. "I love you too, but I think you need a little more sleep. You're sounding awfully pessimistic."

"I don't think sleep is what he needs right now," Colin said abruptly.

I frowned at him. "Well it couldn't hurt."

"You're right, but I'm pretty sure he needs something else first." I was shocked when Colin grabbed a handful of Julian's hair and pulled his head backward. Leaning down until his face was bare inches from Julian's, he said, "Don't you, Sir?"

Julian swallowed but didn't answer.

"Just get it over with and tell her," Colin said flatly.

"Colin, what the hell?" I protested. "Leave him alone."

They both ignored me as Colin's expression grew cruel. "Are you going to make me beat it out of you, Julian?"

I gasped. "Colin!"

Julian closed his eyes as a sigh shuddered through him. "Please do."

"Very well." Colin put a hard kiss on his lips. "Be waiting for me in the punishment room in one hour. You know how it works."

Julian shuddered again. "Yes, Sir."

An hour later, my stomach was rolling with anxiety when Colin and I entered the dungeons through the door directly across from my room. I'd begged him to tell me what was going on, what he thought he was doing, but as usual he said it was something Julian would have to tell me himself.

When Colin flipped an externally wired wall switch, half a dozen clear incandescent bulbs hanging from the ceiling flared to life, starkly illuminating the more traditional-looking dungeon. There were crosses, stocks, cages of different sizes and styles, a variety of padded sawhorses and benches, and an entire long wall hung with instruments of torture. And everywhere above us, chains dripped from the ceiling like streamers at a kinky prom.

My heart stopped when I saw Julian kneeling naked on the stone floor, his head down, his hands behind his back.

"I hate this, Julian," Colin said shortly.

"I know," Julian whispered. "I'm sorry."

"We'll see, won't we? As you're so fond of telling me, real repentance is expressed through actions rather than words."

"Yes, Sir."

My tummy twisted with fear. Was this just another mind fuck, an intense role-playing scene, or had Julian truly done something wrong?

Had he cut some legal corners to make his brother's surgery happen? It had crossed my mind more than once that donating his body to the experiment was an awfully altruistic gesture for a serial killer, whatever concessions he might have been granted. If Julian hadn't obtained permission from the "donor", it would be the modern-day equivalent of body-snatching.

I shuddered. *God, please don't let that be it.*

Colin nudged Julian's thigh with the toe of his shoe. "Up."

Julian climbed awkwardly to his feet and stood there with his head down, his hands still behind his back. His long, pale body and heavy, flaccid cock looked unreasonably vulnerable.

"Come with me." Colin led him to a heavy wooden stock in the corner with leather-padded neck and wrist holes and a similarly padded low platform. While Julian stood there, Colin lowered both neck boards until the openings were at knee height and then raised the upper one. "In."

Once Julian had knelt on the platform and placed his neck and wrists into the openings, Colin slid the top board down and latched it so that Julian was locked in place with his head only a foot from the wall. Then he picked up some kind of mini-stock with just two holes and kicked Julian's ankles farther apart. Crouching, he opened up the stock and locked it around Julian's ankles and then hooked the ends to the side rails.

Julian jerked a little in his bonds. "I'm sorry, Colin."

"Quiet. Unless you're ready to tell Rachel what you did?" When Julian didn't reply, Colin said, "I didn't think so. The next time you speak without permission, it had better be to tell her the truth or you'll wish you were standing."

Julian quieted at once but his feet twisted restlessly.

Colin went to a cabinet and pulled out a rolled-up mat. "Rachel, you sit on the floor by his head and keep an eye on him. No touching, please, no matter how badly you want to. He has to do this by himself."

I took it with a nod and unrolled it on the floor right by the wall. God, I hated seeing Julian like this. It was so wrong, I felt like I should avert my eyes.

My stomach clenched when Colin went to the wall of torture implements and came back with two different canes, one white with a black handle, and a thinner one of wood, curved at the end like a walking cane.

"I'm not going to give you much of a warm-up, Julian, and you have no safe word. You know what you have to do to make it stop."

I was shocked to see a tremor run through Julian. Suddenly I was very afraid. I didn't want to be here.

"Please don't do this," I said unsteadily.

"Rachel, Julian needs you beside him, but if you can't be quiet I'll have to gag you and put you in restraints."

Stomach churning, I wrapped my arms around my drawn-up knees and bit my lips.

Colin set the white cane on a nearby bench. Then he took his place behind Julian and rolled his neck and shoulders before blowing out a breath.

"I love you, Julian," he said.

Julian took a deep breath and then gasped when the first strike landed on his butt. It didn't look like Colin was hitting him very hard, but Julian flinched and gasped with every blow, the long muscles in his legs twitching like a racehorse's. After about twenty, spaced less than five seconds apart, his gasps turned to grunts.

At forty, Colin stopped and leaned down to rub his hand roughly over Julian's butt cheeks and thighs, and Julian groaned, keeping his eyes tightly closed.

Colin sighed. "All right, let's get down to it."

My eyes widened in horror. That was the *warm-up*?

He drew back his arm and laid the cane across Julian's thighs, drawing a yelp from him. He did it again and again, and when Julian arched his back, drawing his knees closer together, Colin hit him harder.

After the echo of Julian's shout died, Colin ordered, "Get your back down. Don't try to protect your nuts or I'll go after them."

Julian reluctantly straightened his back and spread his knees, breathing harshly.

Colin hit him hard across both thighs again, and this time Julian screamed.

I burst into tears, shaking all over. "Colin, please stop."

"No," Julian said through clenched teeth. "It's okay, Rachel. I need this."

Colin leaned down to tap the bottoms of Julian's feet repeatedly and Julian howled like an animal, bucking and

Julian swallowed and closed his eyes, his expression one of such undiluted dread, I decided against pushing him further.

When Colin returned, his face was pale, his eyes red-rimmed, and I felt like I'd been kicked in the chest. Oh God, how selfish could I be? Inflicting so much pain on the man he loved had to be ten times worse than watching it.

"Any infractions, Julian?" he asked with unbelievable calm.

"No, Sir."

"Good. Thank you both." He picked up the white cane and whipped it around in the air, looking as sick as I felt. "Julian, I want you to think about this while you're being stoic—every stroke I give you punishes Rachel and me as much as it does you, and even if you deserve it, we don't."

Julian's face crumpled and he sobbed once but didn't say anything.

"Have it your way."

It took thirty-two strokes of the mean white cane to break him.

"He said no!" he finally screamed.

Colin dropped the cane immediately. "Thank God."

Horror gripped me. "You *did* steal the body?"

"No," Julian gasped. "My brother. He said no. I didn't have Jordan's permission for the transplant. He said he'd rather die than live as my monster, but I just...couldn't let it take him too."

I covered my mouth with my shaking hands. "Oh my God."

And I'd thought body-snatching was the worst possible scenario. At least that, the donor wouldn't have had to live with—he was dead either way. But Jordan might have fifty or sixty years to live with the results of Julian's highly unethical action.

"He's only twenty-eight," Julian ground out. "He hasn't begun to live yet. He's never even been in love. How could I just let him give up without a fight when I could offer him the chance to live a full and happy life?"

Numb with shock, I watched as Colin released the boards one by one and pulled Julian's limp, naked body into his arms, cradling him against his chest.

"It's all right, Julian." He kissed Julian's stubbly jaw, his wet eyelashes, his sweat-soaked hair. "You did what you had to. If it were you, I'd have done the same thing."

"So Pohlson *did* consent to the donation," I said dully.

"Yes," Colin told me. "All the terms of their agreement have been fulfilled. Within minutes of the execution, an escrow deposit in the amount of ten million US dollars that Julian had made under the guise of an anonymous abolitionist was released to his family."

I sagged against the stock, relieved that, that much, at least, had been true.

Then Colin clutched Julian tighter and whispered against his ear, "Tell her the rest."

"Oh shit, there's more?"

Julian turned his face into Colin's neck. "I can't."

"You have to. She deserves to know everything."

Julian swallowed hard and took a deep, shaky breath before opening his swollen, red eyes. He didn't look directly at me, a fact that chilled me.

"Pohlson wanted to fuck," he said harshly, "preferably teenage boys. He wouldn't even discuss any other terms until we'd reached an agreement on that one."

I covered my mouth. "Julian, you didn't..."

"No, Rachel, I didn't," Julian hissed, finally focusing on me with tempered steel in his eyes. "I would never have allowed anyone else to submit to that monster."

The rest of the world ceased to exist as the implications of that statement crashed down on me.

I don't bottom. Ever.

"Oh, Julian, no," I said faintly.

"Oh yes. I spent thirty minutes a week locked in that godforsaken cell with Augustine Pohlson after the agreement was finalized four months ago. Yesterday afternoon was the last time, a full hour, and he made the most of it. He toyed with me, telling me he'd changed his mind, making me beg, making me..." His voice broke, and he closed his eyes, shuddering. "I'm sure that sick fuck died smiling, replete with the knowledge of how completely he'd degraded the great Dr. Julian Xavier Kilmartin."

I sat there shaking, my mind a wasteland, my breastbone aching with the force of emotions too complex to sort out and too volatile to risk venting when Julian was in such a fragile state.

Colin looked at me, defiance and hope and dread mingling on his face. *Don't hurt him,* his eyes pleaded.

"That's it?" I demanded. "That's the whole truth?"

Colin nodded. "Everything else about the operation was completely aboveboard."

Making use of my hard-won ability to compartmentalize, I stuffed everything I'd just learned into a mental drawer, slammed it shut and locked it before standing up stiffly. "We need to take care of his wounds."

Colin's eyes fell to Julian's flanks, which streaked with too many livid welts to count, several of them welling with blood. He nodded, swallowing visibly. Between us, we got Julian up to his feet and half carried him to my room, since it was closest. He grunted with every step.

"Dammit, why did you talk?" Colin said as we laid Julian facedown across the bed. "I didn't want to hit your feet."

"Better my feet than my nuts," Julian mumbled into the spread.

Colin snorted. "You don't walk on your nuts."

"No, but I might," I said under my breath. I'd seen enough cock-and-ball torture in my online explorations to know how to administer a little discipline of my own.

Apparently I hadn't compartmentalized the anger quite as effectively as I thought.

Colin looked at me sharply but didn't say anything. He left and returned with a bottle of water, a handful of capsules and a jar of salve. He made Julian take the capsules, and then together we applied the salve liberally to Julian's poor blistered butt and thighs. Julian flinched and moaned the whole time, but the moment we were finished, he seemed to fall into a deep sleep.

Colin crawled onto the bed to gently kiss his cheek and then wrapped the top and bottom ends of the quilt over him.

"He'll probably be out until tomorrow, but someone should check on him," he said, closing the door behind us. He pulled out his phone and called Dirk, quickly letting him know the situation and asking him to check on Julian periodically.

Then he took my hand, and though I wanted to be alone, *needed* to be alone, I let him pull me down the hall into another bedroom. It must be his—though it was very clean and everything was neatly put away, the closet door was open and I could see his clothes on the bar and shoes on the floor.

He started stripping off his clothes as fast as he could.

"I need you," he said with a shiver.

Noting his lack of erection with relief, I stripped off too and climbed under the covers with him. He was ice-cold and shaking when I pulled his head against my breasts.

"Please, God, let me never have to do that again," he said, clutching me tightly.

"Have you done it before?"

"Every week for the last seventeen weeks. After he returned from the prison, he'd disappear into his bathroom for an hour, scrubbing himself raw inside and out, and then make me beat him until he was able to scream out whatever that sick bastard made him feel. This time was the worst."

A shudder rattled through him, and then another. "I don't think I can do it again," he choked out before a sob was torn from deep in his chest, and then another.

I held him for quite a while, keeping my eyes wide open and my mind blank so the lid didn't fly off the pressurized compartment where I'd stuffed everything.

When I was sure he was asleep, I carefully extracted myself from his arms and dressed. I stumbled down the hall, opening doors until I found a vacant bedroom, and then cried until I vomited.

Chapter Fifteen

November 6

My bags had been packed and waiting by the door for the last three days while I floundered in a morass of dread and yearning. For once, my inner good girl and bad girl were completely silent, as if both of them were as conflicted as I was.

The day after Julian's shocking revelations, I'd told him I needed some time off to think—and the key to my room so that I could lock it from the inside. He'd granted both without hesitation. That afternoon, Colin knocked on my door and handed me a flash drive.

"This is the only remaining copy of the footage Vince took during your first scene in the dungeon."

"Footage?" I gaped at him, prickling all over with a now familiar blend of dread and secret arousal. "You mean Vince made a *movie* of me? *Naked?*"

"You agreed to it," he said shortly. "Look at section 12 in your personal conduct agreement."

Gasping with outrage, I slammed the door in his face. At least that explained where my employee ID photo had come from. God, how high had I been flying not to have noticed a man aiming a video camera at my nude body?

I almost threw the drive into the fire, but something stopped me. Who'd already watched it? Did I want to know? Did I really even care at this point?

Deciding I might one day need it, I dropped it into my computer bag, not the least bit interested in seeing myself so completely vulnerable and losing all control.

The next day it had warmed up enough for me to go outside without a winter coat, and I tromped down the slushy driveway in just a red hoodie, breathing the crisp, clean air and soaking up the bright sunshine. I didn't even try to think, but just opened myself to the world around me. I walked down the narrow paved road for quite a while, and when a couple of compact cars gave friendly honks as they zoomed past, I waved and smiled, glad to finally be grounded in reality again, if only in a small way.

It was at that point I realized how very disconnected I'd become in the last three weeks. When I got back to my room, I turned on my cell phone for the first time since the night I arrived and called Bree. She laid a ten-minute guilt trip on me and then immediately asked if Colin was as good as ever in bed.

"Better," I told her honestly. The bold pronouncement distracted her enough that she didn't even mention Julian or ask about the project. She did ask about Bangenschloss, and I took the opportunity to distract her further with a vivid description—leaving out, of course, any mention of the dungeons. Horribly homesick now, I asked her about Mom and Dad, and she filled me in on the little routine things I'd missed. By the time she finished, I was nearly in tears, I wanted to go home so badly.

"Rae, are you okay?" she asked.

"Yeah," I told her with a tremulous sigh. "I just didn't realize how hard it would be to live so far away from all of you."

She promised to come see me at Christmas. She was so excited I didn't tell her it might not be wise to book flights since I might not be here then.

This morning, I finally watched the scene on the flash drive, and it shredded my heart to pieces. It reminded me how desperately I wanted Colin and Julian back, how hollow and lonely I was without them. I missed working with them. I missed having meals with them. I missed playing with them.

But I just couldn't be around them right now or I'd do or say something I might regret, and I'd have no idea what that something was until it came tumbling out of me and I couldn't take it back.

Ready to jump out of my skin, I went across the corridor into the punishment room and turned on the lights. Without a naked Julian or a cane-wielding Colin to bring it to life, it was back to being just a BDSM stage with a bunch of lifeless props in it. I disliked the way it smelled now—the hints of leather, antiseptic and damp stone brought the memories of Julian's beating too vividly to life.

Feeling as though I were trespassing, I walked slowly around the room, trailing my fingertips over the various leather-covered pieces of furniture and trying to imagine myself draped over them, or locked in one of the very sturdy-looking cages. I wasn't successful.

Approaching the wall with trepidation, I threaded my fingertips through the flat, black tails of a flogger much like the one Master Rod had planned to use on me once upon a time. Suede, I thought, soft and fine. Would it have hurt? Probably not much, unless he'd swung it really hard. Would pain alone do it for me? Would it send me to the same place that playing kinky games with Julian and Colin did? Or did I need them to get me there?

The rush of intense yearning startled me. I wanted to try it. I needed to see if I could reach that headspace, where everything was suddenly easy and clear, without the men I loved so much.

"May I help you with anything, Rachel?"

I turned to find Vince in the doorway to the mad scientist's lab, leaning against the wall with his arms crossed. How long had he been watching me?

After biting my pursed lips for a moment, I told him, "Possibly."

Turning back to the wall, I sifted my fingers through the sparse tails of a multicolored flogger. They were braided, and knotted near the ends. I imagined those probably hurt quite a bit, especially in the hands of a ruthless sadist.

The tickle of desire I experienced at the idea startled me.

Fighting the feeling I was somehow cheating on Julian and Colin, I said, "Tell me about these, Vince."

"All right." He came to stand beside me, taking down each of the floggers one by one and explaining the differences between them—which were stingy, which were really stingy, which could be thuddy, and which would make me seriously consider safe-wording. As I'd suspected, the soft one was more for sensation than real pain play.

Then we moved on to slappers, crops, paddles and canes, which, once he started talking about them, I found even more fascinating. I was irresistibly drawn to the ones Colin had used on Julian.

"Have you ever had any of this used on you?" I asked.

He grinned. "All of them, some just about every day. I'm not actually a badass Dom, you know—I just play one on TV."

"You're a sub?" I asked, wide-eyed.

"To the bone. Pun intended, of course."

I smiled. "Well you certainly had me fooled. You're a better actor than the real Vincent Price."

"I'm as real as he is, Rachel," Vince said dryly.

"Sorry, you know what I mean." I tilted my head. "So do you have a Dom—or is it Domina?"

"I do," he said with a coy look. "He's a mean-ass German surgeon named Dirk Hauptman."

"Dirk?" I blinked. "Does that mean you're..."

"Lovers," he confirmed. "I'm mostly gay. He'll fuck anyone

who can't get away."

"Is anything I thought I knew about you true?" I asked with wide eyes.

"I *am* Julian's personal assistant, if that makes you feel any better."

"Well thank God." Then I thought of the flash drive. "So you're the one who recorded me, huh?"

"Does that bother you?"

I considered it. "Actually, no. I mean, it's not like you'd be jerking off to it or anything."

"What makes you think that?" he asked with a slight smile. "I'll jerk off to just about anything, and power exchange does it for me, no matter who's topping whom. Frankly, Rachel, watching Dirk turn you on while he scared the shit out of you was off-the-rails hot, and your submission to Julian was something I felt privileged to witness. I'm hoping you'll give me a copy of that night. You have my word it will never wind up on the Internet."

My heart squeezed uncomfortably. "I'll think about it."

"So what are you really here for, Rachel McBride?" he asked with a penetrating look. "What do you need?"

I glanced up at the wall. "Have you ever used these on anyone?"

"As a matter of fact, yes. As a masochist, I have no problem dispensing pain to those who enjoy it." His eyes narrowed a bit. "Julian isn't much for whips but I'm sure Colin would be more than happy to administer your first flogging."

"He might," I said, though I wasn't so certain after his ordeal with Julian. "But this is something I think I need to experience on my own. Without them."

"They might not agree."

"They're not in any position to agree or disagree," I said flatly, refusing to feel guilty. "I need this. My head is buzzing with all these conflicting voices, and I just can't seem to relax or focus on anything."

"You need to feel more centered?"

I sighed. "That's it exactly."

Vince regarded me silently for a moment. "I'll have to talk to Dirk first. I assume you want to do this fairly soon?"

"Now wouldn't be too soon for me. I'm going out of my mind."

"Not necessarily the proper headspace for agreeing to your maiden beating," he pointed out.

"It's the only headspace I've got at the moment. Please," I added.

He pulled out his cell phone and called Dirk, explaining briefly what I wanted and then listened for a couple of minutes while I vibrated with tension. Finally he hung up. "Dirk said it was okay but to wait for him. He'll be here in twenty minutes."

Finally I relaxed. "That's fine."

"He'd do it all, if you'd rather. He's a hell of a lot more experienced than I am."

Something in me balked. "I'd rather have you," I said quickly.

Vince smiled. "Excellent. It's about damn time I got off the sidelines."

"Are you certain this is what you want, Rachel?" Dirk asked, standing before me with his arms crossed. He still looked forbidding, but knowing he was Vince's lover reassured me somehow. Fun, easy-to-talk-to Vince wouldn't sleep with anyone too cruel, right?

Ignoring a little niggle of guilt, I said, "I'm positive."

"All right then, pick out everything you want to try and bring it to me."

I picked out a couple of floggers, including the one with the knots in it, a leather paddle, a slapper and the two dreadful canes.

Vince shook his head. "I won't use the canes on you. I haven't had enough experience and I don't think you're ready."

"One from each would probably be enough," I said. "I just need to know what they're like."

"I'll handle those," Dirk said.

"Fine." I looked around a little self-consciously. "Do I need to be naked?"

"Naked is best if you want to get a true feel for all of these, but you can leave your socks on if you want to," Vince said, plucking yet another flogger off the wall. "And I'd suggest that you be bound. If you're going to fly, that's probably the only way you'll get there."

I undressed quickly, and then at the last second, took my socks off too—I felt more conspicuous with them on. My good girl and my bad girl were singing a bad-idea duet, but I shut them down. If I didn't, I'd never have any clarity.

Vince wasted no time cuffing my wrists into a large metal frame and drawing them up with a rope pulley until there was just a little play. When I asked why the frame instead of one of the crosses, he explained, "Since you want to try so many different implements, it's best for me to have access to both sides."

That made me bite my lip. My sensitive nipples still hadn't forgotten their introduction to the violet wand.

Vince cuffed my feet far enough apart on the cool stone floor that I felt vulnerable but not physically uncomfortable and then rubbed my back reassuringly. It was different, being nude while he and Dirk were both dressed, especially knowing they were a couple. The awareness that nobody was waiting to get it on with me took the edge off, and not necessarily in a good way.

Standing where I could see him, Vince stretched his arms and shoulders and then took a few practice swings with the flogger he'd picked up. "This one's deerskin. Makes a better warm-up. Floggers work best on the upper body in an upright position, especially since I'm taller and you're not wearing fuck-me heels."

"Gotcha."

"Ready?" he asked.

I nodded.

"Dirk will keep an eye on you to make sure you don't fly off too far to safe-word."

Rather than hitting me, he dragged the flogger across my skin, trailing it over my shoulders and arms, letting the tails trickle over me like water. At his instruction, I'd gone back across the hall and put my hair up in a clip while we waited for Dirk, and now the feel of the cool leather sliding over the nape of my neck gave me chills.

Then the tails sprayed across my back, and though it didn't really hurt, I jumped at the sound.

"This one's bark is much worse than its bite." He started with very light brushstrokes on my back, working in a slow, steady rhythm that I found distinctly enjoyable. When he put a little more strength into the blows, painting warmth across my shoulders and back, I sighed, closing my eyes and sagging into the cuffs just a bit. If it were Colin behind me, doing this to me, I'd be in heaven.

Then the tails snapped around my ribs and I gasped at the sting.

"That was just an example of why you want to be careful not to let the tails wrap around," Vince said.

He moved around to the front to tease the tender skin of my underarms, making me jump and giggle until the skin began to heat. When he moved down, I bit my lip, trying not to moan as the soft tails repeatedly licked over my nipples. It was embarrassing to realize I was very wet already. When had that happened?

Vince hummed thoughtfully, maintaining a smooth, even rhythm. "You have lovely breasts, Rachel. Dirk's got a big hard-on for you right now."

He'll fuck anyone who can't get away. "Uh..."

"Actually, it's for you and your little whip, my boy," Dirk drawled. "I should let you top pretty girls more often. Why aren't you naked? Rachel should have a thing of beauty to appreciate too."

Vince immediately set down the flogger with a happy grin and tugged his T-shirt off over his head. "I feel better naked."

"I guess so," I murmured, flushing when he bared his stiff cock.

His grin broadened. "Told you power exchange does it for me no matter who's playing."

Well that put a little edge back into the event.

He switched to the flat, narrow slapper, tapping me at random spots, giving me just a little bit of sting. That was fine until he aimed it at my clit. Then I jumped, hissing at the burn.

"Vince!"

"Rachel!" he teased.

"You're gay!"

"We're both naked, I've got evil toys and you can't get away," he said. "I'm not supposed to play with your fun girl parts?"

"No!"

"Too bad. Safe-word if you can't take it." He did it again, and I swore, trying in vain to pull my knees together. If he kept that up, I might embarrass myself completely.

"That will be enough of that," Dirk said severely. "If anyone gets to play with her defenseless little cunt, it's me."

"You never let me have any fun," Vince complained without heat. He traded the slapper for the sparse, knotted flogger. "This one's got quite a bit more bite but I'll go easy on you. Try to relax," he added when I braced myself. "Bite can be very good when you're sufficiently warmed up."

He returned to my back and shoulders, waiting a few seconds in between strikes to let the sting roll through me. It wasn't long before I began to move in my restraints, biting my lip and dancing a little after each blow.

"A little different sensation, isn't it?"

I blew out a breath. "Just a little."

When he moved around to my front again, he showed me yet another flogger, one with flatter, wider tails and more of them. "Getting more into thud here," he warned.

I nodded, bracing myself and trying to relax as he started in on my back and shoulders again. This one wasn't as loud as the first one but it definitely packed more of a punch, reaching under my skin and into the muscle. It was like a hot, slapping, deep-tissue massage that made me gasp and moan in an embarrassingly sexual way.

"Had enough of that?" Vince asked.

"Just a little more, please."

Though I was relaxed and thoroughly aroused, I didn't feel like I was even close to sinking the way I had with Julian and Colin. When he used an oval wood paddle on my butt, the sting sent me up onto my toes several times, laughing at the stress of it to keep from crying.

Dirk reached over and scrubbed his smooth hand over my buttocks. "You pink up very nicely, slut."

Like he'd thrown the magic switch, I started to sink. God, what did it for me? Was it the word *slut*? His proprietary touch? His guttural accent? Or just the knowledge that he was a "mean-ass" Dom?

Whatever it was, I responded to it in a big way. Did I want to sink with Dirk? Did I trust him enough?

Maybe it was time to find out.

writing in the stock. I sobbed silently into my jeans-clad knees.

"I told you not to speak until you're ready to spill, Julian. Don't do it again or you won't be able to walk tomorrow."

Julian blew out a couple of hard breaths, as if bracing himself, and I wished desperately to hold his clenched hands, stroke his sweat-beaded face. Part of me wanted badly to run away, to do anything but watch him take this punishment, but I couldn't leave him to face it alone.

Colin hit him a dozen more times, and though Julian yelped after several of them, he seemed to be in better control of himself.

"That's fifty," Colin said, rubbing Julian's butt and legs again. "You have five minutes to come clean and then I'm switching from the rattan cane to the Delrin."

Then he looked at me. "I'll be right back. You can talk to him, but don't touch him. When I get back, I'll ask if either of you violated my orders and he'll tell me the truth."

He set the cane down by the other one and walked out, leaving me alone with Julian.

"Please tell me," I whispered, wiping my runny nose with the sleeve of my sweater. "I can't take this anymore."

He shook his head.

"I love you, Julian, and I will love you *forever*, no matter what. Please tell me."

Julian shook his head.

Gathering my nerve, I asked, "Did you lie about having permission?" When his eyes widened, I gasped. "Oh God, that's it, isn't it? You stole the body."

He hesitated for a moment, looking torn, and then shook his head again.

I slumped against my knees in relief. "Oh thank God. I don't know if I could have lived with that."

Chapter Sixteen

"Master Dirk, will you finish me, please?"

"It would be my pleasure, little slut. But first let's make a slight adjustment." He turned the crank, lowering my wrists to about waist height. Then he unhooked my cuffed ankles from the frame and tugged my hips back until I was bent over, making me feel even more exposed.

"It's easier to target the amusing bits this way," he told me with an evil grin.

For some reason I grinned too. What was I thinking?

Vince nudged my ankles shoulder-width apart and attached a black spreader bar to the cuffs, ensuring they'd stay apart. Then he stood beside me, sliding one hand under my stomach and resting the other on my low back. "I'll help you stay in place, okay?"

I took a deep breath. "Okay."

"I think you need an intermediary step before you play with the big toys," Dirk informed me. "The paddle you picked is all sting, no thud."

He went over to the wall, picked up a rounded oak paddle and showed it to me. "Good?"

I nodded, my stomach curling just a bit in thrilled anxiety. So far nothing had hurt nearly as bad as the spanking Julian had given me, but I had a feeling that was about to change. And I wanted it. A lot.

"Sting first, then thud. Ten of each."

I looked at Vince. "Did he say *ten*?"

The only warning I got was the whoosh of the leather

paddle flying through the air the instant before it slapped my right butt cheek. It took a second for the hot sting to kick in, but when it did...

"Yeow!" It felt like a swarm of angry ants was biting my skin from the inside.

By the time he delivered the last two stingers along the lower edge of my butt cheeks, tears streamed down my face and Vince was actively restraining me while I laughed and swore and shifted my weight from foot to foot.

"How did you like that, slut?" Dirk asked, stepping up to rub my butt again. This time it hurt.

"Call the fire department," I gasped. "My butt's blazing." And the sinking sensation was gone as if it had never been.

"The surface is a very pretty shade of red," he agreed. "Now let's see if we can add some depth to your discomfort. Your safe words, slave?"

"Red and yellow."

"Use them when you reach your limit. That's an order. I'm going to go lightly, but I've no doubt you'll show a little bruising regardless."

I swallowed nervously. "Yes, Sir."

The first three or four weren't as bad as I expected. They startled me, then they stung, then they ached and then a burn built inside the muscle. It seemed like he hit the same areas over and over, and at five I started to moan and flinch, bracing myself for the next one.

"Don't tense your buns or they'll bruise more," Vince warned me, smoothing his palm over my back and hips.

I ignored him. There was no way I could relax when I knew what was coming, and I was actually kind of excited at the idea of having marks that would last for a while. They might be the last marks I got for a long time.

Oddly, looking forward to seeing the marks made me relax, and I took the last four or five with only a few whimpers. My butt was still on fire and felt swollen to about five times its usual size, but the end was finally in sight.

"You have two left. The rattan first," Dirk said.

This was the one Colin had warmed Julian up with last week.

Dirk walked in front of me and gave me a light tap on the thigh. It didn't feel too bad but a second later, an intense sting flared and I flinched. "Ouch!"

"Any sadist will tell you that's not a safe word," Dirk grinned.

"I didn't mean it as one."

"Do you still want to feel it on your ass?"

I deliberated for a second. "Yes."

He walked behind me and gave me two across the butt in quick succession before I had a chance to brace myself.

"Son of a bitch!" I said through my teeth.

Then two arrows of fire streaked across the back of my thighs and I jerked hard, screaming, "Red, you bastard!"

"Had enough of that one, eh?"

"I said *one* from each of them," I forced out bitterly, writhing as my body tried to process the pain into something my brain could cope with. It helped when Vince rubbed the marks vigorously.

"One stroke is hardly enough to get a good feel for any impact toy, slave."

Still panting, I scowled at the sneer in Dirk's tone. "It would have been enough for me."

"So you don't wish to experience the Delrin then."

Ah, so that was his game. "I can take it."

He chuckled. "In that case, you will take it until I hear your safe word again. Agreed?"

Oh hell. "Fine."

"You hide more fire than I realized," he told me.

"Is that a good thing?"

"In certain contexts, a very good thing."

I heard the cane whip through the air behind me and sucked in a breath, closing my eyes tightly.

Nothing happened. Shit, he was practicing?

I sagged, and he struck two, three, four times. The pain wasn't coy—it screamed across my butt like grazing bullets and reverberated right down to my bones—but I took it as long as I could stand it. Whimpering, I writhed in my bonds, frantically trying to get away from the blossoming mushroom cloud of agony. After eight, I burst into tears.

"Red, red, red!" I sobbed.

An instant later my hands and feet were free, and Dirk swept me up in his arms, still writhing and sobbing and trying to hold my abused butt. He laid me facedown on a padded leather table and took my hands, and then someone else's hands started massaging my butt firmly with oil. It made the pain even worse, and I fought for a couple of seconds—and then went under.

I drifted for a long time as the pressure and warmth worked their way up my back to my neck and down my legs to my feet and toes. A series of images flashed through my mind: Julian watching me from afar; Julian looking up at me between my breasts as he hugged me in the mad scientist's lab; Julian surrounded by a platoon of dedicated surgeons; Jordan lying on the operating table with his head completely severed from his body; Julian cradled in Colin's arms; Colin sobbing in my arms...

Julian naked on his hands and knees, being sodomized and tortured by a faceless condemned killer.

Was there anything Julian Kilmartin wouldn't sacrifice for his research?

I didn't even realize I was weeping silently until Dirk asked,

"Good tears or bad, little slave?"

My sigh was almost a sob. "Both, I guess."

"My Vince is a talented masseur. I promise, your aching body will feel much better for his deep-tissue torture."

I sighed again. I'd finally sunk deep enough to find the clarity I'd sought, but it hadn't brought me the verdict I wanted.

"Is there anything he can do for my aching heart?" I whispered.

Dirk sighed too. "I wish there were, my dear."

"Will you drive me to the airport tomorrow?"

"If that's what you wish."

No, it wasn't what I wished. But it had to be done.

Early the next morning, Julian and Colin met me in Julian's little sitting area, as I'd requested in my text to Colin the night before.

Judging by their expressions as they sat side by side on the sofa, they knew I was leaving. Of course Dirk would have let Julian know my plans. Colin looked distant, cold, with his jaw clenched and his arms crossed. Julian just looked...resigned.

I took the chair opposite them, wringing a tissue between my damp hands. While part of me wanted to see Julian get down on his knees and beg me to stay, to hear him swear to never again do anything to jeopardize himself or another human being, I hoped he wouldn't. It would just make it harder to leave.

Drawing a trembling breath, I said the only thing I could.

"You both know I've always been almost fanatical about following rules. It's probably a big part of my being a submissive. I believe there are reasons for rules. They make me feel safe. They *keep* me safe. Without rules, there'd be anarchy."

I had to pause and take another calming breath before I

could continue. "What you did, Julian, runs counter to every moral, ethical and legal rule for medical care in the world. You performed an experimental procedure on your own brother without informed consent. You denied him the right to refuse treatment. You jeopardized the career of every single medical professional who had anything at all to do with this surgery, including Colin and me. You deceived and manipulated me every step of the way. And you allowed a stone-cold killer to assault and torture you in exchange for his body. All in the name of your almighty research."

He flinched, looking at the window and blinking repeatedly. His Adam's apple rose and fell before he said, "I know."

"I love you, Julian, and I understand your wanting to save your brother. But when I think about staying with you, I have to wonder what you'll sacrifice the next time someone you love is dying. *Who* you'll sacrifice. You seem to be answerable to no one here. You're a law unto yourself, a veritable god among men, and the rest of us are nothing more than pawns for you to manipulate and control. Is there any rule you won't break, Julian? Any line you won't cross to get what you w-want?"

Julian shut his eyes tightly and, God, I wanted so badly to stop hurting him, to stop hurting myself. But if I'd learned nothing else from my time with him, it was that there was no way around the pain—I had to go through it. And so did he.

Wiping my eyes, I pulled myself together and finished it. "I always thought you *were* a god, that you could do no wrong, and now I know you're only human and just as flawed as the rest of us in your own way. And believe it or not, I love you even more for it. But right now, I don't trust you, and without trust...that love just doesn't work. At least not for me."

I forged on before my determination could waver. "And, Colin, you lied to me, if only by omission. You brought me here, and you were every bit as willing to risk my career. I know you did it out of love and concern for Julian, but that doesn't make it any easier to accept. If anything, it makes it worse—now I know you'd throw me under a bus for him."

Colin's heel began bouncing, as if he were about to explode, but he looked right past me, still clenching his teeth.

I sighed, wishing he'd say something, anything, even if it hurt. "I love you, Colin...so much...and I wish—"

My voice broke again, and I stood up abruptly. I had to leave while I could, before I broke down and begged him to come with me. Or worse yet, threw myself into both their arms and begged them to tie me up and make me stay.

"Rachel..." Julian looked at me then, his eyes so filled with bitter knowledge and regret I almost relented. "Please. Just go."

Chapter Seventeen

March 29

Exhausted and achy after twelve hours on my feet, I slammed my locker door and laid my forehead against it with a groan. Never again would I take three months off work. I'd been regularly covering shifts in the ER for almost two months now and had yet to adjust to the hours and the physical demands. There was a shortage of emergency physicians in Seattle, and taking the temporary job at the university medical center had seemed like the right thing to do until I figured out where I wanted to go next.

I would have gone back to work a lot sooner, but less than a week after arriving at my parents' house, I received a check from Julian for the full term of my contract. In the cover letter, he said he couldn't in good conscience offer me anything less since his misrepresentations had cost me the EVI fellowship.

He also said I was still entitled to a percentage of any patent income resulting from the surgery, but I immediately fired off a letter renouncing my share. The last thing I wanted was to profit from Jordan's misfortune.

The check, though, I felt fine about keeping. I paid off my student loans and deposited the rest, then did nothing but lie around my parents' house plucking out depressing songs on my guitar. I longed for Julian, but it was Colin I missed with a bone-deep intensity I'd never experienced before. While Julian was my Master, Colin was my companion, my other half, and at first he felt like a limb that had been amputated from my body. I'd wake sometimes in the night and reach for him, only to realize he wasn't behind me. Then I'd hold my pillow to my face and weep into it, sick with misery. Despite my efforts to muffle my sobs, Mom would usually come in and sit behind me in the dark, rubbing my back, letting me know without words she was there if I wanted to talk.

After six weeks of that, she told me sternly at the breakfast table one morning that my life wasn't going to get any better until I started living again. It was time for me to pull myself together and get a job. It was kind of humbling, and yet strangely enjoyable. Rather than making me feel bad, her scolding made me feel loved in an unexpected way, like I was worthy of this kind of attention from her. I *was* worthy of her worry and concern.

It was startling to realize that Julian and Colin had helped me resolve a self-esteem issue I wasn't even aware I had.

Warm hands landed on my shoulders and thumbs dug into my stiff trapezius muscles, massaging gently. "You look exhausted. Would you rather skip dinner tonight?"

I groaned as chills of ecstasy slid down my back and arms. There were definite advantages to dating another doctor. "No, of course not, Adam. I'll never toughen up if I keep babying myself."

"Come home with me and I'll baby you all night," he murmured against my ear.

A rueful chuckle escaped me. "That's a lovely offer but I think we'd better stick to dinner for now."

Without letting up on my sore muscles, he sighed. "When are you going to tell me about him so I know what I'm up against?"

"You wouldn't believe me if I told you," I said without opening my eyes.

"Try me."

This time I was the one who sighed. "Ply me with enough decent wine and maybe I'll give you a hint. Maybe."

"You're on." He slapped me on the butt. "Let's go."

Startled, I spun around and he reddened a bit. "Sorry, a leftover habit from football. And my ex-wife," he added with a grimace. "It won't happen again, I promise."

I eyed him suspiciously. Surely Julian wouldn't have the nerve to interfere in my love life again?

"See that it doesn't," I told him sternly.

He grinned. "Yes, ma'am." Then he held up my coat. "Shall we?"

All the way to the restaurant, I watched the all-American-looking Dr. Adam Bigley unobtrusively. He was tall, dark, confident and aggressive, both in the ER and in his personal life, but he'd never once set off my Domdar. He just didn't seem that...complex. Adam had told me that he was divorced when he first asked me out last month, that he and his ex-wife had married young and his medical education had taken too big a toll on his time for the marriage to last. It wasn't an uncommon tale in our line of work, and I'd accepted it without thinking twice.

"I truly am sorry, Rachel," he said, glancing over at me. "I did that without even thinking about it. Probably because I'm so comfortable with you already."

"I'm comfortable with you too," I replied thoughtfully. I still believed he was exactly what he appeared to be, an uncomplicated guy who liked to swat someone on the fanny once in a while.

Why did I have a feeling that rang the death knell for any kind of romantic relationship between us? Not that I was looking for romance per se—I'd started dating him with some vague idea of becoming friends with benefits, but so far the only benes I'd allowed myself with him, beyond a friendly cheek kiss at the door, were meals and good conversation.

It sucked. My body craved sex now—rough, passionate,

uninhibited sex—and it wanted badly to move on with another man. A more average man, maybe one with just a few mild kinks. Adam appeared to fit that description to a tee.

But my heart just wouldn't let me take that next step. It needed…more.

As we were settled at our table with drinks, he said, "So tell me about this guy you're not over yet."

"Did I say that?"

"No. You didn't have to."

"Hmm." I sipped my wine, wondering how he'd react if I told him there was more than one guy. Deciding not to test the limits of his social tolerance yet, I said, "We worked together for a while."

"Another doctor?" When I hummed in confirmation, he rolled his eyes. "Great."

"Don't worry. You're nothing like him otherwise."

"Is that good or bad?"

"Probably both."

"You're not giving me much to work with here, Rachel," he complained, popping the olive from his martini into his mouth.

After deliberating for a moment, I said simply, "He played God."

Adam sipped his drink. "Don't we all do a certain amount of that every day?"

"Not like this. His patient was a family member in the late stages of a terminal disease, and he devised a radical experimental procedure that might give the patient a chance at life. When the patient refused to consent, he performed it anyway."

"How close a family member?"

"Sibling. Young, in his twenties."

Adam leaned back, nodding. "That would be a tough call. What was the outcome, if you don't mind my asking?"

"I'm not sure. The patient survived the procedure, against what most would consider impossible odds, but he was still comatose when I left. He may remain that way forever, or be trapped in a body that he has absolutely no control over."

"And so you left because...?"

Surprised, I asked, "Isn't that enough?"

He frowned. "I don't know if it would be for me."

"Why not?"

"Well, because I have a kid brother, and if it came down to a choice between his life and my career, I hope I'd make the same choice." When I just stared at him, he said, "You have a little sister, don't you? What if it were her?"

"I'd respect her right to decide her own treatment," I said in a tone more defensive than I'd like.

"What if your parents disagreed? What if they'd blame you for letting her die when you might have saved her?"

I scowled at him. "Whose side are you on here?"

"I'm not on any side," he said mildly. "Just playing devil's advocate. I'm kind of famous for that. It might be why I don't have a girlfriend," he added with a grin.

Our server arrived with yeasty rolls and dinner salads. Once she'd gone, I leaned forward, determined to make him see reason. "The thing is, Adam, it wasn't just *his* career at stake. He deceived and manipulated a whole team of medical professionals, including me. Most of us had no idea the patient hadn't consented."

Picking up his fork, he shrugged again. "In for a penny, in for a pound, I guess."

I sat there and watched him butter a roll and take a few bits of his salad, hardly believing the entire conversation.

"Let me tell you about something that happened to a friend of mine," he said abruptly. "A pediatric oncologist. He had a patient with Ewing's sarcoma, a large femoral tumor with lymph node involvement. The girl, a bright, energetic cheerleader and dancer, refused to have her leg amputated. Her father was in favor of the amputation but her mother wanted her to have a chance at a normal life, so they finally agreed to honor the girl's wishes. My friend excised the tumor and treated her with a long course of chemo followed by radiation.

"Less than a year later, the cancer returned and once again, she refused the amputation, saying she'd rather be dead. Her parents let her make that call, even though she was clearly depressed and hadn't fully recovered from the previous round of treatment."

He took a bite of salad, leaving me in suspense while he chewed.

"So my friend operated again," he finally said, "and while he was in there, he gave serious thought to just amputating anyway. He wouldn't have to look too hard to find a legitimate reason to make the call—she actually started to hemorrhage on the table, and the fastest way to save her would have been to just clamp off the artery and remove the leg. But visions of lawsuits and disciplinary hearings danced in his head, so he stopped the bleeding, excised the tumor and closed her up, putting her through more chemo and radiation.

"The girl died six months later in terrible pain, and my friend had a hard time looking himself in the eye for a long time afterward."

"He made the right decision," I said uneasily.

"Did he?"

"Yes! That's why we have a code of ethics, so doctors aren't forced to make choices like that for their patients. Her parents were supposed to be advocating for her—if that girl was too sick and depressed to make an informed decision, they should have manned up and done it for her."

"What if they couldn't agree with each other? What if they were too overcome with their own grief and prejudices and fears to see what was best for their daughter?"

Adam pointed his fork at me. "And what about your patient? Who was advocating for him? I assume, if he was in the late stages, that he was exhausted, depressed and possibly suffering debilitating pain. Was there anyone else to fight for him when he was too weak to fight for himself?"

I stared at him, my stomach churning.

"No." A tear streaked down my cheek before I could check it and I wiped it away self-consciously. "Just Ju— Just his brother. Their parents are dead."

He sighed. "Rachel, you must know that our code of ethics is just a framework for helping us understand conflicts. It can't always tell us how to resolve them. Sometimes we're placed in a situation where there *is* no good answer, and we just have to do whatever we feel is right and hope for the best. If this guy was his brother's only advocate *and* his only hope, what other choice could he have made?"

Another tear escaped. "I don't know."

"Shit, I'm sorry," he said quickly, reaching for my hand and squeezing it. "Sometimes I don't know when to quit."

I wiped my eyes. "It's not your fault, Adam. In fact, I wish I were more like you."

"Opinionated? Oblivious?" he asked with a grin.

I couldn't help smiling. "I suppose both would make my life easier. At least I wouldn't agonize over every little thing."

"You gotta learn to let go, Rachel," he said. "The stress will kill you if you don't."

Sighing deeply, I said, "I know."

"And I'm sensing a deep and abiding platonic friendship developing between us," Adam said dryly, rubbing the back of my hand with his thumb.

"You're probably right. For the time being anyway." I sighed. "I apologize if I've led you on."

Adam grinned. "I'd sound like an ass if I said you did but I'd get over it, wouldn't I?"

"Probably, but friends can get away with sounding like an ass occasionally," I told him ruefully.

The server came back with our entrees. "Are you done with that?" she asked, looking at my untouched salad.

Realizing I was hungry after all, I told her to leave it. I obviously had a lot of soul-searching to do and I couldn't do it on an empty stomach.

Three days later, I finally made it to the post office and checked my mail for the first time in weeks. I'd managed to squeeze in a lot of thinking around my last few shifts, going over everything Julian had said to me again and again, and I still wasn't any closer to having the answer I needed.

Yes, his brother was young and, yes, his father had died of the same disease and, yes, he'd dedicated his life to finding a cure. And, yes, he'd even found one and it'd been frustrating as hell that his brother wouldn't accept it.

But even taken all together, those facts weren't enough to justify what Julian had done, what he'd risked. What he'd sacrificed.

So why did it feel like I was missing some vital piece of information? Why did it feel so utterly wrong that I'd left him? Left *them*?

"Bad Rachel," I scolded when I opened the box and found it stuffed with envelopes. The last time I'd gone this long without checking, my electricity was on the verge of being shut off for nonpayment of the first bill. Not a good way to renew my relationship with the power company.

Setting the pile down on the lobby table, I sorted out all the junk and threw it into the recycle bin. There was a plain white envelope postmarked Coppell, Texas, with no return address, just my name and address on a computer-generated label. I didn't know anyone in Texas and thought about tossing it away but then decided it was better to be safe than sorry. Maybe I'd just inherited millions of dollars from some distant relative I'd never heard of and this was my only chance to claim it.

Instead, it was a photocopied newspaper article, dated more than fifteen years ago, about a commercial jet crash that had killed twelve passengers and injured fifty more. The name Kilmartin jumped off the page at me.

Among the dead is Elaine Kilmartin, 43, who was on her way to lobby the National Institutes of Health for increased funding for Bain's atrophy research. Mrs. Kilmartin founded and was a tireless supporter of the Bain's Research Project after her husband, Dr. Stuart Kilmartin, died of the neuromuscular disorder four years ago. She was dedicated to finding a cure before it cut any more lives tragically short. Elaine Kilmartin is survived by two sons, Julian Kilmartin, 20, and Jordan Kilmartin, 10.

My chest hollowed out as I stared at nothing, letting the article fall to the post office floor. Julian hadn't just lost his father to Bain's—he'd lost both his parents. And Jordan...

I couldn't let it take him too.

If he'd let Jordan go, Bain's would have cost him his entire family.

"Oh my God," I whispered.

Without giving myself time to think, I hurried to my car, dug out my phone with shaking hands and hit Colin's speed-dial number. His service had been disconnected. I tried Vince's number next and it was also out of service.

What the hell?

I rolled several stop signs in my race to get home and scoured the Internet looking for information, but there was nothing current on any of them that I could find.

"Shit," I whispered.

After dithering for two hours, I finally picked up the phone again, totally forgetting that Bree was on night shift. When she answered in a sleep-roughened voice, I took a deep breath. "How would you like to go to Montaneva with me?"

We pulled up in front of Bangenschloss three weeks later, this time in a terrifying little excuse for a taxi. The terrifying little excuse for a driver dumped out our two small bags with an indecipherable grunt and then zoomed away like he was afraid I was going to demand a refund of his tip, which I'd paid in advance along with the fare.

"Charming," Bree snorted, gazing up at the castle, which looked even grimmer in the bright light of a sunny spring afternoon.

"The driver or the castle?" I asked.

"Take your pick."

"Well you can't say I didn't warn you about the castle." I picked up my bag. "Come on. The entrance is this way."

I'd finally broken down and told her everything the evening after I woke her out of a sound sleep to invite her to Montaneva. Okay, not everything—nothing too specific about the patient other than his identity, nothing at all about the donor, and certainly nothing about the dungeons and what I'd gotten up to in them with various and sundry men. I'd signed a confidentiality agreement, after all, and I was walking a very fine line by telling her that much.

But I'd finally admitted to having a three-way sexual relationship with both Julian and Colin, something that, much to my surprise, hadn't surprised her at all. What surprised me even more was how cool she was with it.

"I mean, really, how could you choose between two men you love?" she asked reasonably.

She wasn't so cool with Julian performing an unauthorized organ transplant on his own brother, or involving me in his little conspiracy. In fact, not to put too fine a point on it, she lost her shit.

"That is so many fucking shades of wrong!" she'd raged, storming around my apartment like she was looking for something to break. "I'm going to kill him. Slowly. And painfully. With nothing more than a Foley and my bare hands."

I stifled a smile. "As much fun as that would be to watch, I really wish you wouldn't. I still love him."

"You'll get over it."

"Bree, he had no other choice, and I know he's paid over and over for it already. If Jordan survived, he probably hates Julian."

Bree's eyes went wide. "*If* he survived?"

"It was a pretty drastic experimental procedure," I told her uncomfortably. "But it was the only possible way to save him. Jordan would be dead without it."

"God, I can't believe you didn't tell me about all this sooner," she said.

"Sorry, but I signed a confidentiality agreement and I really didn't feel right saying anything more than I had to."

Then I told her about being unable to reach anyone at the castle. She looked both worried and intrigued. "Really? We're dashing off to the Castle of Fear because everyone has *disappeared*? Doesn't that scream too-stupid-to-live horror-movie heroine to you?"

Nevertheless, she'd jumped on the opportunity, arranging for two weeks off work just in case I needed her. Since I was just a temp, it hadn't taken much haggling to get me the same two weeks off.

When we rounded the corner of the castle, I was startled to see that the wheelchair ramp was gone. Oh God, did that mean Jordan had died, he'd left the castle, or he didn't need a ramp anymore? I rooted for the last option with everything in me.

No one answered when I rang the doorbell.

"Are you sure it's working?" Bree asked, leaning back and shading her eyes with her hand to look up the side of the castle. "I don't hear anything."

"I didn't the last time, either, but Vince came right down."

"Hmm." She reached over and turned the knob. It was unlocked.

When she looked at me with wary eyes, I shrugged. "We're way out in the country. They probably never lock the doors."

"If you say so."

Pushing past her, I walked down the dark hallway and into the tower room. No one here either, not that I expected there to be. I pushed the button and had to wait for the elevator to open, which meant it had last been used to go up. Hopefully that meant there was someone upstairs—if not the someones I sought, then someone who could give me information about them.

Bree joined me in the elevator with a doubtful look. "Are you sure this is a good idea?"

I tugged her dark-brown ponytail with a grin. "What happened to Bree, the buff nurse who could kill a man with a single bubble of air?"

"I left my infamous hypos of horror at the hospital," she said wryly.

The door opened on the second floor and I stepped out into the tower room. No lights were on, but the narrow windows let in enough daylight for me to see at least partway down the corridor. I thought I heard a faint clinking sound from that direction.

"It looks like no one's—"

"Shh!" I cocked my head. "Do you hear that?"

She listened too, and her eyes widened. "Chains? Really? What's next? Moaning and shuffling footsteps?" She looked around. "You're playing some kind of practical joke on me, aren't you? Come on, Rae, where are the cameras?"

"Breanna, when have I ever played a practical joke on you or anyone else?"

"Never, which makes this the perfect setup," she declared. "I'd never suspect a thing."

I rolled my eyes again. "And Julian said *I* had a vivid imagination. Let's go."

Setting my bag down, I started down the hall, and Bree quickly followed. When the rattling chains and clanking noises grew louder, she grabbed the back of my windbreaker and stepped on my heel, pulling my canvas sneaker off.

"Get off me," I hissed, bending down to tug it back on.

"Sorry."

There was another loud clank. And then a deep moan.

Followed by the sound of shuffling footsteps.

"Oh please," Bree whispered. "This is getting ridiculous."

"Shh! It sounds like it's coming from the dungeon."

"The *dungeon!*" she squeaked.

"Not that kind of— Never mind. Just stay here for a minute."

"No freaking way, sister. Not on your life." She grabbed my sleeve this time. "I'm coming with you."

"All right then, but prepare to see some stuff that may shock you." When I realized how that sounded, I added, "Kinky stuff, not blood-and-guts stuff."

She paused. "Kinky? You mean *that* kind of dungeon?"

"Yes. And how do you know about *that* kind of dungeon?" I demanded quietly.

"How do *you* know?" she countered.

"Shh!" I stopped outside the punishment room and realized the sounds were definitely coming from inside. There was a sliver of light bleeding from beneath the door. Crap, what was going on in there? I hated to interrupt somebody's scene—unless it was Julian and Colin. It made my heart hurt to remember they'd probably done plenty of scening without me in the last few months.

The light under the door suddenly disappeared and the shuffling footsteps grew louder. Acting on some childish instinct, Bree and I both darted away from the door and flattened ourselves against the wall, holding each other's clammy hands. The doorknob turned and I assumed the door opened, though it was hard to tell with the castle's well-lubricated hinges. A tall figure stepped into the corridor and went directly across to open the door of my room. The curtains must be closed because I could barely make him out as he went inside, leaving the door ajar.

A light, probably the bedside lamp, switched on. Taking a deep breath, I peeled myself away from the wall, disentangled my hand from Bree's and tiptoed over to peer into the room. A tall, lean blond man, dressed all in black, leaned over the nightstand.

My heart did a sickening flip in my chest.

"Julian?" I said without thinking.

His head jerked toward me, revealing blazing blue eyes.

No, not Julian. Someone younger.

Someone much, much angrier.

"Who the bloody hell are you," he demanded in a stiff British accent, "and what are you doing in my castle?"

Chapter Eighteen

I gasped. "Oh my God, *Jordan*?"

His eyes narrowed. "I don't believe I've had the pleasure."

"Oh, I'm sorry," I said, stepping fully into the room and holding out my hand. "I'm Rachel McBride."

He straightened and turned toward me, crossing his arms. "Dr. Rachel McBride?"

I dropped my hand. "Yes, that would be me."

The man stood there staring long enough to make me squirm, but I couldn't help staring back. Jordan Kilmartin was not just alive, he was *functional*. Six months after having his head transplanted, he was actually walking and talking. It was unbelievable. He was still pale and looked older than his twenty-eight years, but that was to be expected, especially considering he'd suffered from Bain's for five years before the transplant.

"You look— I mean, you've made an amazing recovery," I said. "The last time I saw you, you were—"

"Decapitated?" he asked pointedly.

"Nooo..." I swallowed. "I believe comatose would be a more accurate description."

He sneered. "I suppose you're waiting for me to thank you for restoring the blood supply to my brain."

"Not at all." God, could this possibly get any more awkward?

"Good, because you'd have an interminable wait."

"Trust me, I understand. Completely."

"Oh, I hardly think so but believe what you like. Would it be too much trouble for you to tell me what you're doing in my bedroom?"

I looked around quickly. Except for the bed, which had been replaced by an ordinary king with no headboard, everything looked just as it had when I left. "Your room?"

"Yes. Why, was it your room when you stayed here?" he asked, cocking his head to the side.

"Er, yes," I admitted, unable to help blushing.

He smiled, and it wasn't pretty. "That would explain a great deal, Dr. McBride. Or do you prefer *McBride of FrankenDom*?"

Oh hell. "I didn't have anything to do with that."

"I'm quite sure you didn't. You seem entirely too sensitive, and it has all the earmarks of Julian's twisted little sense of humor." He glanced around the room. "However, the room is all you, isn't it?"

"Actually, it was exactly like this when I arrived."

"He created this little pampered slave chamber and filled it will all sorts of amusing toys just for you, though."

My face was blazing. "Probably, yes."

He prowled toward me—not quite evenly, but still a prowl. Wearing a long-sleeved black turtleneck, loose black pants, black sneakers and even black leather gloves, he reminded me of a panther about to pounce.

"I wondered what sort of female it would take to capture Julian's attention," he murmured, letting his flame-blue gaze slide down my body. "I always thought he was gay."

"That would be a reasonable assumption, I guess." I cleared my throat. It was time for me to get the hell out of Dodge. "Actually, I was looking for Julian. Perhaps you could tell me where to find him?"

"Perhaps," he agreed, stopping right in front of me. He leaned down until I could feel his warm breath gusting on my lips when he added, "For a price."

"All right, I've heard enough," Bree declared, marching into the room. "Back off my sister now, you asshat, or I'll make you wish you had."

Jordan didn't move, but his eyes flickered to her briefly. "Go away, little girl. You're not wanted here." When I started to step back, he barked, "Rachel, stay."

I froze, my heart pounding, and his lips curled in a sensuous smile. "Such an obedient little slave. I'm sure my brother enjoyed the fuck out of you. I'm sure I would too. What do you say, Rachel? Would you like to shag FrankenDom's monster, perhaps in the dungeon across the corridor?"

"Rachel, would you get the hell away from this guy!" Bree grabbed my wrist and yanked hard, jarring me away from the awful spell of Jordan's burning eyes. "He's clearly batshit."

He focused on her. "Oh, I am. Certifiably batshit, as a matter of fact. Perhaps I'll chain you both up and have some fun with you."

She rolled her eyes. "Good luck catching us if you're six months post-transplant. Now quit trying to scare us or we'll chain *you* up and force you to watch a SpongeBob marathon—the new episodes where he's lost all his charm and every word he says makes you want to gouge out your own eardrums with an icepick."

Jordan looked at me. "Is she always like this?"

"Pretty much. She's a nurse," I added, as if that explained everything. For some people, it would. "Jordan Kilmartin, my sister Breanna McBride."

"Delighted," he sneered.

"Decapitated," she sneered back. When he stiffened, she taunted, "What's the matter, Jordan? Did I hit a sore spot?"

"Get. Out."

She shook her head. "Not before you tell us where Julian and Colin are. Rachel's been trying to reach them for weeks."

The way he burned holes through her with his laser eyes would have had me on my knees, but my ballsy little sister didn't back down.

Finally he turned to me. "You know where Julian's rooms were?" he bit out.

"Were?"

"Were."

"Okay, yes."

"Then wait for me in his sitting room. I'll be down to discuss the matter with you as soon as I've cleaned up a bit."

"Are you crazy?" I hissed as she closed the door behind us. "What were you thinking, baiting him like that?"

She pressed her ear to the door. "He deserved it."

"*Now* what are you doing?"

"Shh!"

I scowled but held my tongue.

"Okay, he's in the shower," she said, tiptoeing across to the punishment room. "I want to see what he was doing in here."

I would have taken her to task for nosiness but I was curious too. When she opened the door, I reached inside and flipped on the light.

Then I choked back an incredulous laugh. "He was working out?"

Some of the dungeon furniture had been shoved aside to make way for another type of torture equipment—there was a treadmill, a stair climber, a rowing machine and an elliptical trainer, no doubt lifted from Hans's torture chamber. Beyond them was an impressive set of weights and chains on a stand. He must have been bench-pressing. Without a spotter, which was very dangerous, especially for a man in his condition.

"Dressed like that?" Bree asked doubtfully, wandering around.

"Maybe he's self-conscious. He's awfully thin."

"He is." She turned in a full circle and then pinned me with her dreaded nurse stare. "Rae, what the hell is going on? Why are we in a dungeon? And why did he say he'd been decapitated?"

I sighed. However unwittingly, Jordan had let that cat out of the bag himself and there was no stuffing it back in. "If you know what a dungeon is, it should be self-explanatory. And Jordan's operation was actually a full-body transplant."

Her stare didn't waver. "That's insane. You can't cut off someone's head and just plop it onto a new body. Where in the hell would you find a donor?"

"Well clearly Julian can, and the procedure involved much more than just plopping. It took a surgical team of more than seventy people almost thirty hours to complete."

"You did the vascular surgery."

"Yes, on his left side. Another surgeon did the right at the same time."

"And the donor?"

"Confidential. But entirely legal, I promise."

"I take it Jordan had Bain's?"

I nodded. "That's one reason it was so hard for Julian to let him go. It had already killed his father, and his mother died trying to raise money for Bain's research."

"God, what a freaking mess," she sighed. "He could have you all tied up in court for decades."

"Don't you think I know that? I've been biting my nails for months, waiting to be served with a lawsuit." I looked at my watch. "We should probably get down to Julian's rooms before Jordan comes looking for us."

Ten minutes later, Jordan joined us in Julian's sitting room, dressed in another black turtleneck and jeans, and laid a thick sheaf of papers on the coffee table in front of him. He still wore the gloves. Had something happened to his hands? God, had we missed something, somehow failed to restore proper circulation to them?

"I'll get right to the point, Dr. McBride," he said with a direct look. "Bangenschloss and just about everything else my dear brother owned now belongs to me."

My stomach sank.

"When I woke after the surgery, still on a ventilator and unable to speak," Jordan continued, "Julian apologized for what he'd done. He said he wouldn't ask for my forgiveness because what he'd done was unforgivable, but if there were anything he could do to make amends, anything at all, he would do it without hesitation. When I was finally able to speak, I demanded his controlling interest in Kilmartin BioTech, along with his interest in all its patents and all his real property. Otherwise I'd file criminal and civil charges against him."

Though my heart hurt for Julian, I nodded.

"Do you know what he did when I made my demands, Dr. McBride?"

Biting my lip, I asked, "What did he do?"

Jordan's gaze intensified. "He sighed and said 'thank you' in a heartfelt tone, as if I'd just lifted the weight of the world off his shoulders. Then he set about quietly transferring everything over to me."

My eyes filled and I couldn't speak.

"Of course his apparent penitence means nothing to me. If there were any way I could take both—all his worldly goods *and* his freedom—I would. But making his unconscionable actions public would ruin the company, and if I'm going to live another fifty years, I'd just as soon live them with a vast fortune at my disposal."

He shoved the papers at me.

"You needn't worry about my pressing suit against you, Doctor. Julian assured me that you and all the other surgeons were unaware of my lack of consent at the time of the procedure, so I can't in good conscience hold you responsible for my current condition."

"What's wrong with your current condition?" Bree challenged. "You look better than you have any right to under the circumstances."

Jordan's expression hardened. "I've heard enough out of you, Miss McBride. Be quiet or leave."

Without making a sound, Bree told him very clearly to fuck off.

Ignoring her gesture, he continued, "Among those documents, you'll find a certified copy of my signed release for the surgery." Then he smiled ironically. "I should count myself fortunate to have had you, shouldn't I? In the hands of someone less skilled, I might well be dead now."

What could I say to that?

"So where are Julian and Colin now?" I asked hurriedly.

His lip curled, and not in a nice way. "They're in the US, setting up Kilmartin NeuroMedical Research Foundation. In Texas, to be more specific."

My eyes widened. "Texas?" That was where the article had been mailed from. So who'd sent it? I'd never had a clue before now.

"It's warm in Texas," he explained. "Cold pains me badly, though Julian assures me that will eventually subside."

"I see."

"I need Julian, Dr. McBride, to keep the money rolling in, which is the only reason I haven't thrown his arrogant ass out on the street, but you can rest assured I'll be keeping a close eye on him. A very close eye." He leaned forward, skewering me with that very close eye. "I *own* Julian now, Doctor. He won't be

215

able to spend a penny without my approval, and he won't be able to take a piss in the night without my knowing about it."

It was heart-wrenching to realize that, despite the success of the surgery, that carefree young man in the photos was gone.

When I just kept staring at him, he smiled, and this time there was actual humor in it. "Cat got your tongue, Dr. McBride?"

"I...don't quite know what to say, Mr. Kilmartin," I said slowly.

"Say you'll come work for me."

I blinked hard, shaking my head. "Excuse me?"

"The foundation will require a handful of vascular surgeons to continue with Julian's research, and you'd obviously be a worthwhile addition to our staff."

"You want me...to move to Texas...to work for you..."

"By George, I think she's got it."

I shot him a narrow look. "The last time I accepted a job offer from a Kilmartin, I wound up quitting after less than three weeks. Aren't you worried I'll do it again?"

"Not at all. You quit because your ethical standards had been compromised, something I find quite admirable. You'll have no such reason to quit this time. Julian will be held to the highest possible standards."

My heart tripped, and then began to soar. I stuffed it back into its cage before it could soar too high. "Can I have some time to think about it?"

"Take all the time you need. But do it somewhere else," he added brusquely. "I don't care to have my home invaded. There's a bed-and-breakfast in Kander if you wish to play tourist, or you can return to the States and messenger the documents to me once you've signed them."

"What makes you so sure I'll sign them?"

He gave me a pointed smile. "You're here, aren't you? A

good little slave can only resist her Master for so long." When I bit my lip, he focused on it. "That's not a bad thing, Doctor. In fact, if I thought you'd come willingly, I'd take *you* away from Julian too."

"Lighten up, perv boy," Bree said acidly.

Jordan's expression hardened to stone. "Get her the fuck out of my castle before I toss her out a window."

Bree and I rented a terrifying little excuse for a car and spent three days exploring the Montanevan countryside. We did quite a bit of talking as we trekked between all the museums, churches, monasteries and scenic attractions, and by the end of the second day, she'd helped me come to a few conclusions about myself that weren't necessarily flattering.

In fact, once I'd finally worked out all the reasons why I ran from Julian and Colin, I almost gave up on ever seeing them again. How could I face them? Why would they want anything to do with me?

But how could I *not* face them? How could I let Julian go on thinking he'd failed me when I'd failed him just as badly?

It was Bree who encouraged me to spend the extra time in Montaneva and consider what I really wanted before I made any decisions, and I was more than happy to go along with that plan.

I thought she might be entertaining some regrets about the way she'd treated Jordan. When she kept referring to him as "perv boy", I finally let on that he might have reason to take that particular insult too much to heart and she went uncharacteristically quiet. It made me wonder if she'd connected the dots herself—Montaneva's English-language newspaper, which we both read every morning, was filled with stories about the country's upcoming accession to the European Union, and many of them touched on the abolition of the death penalty and the execution of Augustine Pohlson.

If she did suspect, she didn't say anything, so I didn't either.

By the time we took off from Montaneva's only international airport, I was still up in the air, so to speak, about Jordan's offer. My inner bad girl begged me to just accept it and sort out the mess I'd made of things with Julian and Colin after the fact. My good girl, however, insisted that wouldn't be fair to any of us, and after so many months back in her clutches, I couldn't help but side with her.

When we landed at Heathrow, I made a last-minute decision to change my connection and book a direct flight to Dallas-Ft. Worth.

All Bree had to say was, "Good idea."

We sat in a little Italian coffee shop brooding over our cappuccinos for almost an hour, which turned out to be a bad idea. Between my nerves and all the caffeine, I wound up spending much of the flight in the cramped lavatory, suffering numerous bouts of intestinal distress. Thank God it was a relatively smooth flight or I'd have been throwing up too.

The plane didn't land until almost midnight, and once I'd collected my bag, I took a taxi to a hotel not far from the foundation's offices, the address and main phone number for which were included on several of the documents Jordan had given me. I crashed immediately and woke sixteen hours later, sleep-swollen and groggy, but hungry. After giving myself one more night to recover from the jet lag, I showered and dressed, had a light breakfast in the hotel restaurant, and took a taxi to the foundation offices.

Dallas in May was as hot as Montaneva had been cold in October. As I walked into the humongous building, which according to the literature from Jordan was a hospital undergoing extensive renovations, I blotted the sweat from my brow and upper lip with a tissue. Why on earth couldn't Jordan have picked someplace more temperate, like Seattle?

At the main desk, I asked to see Julian and the receptionist made a quick call before directing me to a suite on the second floor.

I vibrated with nerves as I made my way there. I had absolutely no idea what kind of reception to expect, but I was prepared for the worst.

When I was ten feet from the suite, the door opened and Colin emerged. We both stopped and stared. He looked more edible than ever in charcoal slacks and a lavender dress shirt open at the collar, with the sleeves rolled up to his elbows. I wanted badly to throw myself at him, to clutch him tightly and just soak up the smell and feel of him, but his frown glued my feet to the floor.

"Rachel," he said coolly. "What are you doing here?"

"I..." My brain froze and all I could think to say was, "Jordan offered me a job."

"Oh Christ, you didn't accept, did you?" He rolled his eyes. "Of course you did. That's why you're here. That's just fucking lovely. It wasn't enough for the ungrateful little prick to take everything Julian had—he has to torture him with *you*."

As he spoke, pain unlike anything I'd ever felt before razed my insides and left me trembling. I felt sick. I wanted to run away, to hide from the disgust in his eyes.

But there was no place I could hide from myself.

"I didn't accept," I whispered.

His brows went up in challenge. "No? Then why are you here?"

I swallowed, finally remembering my mission. "I need to speak to Julian."

"Whatever it is you want, you can forget it," he snapped. "I need to go. We're pretty busy."

I ground my teeth. "Dammit, Colin, I want to talk to Julian. Now."

"Why, so you can come crawling back to him?"

The venom in his tone nearly brought me to tears again. "Colin—"

"Because that's what you'll have to do, Rachel," he informed me, his eyes flashing. "If you really want to see Julian again, you can get on your hands and knees and fucking *crawl* to him, because that's the only way I'm letting you in here."

Chapter Nineteen

Anguish swamped me again, along with a healthy dose of humiliation. And fear.

And, God help me, arousal. Colin was *furious* with me. When we were at UW, I'd always thought he probably had a dark side to balance all that brash charm, but I'd never seen his fury before, much less been on the receiving end. In Montaneva, Julian's influence appeared to have smoothed the volatility out of him. But it was clearly still a part of him and it took my breath away. Knowing that I deserved his wrath only increased my trembling excitement.

A little voice inside me whispered, *Finally. Finally, a chance to see what you're made of. How much you can take. How far you can fall. And what it truly means to be broken.*

Because that's what I'd be if they sent me away. Part of me almost hoped it would happen so I could finally quit dreading it.

Knowing I had no other choice, I said, "Fine."

"Fine." He pulled open the door and held it for me.

Glancing around nervously, I took a shuddering breath and sank to my knees, thanking God I'd worn slacks as I leaned forward on my hands. My shoulder bag immediately dropped to the floor. When Colin just continued to stand there with his brows raised in expectation, I pulled the strap over my head and carried my purse around my neck.

"I don't have all day, Rachel. Crawl in or crawl away."

Trying to shrug off the paralyzing effect of his indifference, I started forward, crawling over the hard, cold marble tile. I was relieved to see that the office itself was carpeted. I was even more relieved to see that the waiting area was empty and there was no receptionist behind the desk. Keeping my head down just in case, I followed Colin through another door into a long hallway. Why did people think this was sexy? I'd never felt so ridiculous and undesirable.

Just when I thought the journey would never end, Colin stopped and rapped on a door.

"Come."

The sound of Julian's voice made my heart flutter with fear and longing. God, how I'd missed them both. What if they couldn't forgive me? It would kill me to leave them again. Just imagining it made me weep silently.

Colin opened the door and I crawled into the quiet office, dripping tears on the carpet. He led me around the desk, to the side of the occupied executive chair.

"Stay," he ordered

I stopped, breathing harshly and trying not to sob.

"I think Rachel has something she wants to say to you, Sir. Rachel, sit up."

Feeling very much like a misbehaving puppy brought to heel, I sat back on my heels and pulled my purse from around my neck, dropping it on the floor behind me. I wished my hair was down so I could hide my tear-stained face behind it, but I'd clipped it up in deference to the heat.

I couldn't bring myself to look at Julian, so Colin placed a hand on top of my head and urged it back so that my face was clearly visible. "Rachel, speak. Tell Julian what was so important that you had to come all the way to Dallas to say it."

Oh God, I'd rehearsed this a hundred times on my way here, but now that the moment had arrived, my thoughts were too chaotic to get a handle on them. Closing my eyes, I tried to focus on the single most important thing I had to say, the one thing I couldn't leave this room without making sure he understood.

When it finally came to me, I opened my eyes again to find

Julian watching me with soft curiosity.

My face crumpled as I tried to fight back more tears. "I'm very ashamed of the way I judged you, Sir. You had every reason to fight for your brother's life and the courage to do the right thing, no matter what the consequences to yourself. I admire you for it more than I can say. If I'd been in your situation, if it were my sister with Bain's, I probably would have hidden behind ethics and rules and just...let her *die*."

"Rachel Anne McBride," he said sternly, "stop right there."

The tears fell anyway. "I'm sorry, Sir," I sobbed. "I was so wrong."

Turning his chair so that he faced me, Julian leaned forward and took my jaw in a bruising grip. "Rachel, *silence*."

Shutting my eyes to block out his anger, I bit my swollen lips.

Julian gave me a little shake. "Look at me."

I obeyed reluctantly.

"First off, I didn't do *the right thing*. If anything, I did the wrong thing, but it was the only thing I could live with."

"I know that, Sir, and it scared me." When he frowned, I added, "Not because I was afraid of you. But you are *so* strong, Sir, so...intense. So immovable. And I'm so...not. It's like we operate on almost totally different planes of existence, you up there with the gods and me down here with the commoners. I felt—"

His hand moved to cover my mouth. "If you say *unworthy*, I'll have to spank you for being trite and ridiculous, and it won't be pleasant."

My eyes widened. That was exactly what I'd intended to say.

"This is your submission talking, Rachel. It's not uncommon for there to be an element of worship between a Dom and a sub, not because one is inherently better but because our personalities and our desires complement one another so beautifully. Yes, we're different in many ways. My hardheaded, inflexible, devious dominance worships your ability to submit—your openness, your giving nature, your courage and your trusting heart."

Behind his hand, I smiled at his description of himself. It certainly lowered him to a more human, if not exactly common, level.

"But in the outside world, you and I are simply physicians. You are an empathetic, hands-on healer with high ethical standards, while I am an intimidating boor who lives in a lab with lots of rats and disregards my patients' directives when it suits me. Which of us do you suppose most patients would see as the better physician?"

A huff of laughter escaped me but he didn't take his hand away to hear my answer.

"As far as your sister having Bain's, there's no way for you to know what you'd do in that situation so you really can't beat yourself up for it. Respecting her wishes and letting her die might very well be the right thing for both of you. If you'd asked me as little as a year ago, I'd have said there was no way in hell I would ever disregard my brother's wishes, much less compromise my professional integrity so completely. But I could never have imagined this exact scenario, or my brother's being so damn hardheaded."

When I nodded my understanding, he let his hand drop to his lap and leaned back.

"I'm still sorry I said all those horrible things to you and ran away, Sir," I told him. "I hurt you both because I was scared and hurting and I didn't know how to deal with it."

He shook his head. "Sometimes a strategic retreat is necessary when you're too close to the conflict to be objective. That's why I let you go without a fight, and why I wouldn't let Colin speak to you that morning."

I glanced at Colin out of the corner of my eye. So that was

why he'd seemed ready to explode.

"Besides," Julian continued, "it's not as if your accusations were unfounded. Colin had warned me time and again that I was taking too much upon myself, that finding a cure for Bain's wouldn't bring my father back, or my mother, but I dismissed his concerns as a lover's overprotectiveness. My obsession controlled me, and after my brother's diagnosis, I actually believed that I alone was responsible for saving him."

"It must have been awful for you."

"Yes, such a monumental ego is a dreadful thing to carry around year after year," he said dryly.

"It's not ego," I protested.

"That's exactly what it was, and the closer I got to the surgery, the more I realized I was buckling under the weight of the expectations I'd placed on myself. But by then I was trapped and couldn't see any way out until Jordan himself forced me out. I assume you know about our arrangement?" he added.

When I nodded, Julian sighed. "I doubt he'll ever believe I don't resent his removing that weight from me, that I'm actually grateful to him for taking control of my research."

"He will eventually, Sir," Colin said.

This time when I looked up, he was looking down at me, and I was unnerved to see that his fury didn't seem to have abated in the least.

Looking at Julian, I asked, "So what now, Sir?"

"That will be up to you. I believe Colin has a few wrinkles to iron out with you as well. But first..." He rolled forward until I was between his spread knees and crooked his finger at me.

Hope ignited in my chest as I knelt up.

He leaned down and took my face in both hands. "I love you, Rachel, and I'm so very sorry I put you through such hell. Can you ever forgive me?"

"You have to ask?"

Robin L. Rotham

"Yes, I do. In fact, I should be the one on my knees."

"No, Sir, you shouldn't. I forgave you weeks ago, so just...please kiss me."

He pressed his lips to mine and I sighed, breathing in the simple sweetness of it. My heart thumped with joy...and fear that my joy would be fleeting. Colin was so angry.

When Julian backed away, he looked at Colin. "Well, my love, I believe Rachel and I have worked out our issues. What would you like to do?"

Colin stared down at me for a minute, then said, "I'd like to have her for slave training for one full week, Sir. With no safe words and no limits on what I can do to her or require of her."

There was dead silence in the room for several seconds as the world fell away beneath me. I was glad to be kneeling, otherwise I'd have fallen down.

Julian made a sound somewhere between a laugh and a cough. "My dear boy, you do continue to surprise and delight me."

"I try, Sir."

"'No limits' is an overbroad requirement, though."

"Of course I mean no limits except those that protect her basic human rights, which I'd outline in a formal contract."

"A contract that would be no more enforceable than the personal conduct agreement she signed for me."

"I realize that, Sir. This isn't about enforcement. It's about trust."

Julian deliberated for a moment while I watched him with wide eyes, my heart pounding in my throat. Then he looked down at me, his expression inscrutable. "I suppose I can allow that, as long as I get to approve the contract and Rachel signs it of her own free will."

My pulse kicked up. "Sir?"

"Actually, I'm not your Sir anymore, Rachel," Julian replied

226

gently. "The agreement you had with me was signed without full disclosure on my part and I'm unworthy of the honor. You'll have to straighten out your relationship with Colin before we can decide where to go from here."

Sighing raggedly, I nodded.

Then he looked at Colin. "I won't let you break her. If you go too far, I will call a halt."

Colin's expression shuttered. "Maybe she needs to be broken, Sir."

"Colin..."

"I promise, Sir, I won't give her anything more than you gave me."

After a pregnant pause, Julian asked, "Is that supposed to reassure me?"

I cringed, unintentionally leaning closer to Julian.

When Colin didn't reply, he sighed. "All right then, my love. Go ahead. I'll see you this evening."

Driving another Camaro, only much newer and nicer than the one he'd had at UW, Colin took me to my hotel to pick up the rest of my things. He accompanied me to my room and made me double-check that I hadn't left anything in the bathroom, the closet, or the drawers and then grabbed the unopened bottle of water by the coffee pot. Once he'd put my suitcase and laptop in the trunk, he handed me the water and told me to drink it all. Then he got onto the interstate heading east out of the city.

It was a long, silent ride during which my imagination had plenty of time to run riot. I drained the water bottle, hoping it didn't mean we were going to start out with extreme electrical play. What did he mean by slave training? Was it just sexual, or would I be a genuine slave with household or outdoor chores? If he expected me to cook and clean, it was going to be a long,

227

hard week for both of us. I'd never been much of a housekeeper and I'd never had the time to learn to cook.

By the time we turned off an isolated stretch of gravel road onto a winding driveway, I was about to snap from the tension.

My mouth dropped open when we pulled up in front of a beautiful country house with a huge lawn. "I thought Julian had to give Jordan everything."

"He did," Colin said, pulling into the three-car garage and turning off the ignition. "I didn't."

I blinked as he got out. It hadn't even occurred to me that Colin had probably profited handsomely from their research too.

Before I recovered, he'd opened my door and reached for my hand.

I let him help me out of the car. "Does it bother Julian that you're—"

"No," he said flatly. "That's enough questions, Rachel. Slaves are to be seen and not heard. Don't speak unless I give you permission."

Refusing to be hurt by his brusqueness, I nodded and followed him. I had to expect him to remain angry and unreachable until he'd had a chance to get everything that was bothering him off his chest. He had to do that in his own time.

When we stepped into the kitchen entry, he pulled a plastic grocery bag from a cupboard. "Strip and put everything, including your purse and jewelry, in here. Slaves don't have anything their Masters don't provide."

And so it started. I sighed and undressed while he stood there watching me with his arms crossed over his chest. I folded my blouse and slacks before putting them into the bag on top of my shoes. My bra and panties followed, and then my purse, watch, rings and earrings.

"The hair clip too."

I obeyed at once, shaking out my hair as I did so.

Knotting the bag's handles, he picked it up and said, "This way."

I followed him through the gorgeous modern kitchen and into a large, open living room, where he pointed to a spot on the floor beside a large easy chair. "Kneel here with your knees apart and your hands on your thighs. Back straight. Eyes on the floor."

He nudged my knees farther apart and told me to sit back on my heels. "Get comfortable, slave. You're going to be here a while. Now stay."

He left the room then, and I sighed again. Staying and getting comfortable were mutually exclusive propositions, so I followed the one I knew he meant and didn't move from my assigned spot. After a while, I grew bored and began looking around furtively. The clock on the mantel said it was eleven fifteen, which surprised me. It felt more like late afternoon. Obviously this was going to be an incredibly long week.

Eventually I began to squirm a little and realized I hadn't used the bathroom since first thing in the morning. Not good. I'd had coffee, water and juice with breakfast, and then twenty-four ounces of water in the car.

I looked around again. A house this large had to have at least three or four bathrooms, but I had no idea where they were and no permission to look. Colin had better come back soon or I'd have to start out with some sort of horrible punishment for disobeying orders and finding one.

Ten minutes later, I was rocking and squeezing my thighs together. *Colin, please come back. Please!*

As if he'd heard me, Colin walked back into the room from a hallway and sat on the couch, laying a stack of papers on the coffee table before him. He'd changed into jeans and a tight blue tee-shirt, and in his hand was a leather collar.

"Come here, slave," he said, pointing to the floor beside his sneakers.

Shivering in reaction to his overwhelming presence and more aware of my nudity now, I moved quickly to obey. At his command, I held up my hair while he fastened the collar around my neck and locked the little padlock. Its presence would take some getting used to—I'd never been one for necklaces or turtlenecks because my neck was so sensitive.

His eyes lingered on my nipples, which had tightened to hard points, and then he said, "Here's the contract. I emailed it to Julian and he's approved it. I want you to read every single word and make sure you understand what you're agreeing to before you sign it. Nod if you understand."

My eyes widened. There had to be at least twenty pages there, and I needed to pee badly.

"I don't see your head moving, slave. Is there something about my instructions you don't understand?"

I hesitated again and then nodded.

"Speak then."

Relieved he'd phrased it that way, I said in a rush, "I really have to go to the bathroom, Sir."

His eyes narrowed. "That's not a question about my instructions, slave. Apparently I'll have to be more specific in my language. If you understand my instructions, then begin reading. If not, ask me for clarification."

Dismayed, I stared back. He really wasn't going to let me go to the bathroom before I read the contract?

"Read, slave. And don't even think about pissing on my carpet or I'll rub your nose in it and beat your ass."

Steeling myself, I picked up the pages and began to read quickly. The first two pages were a lot of stuff about his rights and responsibilities as Master and mine as slave. It certainly seemed like he had a lot more rights and I had a lot more responsibilities, but that was nothing more than I'd expected. His only responsibilities were my only rights—basically, he had to keep me alive and reasonably healthy, not maim or permanently disfigure me, not damage me emotionally and not jeopardize my career. While that list was somewhat reassuring, it left a lot of room for extreme discomfort on my part.

The ensuing pages contained a detailed explanation of Master/slave etiquette, detailed descriptions of postures, a detailed list of required reading with synopses for all the books, and an extensive list of websites, along with a description of every page I was to visit at each.

"No skimming," Colin barked. "Read every word."

God *damn* it, how had he known? "I'm a fast reader, Sir!"

"Did I give you permission to speak, slave?"

My eyes closed. Oh hell.

"No, Sir."

"Stand up. Now."

I obeyed. Figuring I was going to be punished anyway, I rushed on, "Colin, please, I'm going to have an accident if you—"

"Quiet! No more talking, slave. Bend over the arm of the couch and put your hands on the cushion."

Whimpering with frustration and anxiety, I started to bend over and then paused. What was I doing? There was no way I could live like this for a week.

I straightened and crossed my arms, looking him in the eye. "No, Sir. I've had a UTI before and it wasn't fun. I refuse to suffer through another one just so you can get your revenge. Now show me the bathroom or get out of my way and I'll find it myself."

His scowl turned ferocious, but not before I saw a flash of amusement in his eyes. "Topping from the bottom is not a good way to start out the week, slave."

I didn't budge. "I'm not topping from the bottom, Sir. I'm asserting my right to a healthy urinary tract."

"Very well," he said in a clipped tone distinctly reminiscent of Julian. "Come with me then."

Right on his heels, I followed him to the sliding glass door and out onto the hot flagstone patio. I looked around quickly to reassure myself there were no neighbors. As far as I could tell, there was no one around for miles. Was my room in some sort of guest house? I hoped it wasn't too damn far because it was hot out here and I was seriously about to burst.

He led me across the yard to a wire strung between two tall trees probably a hundred feet apart. Attached to it by a snap hook was a thick nylon cord that reached the ground, and I froze when he picked up the snap hook at the other end.

It was a dog run.

When he went to hook the cord to my collar, I jumped back several steps. "Colin!"

"Rachel!" he mimicked, holding up the hook with his brows raised in expectation.

My heart thundered. That was *my* Colin shining through the mean-ass Master act and I wanted him back.

"I'm not a dog," I finally said.

"No, you're a beautiful surgeon who's being introduced to puppy play."

Puppy play? Really?

Stiffening my spine, I stomped forward. "Fine. But I'm only doing this because I love you, Colin Carter."

He attached the hook under my chin and then yanked me forward, kissing me hard. I didn't have time to melt into him before he lifted his mouth and stared at me with blazing, blue eyes.

"I'm only doing this because I love you too, Rachel Anne. You're mine now. *Mine.*" He tugged on the hook to emphasize the point. "Everything about you is mine, and you will keep no part of yourself from me. Ever. Do you understand?"

Chapter Twenty

Stunned, I nodded. All the bones in my legs had turned to wobbly gelatin. "Yes, Sir."

He held on to me for another few seconds and then let go of the hook and stepped back, spreading his feet and crossing his arms, obviously prepared to wait as long as it took.

Submission poured over me like thick, warm syrup, sliding slowly down my skin in the hot sunlight. The sensation triggered a critical need, and after a quick check to make sure I was facing downhill, I squatted on my toes and released my bladder, keeping my eyes on the ground.

The relief was almost orgasmic, sending chills over my skin in spite of the heat, and I couldn't hold back a soft moan.

"Good girl," Colin said.

I gave him a wry look from under my lashes. Like this was something every person on the planet didn't do several times a day.

"You're not even blushing, Rachel."

I wasn't, was I? "Because it's you, Sir."

"I know. And now *you* know."

"Yes, Sir. Would you really have rubbed my nose in it if I couldn't hold it?"

His lips quirked. "That's something you'll have to find out for yourself."

"God, I hope not, Sir," I said with feeling. I looked around. "Am I supposed to use a leaf?"

"I wouldn't, unless you're sure you know what poison oak and poison ivy look like. You'll have to drip dry. Just give it a good shake. That's what I do."

I sighed with penis envy.

When I straightened, he stepped up and unhooked me from the line. Then he reached behind himself and pulled a leather leash out of his back pocket, and I sighed again.

"Really, Sir?"

"Shh. No speaking unless spoken to now, slave, or I'll make you crawl back."

Feeling as though I were on much firmer ground now, I let him lead me back into the house and returned to my spot by his feet to read the contract. When he told me he'd emailed me a copy of everything and I could go over the reading and website lists at my leisure, I sent him a narrow-eyed look. The devious Dom had set me up with that big bottle of water, extended wait and long-ass reading assignment, hadn't he?

He grinned. "Get used to it, Rachel. I learned from the master of mind fucks."

After I signed the contract, he gave me a tour of the house, still leading me by the leash. There were two lovely guest rooms on the second floor, each with its own bath, but he didn't say anything about either being for me and I wasn't taking anything for granted. There were two other doors at the end of the hallway that he said were his room and Julian's, but we didn't go in those. Instead, he took me back downstairs and showed me the laundry room. I cheered inwardly when he told me it was there if I needed it but they had a housekeeping service that came out twice a week to take care of laundry and other household chores.

I held my breath when we went down to the basement. As expected, the stairs opened onto a torture chamber—one filled with strength-training machines, a treadmill and a stationary bike. Yay.

"I hope you've been keeping up with your workouts," he said severely. When I grimaced, he shook his head. "You've been a very bad girl then, Rachel. We'll have to do something about that."

At the other end of the room was a locked door to which Colin had the key. When he opened it and turned on the lights, I was unsurprised to see a dungeon, heavy on medical technology and light on BDSM furniture. The carpeted section of the room was a minidungeon with a single cross, a padded metal sawhorse, some kind of metal crossbar thing on the floor and a tall, shallow cabinet that I assumed contained toys. At the back was a seating area with a leather couch and a few chairs.

But it was the coldly tiled medical area that captured my attention and made my stomach flutter with excitement. If that wasn't the exam table from Bangenschloss, it was an exact duplicate. And beside it was a dental chair of some sort, accompanied by a rolling cart with the same e-stim machine I'd seen my first night at the castle. The countertop along the wall held lots of equipment I hadn't seen before and had no idea what it was for.

Colin hummed with amusement. "I suspect somebody's getting a little wet right about now."

I flashed him a coy look, glad for once that I couldn't speak.

"Go bend over the exam table, ass facing the cabinets," he ordered.

My tummy twisted with nerves but I obeyed, leaning over the side of the exam table and recoiling slightly when my breasts landed on the cool vinyl. I heard a door slam behind me, followed by the opening and closing of a drawer and the snap of a rubber glove. Then I jumped when Colin spread my butt cheeks with one hand.

"Look at that wet cunt," he tutted. "You're such a slut, Rachel."

I couldn't help smiling. Being a slut for Colin was so much better than being lonely and miserable in Seattle.

Cold, slick fingers slid into my butt and spent a few minutes twisting and tugging while my breath stuttered in my throat. God, I'd missed him and his anal fetish. I almost cried when he pulled out.

"This one has to be big to stay in properly," he warned a second before something cold and hard began pushing into me. After stiffening instinctively, I relaxed and tried to let it in. Just when it became painful, the stretching eased and the plug settled into place. He quickly swiped me, up, forward and back, with what felt like a disposable wipe. I appreciated that very much after my adventure in the yard.

Then something soft twitched back and forth across my thighs and Colin chuckled.

"Very nice, little slut-puppy," he murmured.

Oh hellfire and damnation. He'd given me a tail.

Walking had never been so disconcerting and uncomfortable, and it was a relief when the tour finally ended at the first-floor home office. In the center of the huge room, two large desks faced each other, and behind each were built-in, floor-to-ceiling bookshelves filled with medical and science books. To my left was a bank of filing cabinets. And on the opposite wall, under the wide, sunny picture window, sat a long, low wrought-iron cage with a thin mattress in the bottom and a tasseled throw pillow at one end.

I wasn't surprised when Colin tugged me directly to it and opened the door at the end.

Unhooking the leash, he said, "In you go."

Offering him a long-suffering look, I crawled in, wincing when the door clanged shut behind me.

"Good girl," he said, crouching beside the cage to smile at me while I found a comfortable position sitting gingerly on one cheek. He reached between the bars and touched my face with his fingertips. "You always look beautiful, slave, but you look exceptionally lovely as a puppy."

When I grimaced, his grin widened. "Accept the compliment gracefully or I'll put the puppy hood and mitts on you. A lick or kiss of my hand will suffice, since you don't have permission to speak."

I quickly kissed his long, sensitive fingers, and then licked them for good measure. When he didn't withdraw, I kept licking, watching his face as he watched my tongue slide over his skin. He looked mesmerized. And hungry.

"*Very* good girl," he said roughly before pulling back and standing up. "All right, slave, I have to work for an hour or so and then if you're nice and quiet, we'll have lunch in the kitchen. Take a nap if you wish. You probably could use the sleep."

He sat at one of the desks and went right to work on his laptop, so I lay down on my side with my head on the pillow. For a long time, I just watched his beautiful face as he frowned in concentration and occasionally smiled or chuckled at something. Did he have any idea how thrilling it was to be able to do that after all the misery of the last six months?

Sometime later, I woke to the feel of something tickling my foot and jerked my leg up, banging my knee on one of the bars. "Ow."

"Time for lunch, slave. Did you have a good nap?"

"Yes, Sir." Rubbing my knee, I sat up and realized he'd covered me with a soft throw while I slept.

"You looked beautiful but a little chilly." When I backed out of the cage and stood, he pointed at a ceiling vent. "That vent blows right on the cage, which I enjoy, but I run hotter than you do."

Startled, I cocked my head. "Does that mean—"

"You don't have permission to speak, slave," he reminded me, clipping the leash back on me. "Do you have to go?"

I shook my head quickly.

"Good. This way then."

With visions of a naked, caged Colin dancing in my mind's eye, I followed him to the kitchen. I was surprised to find the table already set—for one. On the floor beside the table were two large, shallow bowls, one filled with water and another filled with what looked like dog food.

This was carrying things just a little too far. I crossed my arms and glared at him.

Clearly fighting a grin, he raised a brow. "Something on your mind, slave?"

I stomped over and pointed at the food.

Colin snorted and plucked his own spoon off the table. Squatting beside the bowls, he scooped up a bite and ate it. "Tastes fine to me. You don't like beef stew?"

Grrrr. Master of mind fucks, indeed.

"Don't growl at me again, pup, or I'll muzzle you until dinnertime," he warned. "Now eat. I have work to do this afternoon."

Sighing, I knelt down in front of the bowls.

"Here." Colin pulled a thick, folded towel from the chair and slid it under my knees, and then tied my hair into a knot behind my neck.

I batted my lashes at him and he smiled. "You're welcome. Eat."

Heaving one more sigh, I leaned down on my hands and sniffed the stew. It smelled all right but didn't look very hot. Which was probably to keep me from burning my face, but that didn't mean I had to enjoy it. Opening my mouth, I tried to neatly pick out a piece of beef but my chin and nose both dipped into the stew before my teeth even got close.

I looked at Colin, who was still squatting beside me, and he grinned from ear to ear.

"You're the cutest damn puppy I ever saw, Rachel McBride," he told me, rising to take his seat.

Well, I was glad he was happy. Deciding there was no neat way to eat with my mouth, I went for broke. The stew was actually pretty good—the parts of it that didn't go up my nose, that is. I ate until I was satisfied, not wanting to contaminate my water with stew until the last possible minute.

"Rachel."

I looked up and Colin took my picture with his phone. I glared at him and he did it again, laughing heartily.

That did it. I lurched up from the floor and dived for him, intending to kiss him until he looked just like me, but he managed to grab my wrists and hold them out far enough away from him to stay clean.

"Bad puppy!" he scolded, standing up. "You made me drop my phone."

He dragged me over to the kitchen sink, then gripped the back of my collar and held my head over one side. When I heard the water turn on and the *zzzzzzip* of the sprayer nozzle being pulled out, I closed my eyes and took a deep breath just in time. Colin blasted my face with tepid water long after the stew was gone, waiting for me to take another breath. He wasn't satisfied until I was coughing and sputtering and fighting to get away.

"You're lucky this is Texas," he told me, wiping my face none too gently with a paper towel. "In Montaneva the tap water is twenty degrees colder."

Long past shyness now, I blew my nose in the general direction of the paper towel, trying to get rid of the last of the stew. Colin took the hint and held it close enough so I could blow harder.

"You're welcome," he said again, dropping it into the trash can. Then he leaned down and picked up—

I finally flushed painfully. How had I not noticed my tail popping out during the struggle?

He hooked the leash back on me and pulled me down to the basement. "You were going to get to take another nice nap in my office while I finished my work, but now you can stay down here until Julian gets home, naughty puppy."

Opening the dungeon door, he pushed me in and then said, "Kneel."

My heart pounding, I knelt beside the crossbar thing and waited with trepidation while Colin dug under one of the medical cabinets.

When he came back, he stood behind me and took off the collar. "Don't move."

I froze. Whatever I was expecting, it wasn't the leather hood that came down over my head, but I managed to hold completely still until he'd tugged it into place and I could see out the eye holes. I felt him tightening laces down the back until the mask conformed fully to my head, and then he buckled a strap around my neck and I heard the click of a padlock. Coming around in front of me, he snapped something on to the flap hanging off to the side of my mouth.

"Open."

Trembling a little now, I opened my mouth. Colin pushed some kind of thick dildo inside as he pulled the flap over and zipped it. My face was now completely covered and I was gagged. The whole world smelled like leather.

Next he took my hands one by one and covered them with mitts that forced them into fists. It was hard to tell from his bland expression if he was really angry with me again, but it didn't matter. I already felt so punished I wanted to cry. And yet I was strangely aroused. God, was having a pretend-penis in my mouth all it took to turn me on? Or was it the dehumanizing experience of being masked and turned into a puppy that did it for me?

When I was locked into the mitts, he made me get on all fours over the crossbar thing, and I finally noticed the cuffs attached to it.

"Prison stockade," he explained. "Less intimidating but more portable."

He pushed down between my shoulder blades until my breastbone rested on a low, narrow pad and locked my collar to something underneath so I couldn't rise. Then he locked my wrists and ankles into the leather cuffs. The back crossbar was twice as wide as the front, leaving my legs wide open. I knew it was too much to hope that he was going to have sex with me, but that didn't stop me from getting embarrassingly wet almost at once.

Colin returned to the medical side and I heard water running in the sink. Then he went behind me and forced my tail back in with only the residual lube from the last placement. I squealed at the momentary sting.

"Naughty little puppies don't get more lube," he informed me.

There was a clank of metal on metal and other sounds I couldn't quite make out, and then my tail was tossed up onto my low back and something thick was pushed deep into my vagina and locked there. I groaned loudly at being so completely impaled and utterly helpless.

"Naughty little puppies don't get fucked either, no matter how horny they are," Colin said behind me. I heard the distinctive click of the camera mode on his phone and groaned. He was taking pictures of me. "You look very hot, horny little puppy, and very much in trouble."

Continuing around me in a circle, he took shots from every angle with his phone. "Be glad this wasn't broken or you'd really be in trouble."

I ground my teeth against the dildo, wishing it were his cock. He should be glad I was wearing this hood or *he'd* really be in trouble.

When he was done taking pictures, he pulled a chair from the back of the room and sat directly in front of me, resting his elbows on his knees.

"I wasn't going to do this today but now that I've got you all trussed up, I can't wait any longer," he said with an impenetrable look. "Julian ordered me not to speak to you that last morning in Montaneva or I'd have given you a big earful then. Part of me wishes I'd disobeyed but he was already on the edge and I didn't want to be the one to drive him over. I knew you'd be fine and we'd get you back eventually."

I bit harder. God, he could be so arrogant sometimes!

"Now I want you to listen to me carefully," he continued. "I didn't deceive you deliberately, Rachel. I didn't find out Jordan hadn't agreed to the surgery until the night before you arrived, when I caned Julian after his time at the prison, or I'd never have involved you. I would have protected you with my *life*. But I couldn't tell you because you might have prevented the surgery and I couldn't let Jordan die when I knew we could save him. I didn't *think* it, Rachel, I *knew* it, and unlike Julian, I think we did the right thing. You've seen Jordan—do you think he would have been better off dead?"

He watched me with his brows raised, clearly expecting an answer, and I hesitated. Right after the surgery, I'd thought he might be better off dead. If living in Augustine Pohlson's body didn't drive him mad, knowing his brother had betrayed him might. But after seeing him walking around, working out, being angry and aggressive and taking control of Julian? I had to admit, I thought he probably had an amazing future in store for him, if he didn't let bitterness eat away at him for too long.

I shook my head from side to side. .

"Good. I don't either. I think eventually he'll adjust to his new body, and it will become his, rather than Pohlson's."

God, I hoped that was true, for Julian's sake as much as

Jordan's.

"But I didn't throw you under a bus for anyone, Rachel, and I never would. After he told me Jordan hadn't consented, he took me to his office and gave me signed affidavits swearing that he was the only one who knew his brother had refused the surgery, that he had deliberately withheld that information from us in order to save his brother's life. Jordan and all his nurses thought he'd come to the castle to spend his final days with Julian, and at the end, Julian dismissed the nurses most afternoons so that he could care for Jordan himself.

"He *loves* him, Rachel. He didn't save him for the sake of his research—he raised him after their mother died, so he's as much a father to him as a brother. No parent could just stand by and watch their own child die when they could do something about it."

By the time he finished, I was almost in tears. There was no longer any doubt in my mind Julian had done the right thing, and so had Colin. If we could do it all again, I'd operate on Jordan without thinking twice, even knowing he hadn't consented. My career wasn't worth his life.

"You didn't know all that, did you?" When I shook my head again, he sighed. "I figured. That's why I sent you the article. I thought you were taking too damn long to come to your senses."

Swallowing hard, I nodded. I wanted so badly to thank him but batting my lashes was just too flirty and superficial under the circumstances, and I wasn't sure he'd see them anyway.

"All right then," he said. Standing up, he walked behind me and I heard the door open. "I want you to stay here for a while, Rachel, and think about us. Think about you and me—everything we said, everything we did, everything we were. Everything we *are*. And I want you to think about what you did to *me* when you left Montaneva that day. Not Julian—me. I'll be back in a little while, just in case you decide you have something to say to me."

243

I heard the door close, and then I was alone with his words ringing in my ears.

Think about what you did to me. Not Julian—me.

My stomach began to churn. What *had* I done to Colin when I left Bangenschloss? The right thing, I thought. Even if I'd known he hadn't deliberately deceived me, that he hadn't thrown me under a bus, I couldn't have asked him to choose between me and Julian. Julian needed him. They'd been together for years, and they loved each other so much. Surely he could understand that.

Jesus, I've missed you so much. I love you, Rachel.

The words came back to me as if he were radioing them directly into my brain, and I whimpered. At Bangenschloss, Colin had been my lover, my companion, and I'd been devastatingly lonely without him. Was that how he'd felt about me? Somehow I'd thought that still having Julian would be an acceptable consolation—or more than I had, anyway. I had neither of them. I'd made the sacrifice so that they'd still have each other. What right did Colin have to be angry?

I've missed you so much.

Oh God, had he really missed *me* that much? I'd sort of assumed he mostly just missed using his cock on someone else.

You went all subbie and hot the very first time you saw him. I know because I was standing right there watching your face. I wasn't even a blip on your radar. You didn't even notice I was alive.

My stomach went painfully hollow. Why had he been watching my face? It hadn't even occurred to me to wonder when he said it. I was a brand-new resident, timid and insecure and anxious to please everyone, and Colin pleased no one but himself back then. Why would he have cared how I felt about him?

I'm his to do with whatever he pleases, and it's made me a better man—and, believe it or not, a better Dom—than I ever thought I could be.

He *was* a Dom, wasn't he? He'd been one from the beginning, or at least felt the urge to be one. He'd tied up girls and wanted to tie me up. Had he gone all hot and dominant for me right away and I just hadn't seen it, hadn't responded to it?

I wanted to be reserved for you. I love you, Rachel.

Chills rose on my skin and I started to tremble. I'd always thought Colin had some hidden agenda when he was with me, and in Montaneva I'd decided it was getting me together with Julian.

But what if it wasn't? What if Colin's whole agenda all along was becoming my Dom?

The minute I thought it, I knew it was true. Colin had been in love with me long before I ever thought about wanting him. He'd loved me even before he loved Julian, and wanted to be better for me. Wanted to be worthy of me. He'd waited and worked for me all those years, and he'd been thrilled to have me back.

And I'd left him.

Tears burned in my eyes, and then I started to sob. I'd been so wrapped up in what I was doing to Julian, it hadn't even occurred to me to wonder what Colin might be suffering. Oh God, how could I have been so blind? Colin was the love of my life, and apparently I was the love of his. And I'd just...given up on it.

Suddenly I realized it was getting hard to breathe. Oh crap, my nose was stopping up and I had a penis in my mouth. I needed to stop crying, stat.

A hand reached down and unzipped the lower part of my hood, releasing the gag. "You're okay, sweetheart—just take a few deep breaths."

Colin rubbed my back and I burst into tears again.

"Colin," I sobbed, shaking in my restraints. "I love you so much, and I was so blind. Why didn't you tell me?"

"Because you needed to see it on your own. You needed to see *me*. And did you?"

I nodded emphatically. "Yes, Sir."

Kneeling at my side, he tipped my chin up.

When he pressed his mouth to mine, I sobbed even harder and tried to pull away. "I'm all snotty!"

"I don't care." He kissed me again with his mouth open, sucking on my upper lip. "Everything about you is mine now, Rachel Anne. Even your snot."

A choked laugh escaped me. "You never did have any limits, did you?"

Colin didn't smile. "None, where you were concerned. I craved every particle of you from the first time I saw your sweet smile. I wanted to hold you, own you...absorb you through my very pores. I needed to be the one who made you tense with submissive wariness whenever I was in the vicinity. But you wanted nothing to do with me."

Sniffling, I cringed. "I'm sorry!"

"You should be."

"Well you have to admit you acted like kind of..."

"An assmunch?"

"Yes! You even said as much."

"That didn't make me crave you any less. And I don't think I was acting like an assmunch when you left me in Montaneva."

"I wasn't leaving *you*," I started. Annoyed by the leather obstructing my vision, I shook my head around. "Would you please take this damn hood off and let me out of here so I can see to talk to you?"

"I don't think so," he said flatly. "And excuse me, but you did leave me. You packed your shit and walked out without even talking to me."

"I talked to you! You're the one who didn't talk to me."

"Because Julian wouldn't *let* me or, believe me, I'd have

had a few things to say about your letting Dirk and Vince top you. I sure as hell had a few things to say to them after you left."

Blinking hard, I froze. "Really?"

A hard slap landed on my butt and I squeaked.

"God dammit, Rachel, yes, really! You're mine!" he roared.

"I'm sorry! I didn't know!" I shouted back at him.

He took a deep breath and then said in an eerily calm tone, "You will after we're done here today."

Chapter Twenty-One

Well he certainly made me tense with submissive wariness now. "What do you mean?"

He stood up and walked away.

"Colin, talk to me, please," I begged.

"Settle down, I'll be right back."

That was enough to calm me for the moment. I took a few deep, shuddering breaths and tried to relax. Colin loved me, and he'd loved me for years. He wouldn't hurt me too badly...would he?

Though he certainly had pinned my wrists so that Julian could beat my butt until it was bruised. And he'd caned Julian black and blue.

A fine tremor passed through my bones. Now that I knew he was my Dom, Colin was suddenly an enigma to me, an unknown quantity, and it threw me off balance. I loved it, and I hated it. He was safety and danger all rolled into one gorgeous, frightening package.

And Jordan though *he* was FrankenDom's monster.

"Well if that isn't a sight for sore eyes."

I twitched. Julian was here. And he was looking at my stuffed rear end.

"I thought you weren't coming home until this evening, Sir." Then I remembered he wasn't my Sir anymore. "I mean Julian."

"Sir is fine, Rachel," Colin said. "Now that you and I have sorted out who your owner is, you may address all Doms as Sir if I've given you permission to speak to them."

"Yes, Sir."

"And Julian's home because things came to a head between us a lot sooner than I expected and I wanted him to be here to protect both of us." The buckle at the back of my neck was unhooked and he started unlacing the hood.

"What do you mean, to protect us both?"

"I mean, you need to be punished for letting Dirk and Vince top you, but I'm so angry, I'm afraid I'll go too far. He's here to make sure that doesn't happen."

The breath rushed out of me. How could I feel better and yet more frightened at the same time?

Colin squatted in front of me, looking serious but not furious as he took off my mitts. "Rachel, I've got all the implements that they used on you and I know exactly how many you took from each. Julian and I discussed it, and I've decided to give you a choice. You can take everything they gave you times two, only I'll probably hit you quite a bit harder with everything except the canes. Or you can take a simple caning. Fifty strokes from the rattan and ten from the Delrin, plus a warm-up."

My mouth fell open. *Fifty?*

Oh. Crap.

My mind worked feverishly, trying to remember how many strokes I'd taken altogether, but it was no use. I was a wreck when I let them top me. All I remembered was that I'd taken eight from the Delrin. Ten was only two more than that. Surely I could take that. But *fifty?*

Then I frowned. "Wait, warm-up? What kind of warm-up?"

"A bare-handed spanking. Without it, the caning will be a lot harder to handle, Miss Tenderbottom."

Oh God, now I was really scared.

Colin took my face in his hands. "Rachel, look at me." When I did, he said, "Not a punishment spanking, like the one you got from Julian—just a warm-up, something to build on.

It's like exercising—if you do it without warming up, you're more likely to perform poorly and get hurt."

Taking a deep breath, I nodded. "Okay. Caning, Sir."

"Good girl." Dropping to one knee, he wrapped a hand behind my head and gave me a Colin kiss, long and involved and emotional. I was a quivering mess by the time he pulled away.

"I'm sorry, Sir," I said unsteadily. "I shouldn't have let them top me and I think I knew it. You're right to punish me. I'll feel better. Eventually."

He grinned. "There's my girl. And yes, you will feel better. We both will."

"And you'll forgive me?"

"If you'll forgive me."

"Always, Sir."

"Then let's get to it."

When Colin moved away, Julian sat down in the chair in front of me, wearing jeans and a dark-gray tee-shirt. "Hello, beautifully bound slave."

"Hello, Sir."

"It feels better like this, doesn't it?" he asked. When I looked at him quizzically, he said, "Colin being mine and your being his. There was something not quite right about having to divide my attention between the two of you. I couldn't do either of you justice that way."

"I think you're right, Sir." I swallowed and said, "Thank you for saving him for me."

He leaned down and kissed me. "It was my pleasure, little slave."

When Colin removed the dildo and tail, I was surprised to feel *too* empty, and even more vulnerable. As if they would have been any protection at all.

"All right, Rachel. Time to warm up."

"I'm ready, Sir."

He started out lightly enough that I was almost impatient. I thought he must have been kneeling behind me, using both hands all over both cheeks until they started to feel warm, and then hot—and I started to feel hot too. I wouldn't mind if he did this all day.

Of course, the minute I thought that, he stopped and stood up.

"Okay, now the rattan," he said, laying a hand on my low back. "I'm going to start lighter and faster, in bursts of five strokes, so they're easier to take. The last ten will be the hardest, and I'll give you more time to process them, all right?"

I took a shuddering breath. "All right, Sir."

The first five taps scattered over my left cheek made me hiss. They weren't as bad as even the first one Dirk had given me on the front of my thigh. The second five on my right were about the same, and I relaxed a bit while he rubbed both sides. Maybe it wasn't as bad as I remembered.

The third five and the fourth made me whimper and writhe, especially after the pain had time to blossom and mature. "Ow, ow, ow!"

"Almost halfway there, Rachel," Colin said, rubbing my cheeks again.

"Yay," I said in a tremulous voice.

Julian smiled and stroked a tendril of hair away from my face.

"I'm going to move to the other side to change my angle so I don't keep hitting the same spots, Rachel," Colin warned me. "No more bursts. You'll need time to process these."

Frightened, I nodded. From there on, I flinched and hummed after every stroke, keeping my eyes closed and trying to let the pain go through me instead of trying to stop it. By the time he reached forty, I was straining against my cuffs and collar, sobbing quietly, but I'd managed to keep from screaming.

Colin's hand on my hot, swollen flesh was almost more than I could take, and I cried out, "Sir, please!"

"Shh," he said, rubbing. "It's almost done, Rachel. Your ass looks amazing. I think you'll be very pleased."

My sobs ebbed and I opened my eyes with a frown. Why in God's name did that make me feel excited?

"Badges of courage," Julian told me.

"I don't feel very courageous, Sir," I mumbled wryly, "but I'll take it."

"Last set," Colin warned. "Don't try to hold back, Rachel. You need to let it go this time. Nothing you say will be grounds for punishment or hurt feelings. If you need to scream you hate me and want to rip my balls off, do it. Whatever you have to do to get through. Got it?"

Oh God. "Got it, Sir."

Molten fire streaked across both sides of my butt at once and I jerked hard in my restraints, growling through my teeth, "Son of a bitch!"

My language went downhill from there, and I probably ground quite a bit of enamel off my teeth, but I made it through without screaming—and Julian was covering his mouth with his hand and trying not to laugh.

Colin felt no such compunction. "I knew there was a seasoned sailor in there somewhere," he chuckled, touching my twitching, flaming flesh again.

"Hands off my *ass*!" I ground out.

He started rubbing with both hands. "I don't think so, slave. In fact, I think I'll leave off the Delrin and get right to fucking this beautiful ass. What do you think, Sir?"

Startled, I looked at Julian and he raised his brows at me. "What do you think, slave?"

I knew I'd probably kick my own ass for this later, but I said, "No, Sir. I want the last ten."

After a long pause, Colin said, "Rachel, I've forgiven you. There's no need to go any further."

"I disagree, Sir. You deemed fifty and ten a suitable punishment and if I don't get them, I'll feel like I still owe them. I don't want them hanging over my head."

He rubbed circles on my cheeks. "If I give you the last ten, I probably won't feel right fucking your ass."

"I'll have no problem fucking yours, though," Julian drawled.

"That," I said immediately. "I want to see that, Sir. Please."

He sighed. "Rachel, I—"

"I had a one-night stand on my dive trip."

Colin gave a bark of laughter. "All right, my slave. I already knew that, but you've just convinced me you do need the last ten."

"Yay." Wait, why the hell was I cheering? I was going to get ten strokes from the horrible, mean cane across my already blistered butt. And how did he already know that?

"Prepare yourself, Rachel—the eight you took from Dirk were on relatively unmarked flesh. This time your ass looks like a checkerboard. These are going to bruise you, and it'll hurt like hell, so I'm not going to drag it out. You were still holding back on the last ten, but don't do it this time. Let it fly."

It was all over in twenty seconds, but it was the longest, most intensely painful twenty seconds of my life. I started screaming and crying and trying to get away, and I didn't stop, even after they'd released me from the stockade and Colin had taken me in his arms. He kissed my streaming eyes and my open mouth while I held my butt, writhing and howling like an animal caught in a bear trap.

"I love you, I love you, I love you," he murmured. "You are so good, Rachel, so beautiful."

"Make it stop," I sobbed.

"Soon," he promised.

As promised, soon cool cloths were laid over my traumatized tush, pulling out some of the pain along with the heat, and I fell into another world.

I had one of those cognitive-leap dreams, where you think you suddenly understand some complex idea normally beyond your reach, like the molecular structure of peanut butter or how your car's engine really works. But then when you wake up, it all slips away.

When I awoke, I was startled to find myself in my bed from Bangenschloss. It was dark, except for the dim bedside lamp and I realized I must have been out for hours. I mean truly out—there was a wet spot on the sheet where I'd drooled.

"Pretty," I muttered, rolling to my side. I winced when I sat up. My butt still felt like it was twice its normal size but the pain wasn't too bad.

The bathroom wasn't as opulent as my bath at Bangenschloss, but it had double sinks and a whirlpool tub big enough for two people. After using the toilet and washing my face and hands, I used the hairbrush on the counter to make myself halfway presentable and then went looking for something to put on.

Then I remembered slaves didn't have clothes and sighed. Guess I'd have to wander the house naked. If Colin planned on this being a permanent state of affairs when we were home, I was going to have to negotiate a robe or something to leave downstairs in case I had to answer the door.

The upstairs was quiet and seemed to be deserted. I looked around the main floor and found no one. Had they gone out? Surely not. Colin wouldn't leave me zonked out after a scene, and neither would Julian.

I found the basement door open and started down the

carpeted steps. About halfway down I heard a rhythmic sound and stopped to listen to what sounded like throaty masculine humming. And was that a flogger slapping flesh? It was awfully fast, but that's what it sounded like.

Biting my lip, I continued down far enough to peer around the corner. The lights in the workout room were off, but the dungeon door was halfway open and inside I could see Colin cuffed naked to the cross, his head hanging forward limply. Hidden by the door, someone—I assumed Julian—was beating his shoulders and upper back with two long-tailed floggers in a smooth, even rhythm.

Now I recognized Colin's rumbles of appreciation, and my mouth hung open as lust blazed a trail from my eyes to my suddenly wet pussy. God, he was so beautiful.

Then it hit me—*was* it Julian flogging him? Colin had said Julian never hit him again after the day everything went to hell five years ago.

My breath came faster and faster as I crept toward the door. Part of me felt like I shouldn't intrude on their privacy, but they knew I was here and they *had* left the door open. And it wasn't as if Colin were shy about anything, especially being watched during scenes. He loved being watched.

But I should let them know I was here, so when I reached the door, I pushed it open slowly...and froze.

It *was* Julian flogging Colin. Still wearing the same jeans and tee-shirt he'd had on earlier, he swung the floggers in almost a figure-eight pattern, his posture relaxed and open. The flexing of the muscles in his arms and shoulders was fascinating, but it was his face as he watched Colin that held me transfixed—he was smiling as he cried.

"Are those shoulders heating up, my fuckhole?" he asked quietly. "They're turning a very pretty shade of red."

"Mmmmmm, yes, Sir," Colin mumbled without raising his head.

Barely holding back tears of my own, I watched as Julian shifted his strike zone to the middle of Colin's back and began working his way steadily downward. When he reached Colin's hips, he spread out again, concentrating on his already pink buttocks while Colin's rumbles grew louder. Julian stayed there for a long while, until the flesh had reached a deep shade of red. Then he changed to an underhand stroke without missing a beat, giving the bottom of Colin's buttocks the same treatment.

When one of his strikes strayed between Colin's legs, Colin yelped and pushed up on his toes. I thought it was an accident at first, but then I looked at Julian's face—his beatific smile had broadened to a grin.

I smiled too. Evil man.

He stayed in the underhand pattern for a long time, hitting Colin between the legs randomly, chuckling with enjoyment as Colin's cries grew louder and his body drew up taut in anticipation of the more painful blows.

Finally he stopped and laid the floggers on the medical table. After he shook his arms out, he smiled at me, placing his index finger over his lips in a shushing gesture. When I nodded, he pointed to a spot on the floor a couple of feet to Colin's left.

I complied eagerly, kneeling beside my lovely, endorphin-drugged Master as he hung in his cuffs and wincing as my butt settled back on my heels. It would be a few days before sitting was enjoyable again, but for a ringside view of this, I'd gladly suffer any amount of discomfort. Colin's skin practically glowed in the soft light of the table lamps, and I longed to run my tongue over the round, red swells of his buttocks.

Instead, I got to watch as Julian pressed his fully clothed body against Colin's naked one and pressed lingering kisses on the back of his neck and across his shoulders. Colin whimpered in clear enjoyment.

"Oh, Sir, I've missed this," he whispered.

"As have I, my sweet fuckhole. So much." Julian's voice grew thick. "You'll never know how sorry I am for depriving you all those years, but I just didn't think I had an ounce of control to spare after Jordan was diagnosed. No, don't speak—I know you've absolved me, but I still want to make it up to you in whatever way I can."

Colin whimpered again, and then his whimper rose to a whine as he strained up onto his toes. I hadn't noticed Julian's hands sliding around his hips, but I noticed them now as one pulled Colin's semihard cock upward. I leaned to see around the cross and gasped at the sight of the other one pulling down ruthlessly on Colin's dark-red, stretcher-bound scrotum. Good God, Julian had been hitting *that* with the floggers?

A laughing groan stuttered out of Colin.

"Rachel, my beautiful slut-puppy, how long have you been here?" he asked, smiling down at me lazily.

"Long enough to see her Master take a good flogging," Julian murmured against his ear before taking the lobe in his large white teeth.

When he ground them in a circle, Colin's laughing groan went up a good octave. "Oh fuck, Sir, you're cruel."

"Be glad it's not your sac in my teeth," Julian said as he moved to the other ear. "Yet."

After a few more seconds of torture, Julian pulled away and Colin groaned. Ignoring him, Julian picked up the floggers and hung them in the cabinet, then came back with the same two canes Colin had used on me. When my eyes widened, he grinned.

"Unlike you, my dear come slut, Colin is a pain slut. If he could see what I've got in my hands, he'd probably come without permission. He'll probably do that anyway, so I might as well just plan on it and punish him in advance."

Colin whimpered and moved restlessly. I knew him well enough by now to recognize anticipation when I saw it. Jesus, he actually enjoyed being beaten with those things?

Julian set the Delrin on the carpet and dived right into tapping the rattan all over Colin's shoulders, buttocks and thighs, maintaining a fast pace. I watched with awe. He must have hit him with the cane a hundred times before he stopped to rub the mottling skin and Colin only moaned like he was enjoying it—which he was, if the state of his cock was any indication. When Julian began adding some weight to the taps and spacing them out a little, still bouncing all over Colin's buttocks and flanks, Colin began to dance in his restraints, biting his lips and hissing.

"Don't come, dear fuckhole, or I'll show you the business end of the Delrin."

Colin whined like he was starving and Julian had dangled a juicy steak in front of him.

Then Julian switched out the canes and moved to stand beside me, laying stripes across his butt and thighs in earnest, rubbing his marks briefly and infrequently and giving him what I considered very little time to process the pain. Colin's closed-mouth whimpers grew urgent as he twitched and jerked and jumped, and when Julian hit a certain level of intensity, he finally let his shouts and pleas fly.

"Please, Sir! Please, Sir! *Pleeeeease*, Sir!"

Julian stepped back and, much to my horror, tapped him twice, lightly, right on his tight, livid scrotum.

Colin screamed, his whole body raging against his bonds, and then he burst into sobs as his semen splattered onto the wall in front of him in long streams.

I was in shock, but Julian watched him with a tender smile.

"There's my fuckhole," he murmured when Colin finally began to wilt. "That was beautiful, my love. You were wonderful." He moved up behind him and began to stroke him gently all over, beginning at his wrists and working all the way down to his calves. Then he knelt to rub Colin's legs and wrapped his hands around his thighs, trailing kisses all over his mark of ownership.

Whoever thought kissing someone else's ass was humiliation had never seen this act of worship. I was in tears watching it.

"I love you, Colin," he said.

"Thank you, Sir. I love you too," Colin mumbled, his head still hanging limply. "Will you please fuck me now? Please?"

Julian looked at me and smiled as I wiped my eyes. "What do you think, little come slut. Would you like to see me fuck your Master?"

I smiled back. "I'd love to, Sir."

Chapter Twenty-Two

Once he'd helped a trembling Colin upstairs to the master bedroom and removed the evil-looking stretchers from his scrotum, Julian pushed a bottle of water into his hand and made him take a couple of pills. Then he urged him onto his stomach on the bed and wasted no time getting naked.

Claiming another prime viewing spot on the other half of the bed, I watched as he went into the bathroom and returned with a tube of ointment. He nudged Colin's legs apart and knelt between them, leisurely rubbing the stuff into the heavily marked flesh of his butt and legs.

"So beautiful," he murmured. "I truly didn't realize how much I'd missed this."

"Does that mean you'll do it again?" Colin asked in a drowsy voice.

"Just try and stop me."

Colin sighed. "Thank you, Sir."

When he was finished, Julian capped the tube and laid it on the nightstand, then reached inside for a bottle of lube and spent even longer preparing Colin for his penetration.

Colin hissed but didn't complain when Julian urged him to his back and put a pillow under his hips, then stretched out over him. Heat washed over me as they kissed lushly, tenderly, even intuitively—they'd clearly been lovers in every sense of the word for years. The sight of Julian's straight blond hair mingling with Colin's brown curls was incredibly arousing. The sight of Julian's hand pulling Colin's up beside his head was even more so. There was something so sweetly vulnerable about Colin's exposed armpit, with its patch of brown hair. I wanted to lick that pale, tender skin.

Then Julian made an adjustment out of my sight with his other hand and Colin groaned, arching his back.

"Are you all right, my love?"

"Yes, Sir," he whispered. "Thank you so much for my marks."

"Believe me, they were my pleasure. Thank *you* for helping me find the courage to give them to you."

Drawing Colin's other arm up, Julian pinned his wrists to the mattress and braced himself up on his spread knees. Then he flexed his hips and I could see that his cock was already buried inside Colin. Between them Colin's cock strained toward his navel, red and needy. Julian moved in and out slowly, drawing it out, teasing us both, and it wasn't long before Colin began to whimper.

"Please, Sir. Please fuck me."

"What do you think I'm doing, my fuckhole?"

"Teasing me, Sir!"

"Isn't that my prerogative?"

Colin shuddered. "Yes, Sir. Please tease me, Sir."

"Reverse psychology isn't going to work, Colin. I'll fuck you into the mattress when I'm damn well ready."

"Yes, Sir."

Julian must have been pretty close to ready already because his pace picked up at once. He slung his hips forward, driving steadily into Colin, and I bit my knuckle at the image they made. I could watch this every single night and never get tired of it.

Colin's moans increased in volume and Julian drove him harder, fucking him like a machine.

"Rachel, if you want his come, it's about to make an appearance," Julian panted.

He didn't need to tell me twice. I scuttled over and

insinuated my head under his arm to capture Colin's cock in my mouth. It was unbelievably exciting to put myself in that position, wedged between them in the midst of such power and vulnerability and love. When Julian put a hand on my head and forced Colin deeper, resting some of his weight on me, I closed my eyes and went under, throbbing with hot arousal.

Colin sobbed like he was in pain, and then started shouting as his come poured into the back of my mouth.

Julian groaned long and low. "So good, beautiful slaves, so good."

His movements grew jerky as his muscles trembled violently, and then he shouted too, driving home and staying there, grinding himself into Colin.

Long after Julian had left the bed, I floated in supreme enjoyment, with my head resting on Colin's abdomen, holding his flaccid flesh in my mouth and caressing it delicately with my tongue while I smoothed my palm up and down his thighs. I would never get enough of this, and I would never, ever leave him again, for any reason.

Finally letting him slip away, I said, "That was incredible, Sir. All of it."

Humming with contentment, Colin stroked my hair. "It was."

"Are you feeling all right?"

"I'm feeling marvelous. How's your ass, my Rachel? Are you hurting yet?"

"Not as much as I thought I'd be."

"The pain pills are still helping then."

I raised up on my elbow to look at him. "You gave me pain pills?"

"Of course. You don't remember?"

"Not at all. Wow."

"You were pretty out of it, little slave. I was proud of you, but we're never doing that again. Are we, Rachel?" he asked pointedly.

I smiled. "No, Sir. I'll never let anyone but you and Julian top me again."

"Without my permission," he qualified.

"Without your permission, Sir."

He pulled me to his chest and hugged me. "And you're never having another one-night stand with a lame substitute for what you really want."

"Never," I said fervently. "That was awful. How did you know about him anyway?" I asked, flushing.

"Julian wasn't kidding when he said he monitored your activities, Rachel. If that guy had exhibited the least sign of dominance, he would have been forcibly removed from your vacation plans."

Unsure how to feel about that, I said, "Please tell me there's no photographic evidence."

Julian came back in, wearing his unbuttoned jeans.

"I had a file with surveillance shots of the Milquetoast," he said, sitting on the edge of the bed by Colin, "but none of the two of you together, if that's what you're concerned about. I destroyed it all when we left Bangenschloss anyway."

"Okay, good."

Julian leaned over and kissed Colin sweetly on the lips. "Good night, my beloved fuckhole. I'll see you in the morning."

Colin caught him behind the head and pulled him back for a deeper kiss. "Good night, my beloved Master. Thank you again."

After Julian kissed me, I grabbed his hand. "Please wait, Sir. I want both of you to promise me something. And I'm asking as Dr. Rachel McBride, not as a slave."

They looked at each other and then Colin said, "It depends on the promise."

"I want you to promise that if I'm ever dying and a head transplant is the only way to keep me alive, you'll let me go." When neither of them answered, I said, "Please. I don't want either of you going through something like this again, and there are some things I just don't want to live with—like having to deal with some other woman's period every month."

They looked at each other again and then looked me right in the eye and promised.

I gave a disgusted sigh. "There's no way you'll keep that promise, is there?"

Colin grinned. "Nope. We'd both better hope he dies first or one of us might wind up with our head attached to a pig or something."

Julian smacked his bruised hip. "Just for that, I'm attaching yours to a jackass."

"Don't forget, Sir," Colin said with a grin, "I know how to transplant a head too. If anything happens to you, I might put your head on a woman's body and you can spend the rest of your life as my Domina Julia."

Julian frowned fiercely...and then looked intrigued. "Now *that* could be a fascinating project. There's a lot of room for improvement in the field of gender reassignment."

Colin rolled his eyes. "Good night, Sir."

"Good night, my dears," Julian said absently as he closed the door, obviously considering a possible expansion on his research.

"I think you've just given him a new reason for living," I said as I snuggled back into Colin's arms. "I hope I'm not kicking him out of his own bed."

He shook his head. "We've never shared a room. He only sleeps a couple of hours at a time, and I like my eight hours when I can get them. That's what I hated most after you left," he added softly. "Sleeping alone again."

"Oh, Colin," I sighed, hugging him. "I'm so sorry. I had no idea. I thought you'd comfort each other."

"He was too much of a wreck about Jordan. But that's all behind us now," he added firmly, tugging my chin up with a finger to look me in the eye. "You're never leaving me again. You're mine, Rachel Anne McBride, and as soon as my ring is on your finger, everyone will know it. I want to meet your family."

My head spun and it took me a moment to catch up. "You want to marry me?"

"No, I'm *going* to marry you, and you're going to marry me. This week. You agreed to be my slave unconditionally and do anything I ordered you to, remember? No safe-wording out of it."

Though tears prickled my eyes, I laughed. "Yes, Sir."

"I'm glad you're able to see reason."

Then I bit my lip. "What about Julian?"

"He's mostly married to his research, Rachel, and we both think it's best this way. If that's all right with you," he added. "You do have some say in this, sweet slave."

"He'll stay with us, though?"

"He couldn't live without us, and I don't want to live without him."

I sighed, snuggling into his chest. "I don't either."

"Maybe someday soon we can have a baby or two and name one of them after his very kinky Uncle Julian?" he said hopefully.

"That sounds wonderful." I looked up at him then. "Doesn't Julian want to have kids?"

"God no. There's no way he'd chance losing someone else he loved to Bain's. He had a vasectomy years ago."

I nodded. That was kind of sad, but it seemed the

reasonable thing to do. Julian might be too obsessive to be a fun father anyway.

"You'll be a wonderful father," I whispered, kissing his chin.

"Now that Julian's whipped me into shape, I think I might just agree with you." He leaned down to kiss me, and then pulled me over to straddle him. "I think I owe you a few good, hard orgasms while our pain pills are still working, my darling little brave slave."

Smiling down at his wonderful face, I said, "I wouldn't dream of arguing with you, Sir."

His hands slid down to squeeze my butt cheeks and I inhaled sharply.

"Are you sure about that, Rachel?" he asked. "I'm still going to fuck this ass tonight. Just give me a couple of hours."

Scowling, I declared, "I think Julian might have created a monster after all."

Colin gave me a delightfully evil grin. "My love, you have no idea..."

About the Author

When I complained of being bored the summer before 7th grade, my mother (who worked at a bookstore at the time) handed me a stripped copy of Victoria Holt's The Shivering Sands--and I was hooked. I became a voracious reader and an aspiring author, bringing home stacks of books from the library every single week. The next year, I did a school report on Ms. Holt and wrote to her asking for information. In reply, she sent me an autographed photo and a lovely two-page hand-written letter in which she encouraged me to follow my writing dreams. Sadly, both the photo and the letter were lost over many moves, but my writing dreams remained.

At 14, I tried to write my first two romances. The first was about a federal agent masquerading as a bank robber, and a smart-mouthed customer who drove a custom baby blue Trans Am named Shark. The "robber" stole Shark as his getaway vehicle and the heroine, Nicki, dove in beside him. That was as far as I got--I could never see beyond their flying down the highway bickering as they were chased by bad guys.

The second was a hot mess of an erotic Gothic paranormal involving an eighteen-year-old governess and the sixteen-year-old eldest son of the house, who made quite inappropriate advances toward her via astral projection while she slept. I wrote 100 pages front and back—in pencil—before I hit that I HATE point in the story and shoved it under my bed. When I retrieved it two years later, the lead was so smeared I couldn't read it. The End.

After that, I set my dream aside to address the more practical matters in life--matters like eating and putting a roof over my head. It took finding my own hero to reignite my passion for romance writing. More than 25 years after my last attempt, I bought a used laptop on eBay and wrote my first erotic romance.

Mr. Robin and I have been married for seventeen years; we live on a farm and have three wonderful kids. I love to hear from readers, so don't be timid about dropping by my website robinlrotham.com to say hi!

When you're down on the farm, things are bound to get dirty!

Carnal Compromise
© 2011 Robin L. Rotham

Joe Remke has just one qualification for his lovers—he wants them gone before sunrise, which makes his new bunkmate AJ about as safe as a woman can be around him. It also makes his determination to sleep with his boss downright stupid, because if Brent ever gives in, he'll be looking for a new job.

Ladies' man Brent Andersen knows sex with his right-hand man Joe is inevitable, but he's not going down without a fight. Putting the new female hired hand in their cramped RV was a stroke of genius, taking the heat off him while protecting her from the horny guys on his custom farming crew.

AJ Pender's hard-bodied roomies may hide their feelings for each other from the rest of the crew, but they aren't fooling her—Brent and Joe are hot for each other, and it's all she can do not to cry at the thought. If they ever found out she fantasizes about being the meat in their farmer sandwich, they'd probably die laughing.

Fortunately for Brent and Joe, fantasies have a way of revealing themselves and AJ's are right up their alley. But even threesomes have their risks, and AJ can serve as a buffer for only so long before the tension between them explodes.

Warning: Flying BOBs ahead—and that's just the warm-up! Strap yourself in for a wild ride complete with ménage, m/m, and a voyeuristic f/f scene hot enough to make three grown men beg for mercy.

Available now in ebook and print from Samhain Publishing.

A Dom double-teamed by two submissives?
He doesn't stand a chance.

Chains and Canes
© *2013 Katie Porter*
Club Devant, Book 2

Wealthy businessman Daniel Baker doesn't have a creative bone in his body, but he knows art and craves beauty. Contemporary dancer Naya Ortiz, his fiancée of three years, embodies both. His protective commitment to her happiness extends to hiring Dominas to satisfy the sexual masochism she craves.

The balance of their relationship is tipped when Naya dances with reckless Cajun choreographer Remy Lomand. His magnetism as a Dom carries over to a backstage encounter that leaves Naya breathless—and Daniel unable to look away.

Remy knows the deal. The fancy people want to play with a disposable boy toy. He's fine with that...but not with letting Daniel remain a bystander. As their sessions intensify, Remy guides Daniel's awakening as a sexual submissive. Their no-strings threesome reveals the physical connection Daniel and Naya have lacked—and the emotional depth Remy fears.

When Remy and Naya tirelessly work to found a professional dance company, Daniel is left on the outside looking in. And although he and Naya are ready to submit to Remy for the rest of their lives, the man they call *Sir* may not want their love at all.

Warning: A sexy-as-hell Cajun choreographer plays slap, tickle, chains and canes with a caliente Puerto Rican dancer and her repressed businessman fiancé. What could possibly go wrong?

Available now in ebook and print from Samhain Publishing.

It's all about the story...

Romance

HORROR

www.samhainpublishing.com

CPSIA information can be obtained
at www.ICGtesting.com
Printed in the USA
FFOW03n1051070414
4719FF

9 781619 217058